The Swan's Song

L.C. Maxie

Spoon Creek Press

WHIPPOORWILL GAP PWF SERIES
BOOK 3

L. C. MAXIE

SPOON CREEK PRESS

Contents

Chapter 1

WITH SHAKING HANDS, HARPER Wood shoved her phone into her pants pocket. The large antique wall clock behind her chimed eleven o'clock. On Monday mornings, that meant two more hours until closing time. Scurrying to the front entrance of her bookshop, the Robin's Nest, she flipped the doorway's sign from "Yes! We're Open" to "Sorry, We're Closed." Then she turned the deadbolt before rushing upstairs to her apartment. Her daughter Olivia had called from a trail while out hiking alone. Though Harper was unable to make out everything she tried to say, her hysterical voice left no doubt that she needed help—fast.

One by one, nine small beings winked into sight like fireflies and followed her to the third-floor landing. Ignoring their questions in her haste, she asked if someone could find Walt and have him meet her behind the building, where her truck was parked. Seven of them blinked from sight.

In her bedroom she changed into hiking shoes, then picked up a worn backpack into which Piper, one of the Fae, had already placed two full water bottles, protein bars, a first aid kit, and a bottle of ibuprofen. Then she locked the door behind her and descended the steps to the basement, following faint traces of glittering light to the building's back door. Through the doorway's thick glass, she cast a hopeful glance toward her truck, hoping Walt would already be there, waiting.

Ever since that strikingly good-looking woman, Delaynie, had shown up in her shop asking for Walt, Harper had felt uneasy. The woman's barely concealed contempt for Harper and her shop had reactivated lifelong insecurities. It had been on a Friday evening in late May, just a few days ago. She and Olivia were chatting amiably, before Olivia headed out for her last night as a server at the winery, when the tall, elegantly dressed woman had walked in. The woman had specifically asked after Walt. She'd even known his last name, "Howell," while most people simply knew him as Walt.

Biscuit, Olivia's beagle-mix puppy, had not only growled but had gotten between Harper and the woman, reinforcing Harper's instinctive mistrust. To quiet the little dog, she placed him in her lap, rubbing his ears to distract him.

At first she attempted to make small talk with the woman, whose expression oozed an unpleasant mixture of annoyance and amusement at her efforts, and who offered little conversational effort in return. From behind the desk, while they waited for Walt to arrive, Harper stole glances at her. Her black hair, boasting dramatic streaks of silver, had been pulled back in a severe bun. With her tight sheath dress, heavy but polished makeup, and burgundy lipstick, she resembled a siren from an eighties music video. Her wrinkle-free face suggested a woman in her thirties, but her demeanor and carriage had Harper guessing her to be in her late forties.

With her attempts at conversation ignored, Harper pretended to focus on her inventory, blindly looking over the list of acquisitions on the checkout counter's computer screen. And when Walt had finally arrived at closing time, his dramatic reaction to the woman, as she unfolded her long legs and walked toward him in her slinky, form-fitting red dress, had shocked Harper into stillness. His tone, as he uttered "Delaynie," sounded timid, almost fearful, to Harper's ear.

"Walter!" the woman had responded in a resonant yet commanding voice. "How lovely to see you again. It has been *much* too long." Then she'd placed a proprietary hand on his elbow and, looking at Harper over his shoulder, brushed her lips across his cheek. He stood stiff and still, all color drained from his face.

Walt's eyes had flickered to Harper. He looked dazed. "Excuse us, Harper. I'll be back in a minute."

As he and Delaynie had exited the door in the direction of Divine Coffee, Harper forced her eyes to stay on the shop's interior instead of out the window, where she might catch sight of them. Though she strained her ears to catch their conversation, she only heard the passing traffic.

Five minutes later, a tense Walt had returned—thankfully alone. Knowing how private Walt could be, Harper kept her voice upbeat, only asking who the mystery woman was. She hadn't been surprised at his vague response, but it had disappointed and worried her.

"We met years ago. It's ... ancient history," he'd said before changing the subject so pointedly that Harper, too, dropped it like an electric wire. She'd hoped he would reveal more in the days to come, but he hadn't been forthcoming.

Why the secrecy? As Walt became increasingly preoccupied in the days since, Harper recognized a familiar feeling growing in her chest. The men in her life had always let her down. She chided herself for opening herself to betrayal once again. But Walt had seemed so different. She'd felt drawn to him from the moment they met. Once she discovered that they were both owl shifters, her confidence in him had been solid.

She had only herself to blame. Here she was again, with another woman threatening to take her man. As with her father when he left Harper and her mother, her husband Tim had betrayed her as well. The thought of repeating the process with Walt was more than she could bear, but what could she do to stop it?

But on exiting the building the following Monday morning after Olivia's frantic phone call, she saw Walt's tall, wiry form waiting beside the driver's door of her truck. Nine robins flitted around him, chirping in agitation. As she circled the truck to the driver's side, he placed his hands on her shoulders, pulled her to his chest, then leaned back to examine her face. "Harp? What's going on?" he asked.

Instead of answering right away, she drew a shaky breath and addressed the robins. "Can you guys fly ahead and see if you can spot Olivia? She's somewhere near the middle of the Sky Ridge Hiking Trail. Do you know the one I'm talking about? Some of you stay with her while the others meet us in the parking lot, and let us know where she is when we get there."

Without a word, the group took flight as a unit. In the space of an in-breath, they disappeared over the treetops.

Harper bit her lip, then looked up at Walt. "I'll tell you what I know on the way."

With Walt behind the wheel, Harper filled him in as they sped along the highway. Walt's carpentry skills were legendary among the locals, though he seldom used them anymore. But he was helping her daughter ready the outdoor adventure business she planned to open in a couple of days. This morning, Olivia had been scouting a hiking trail as another potential guided hike for her customers. At nearly twenty-nine years old, Olivia had experience hiking the local mountains, and she'd had wilderness training. But still, both Harper and Walt worried about her solo trips. Anything could happen in the vast forests of the Appalachian Mountains. Until today, Olivia had insisted they had no need for concern.

Thirty minutes ago, the normally confident and practical Olivia had called Harper in hysterics. In frustration, Harper worked to piece her daughter's story together; reception kept dropping due to Olivia's location deep in the mountains. Harper made out the words "bones," "dead," and "scared," between sobs. She'd tried to calm her daughter and asked where she was.

"Sky Ridge Trail!" Olivia had wailed.

"Olivia ... calm down and breathe. We'll be there soon. Are you okay?" She listened. "Is Biscuit with you? Is he okay?"

The sobs continued from the other end.

"Okay, Darling. Hang tight. We're on our way."

While listening to Harper's recount from behind the wheel, Walt kept a grim face to the highway, but then he reached over to squeeze her hand. "It's okay, Tweet. We'll be there soon. The others are likely with her already."

Harper tried to relax. As they passed the parking lot at Olivia's renovated service station, Bright Cloud Adventures, the lot was empty, so they continued to the trailhead about two miles further up the road. Harper hoisted her backpack and fell in line behind Walt on the trail. At the top of the ridge, they heard voices but were unable to ascertain the direction from which they came. Finally, the pale green water sprite, Alida, swooped above them. "I was just coming to find you! We found her! She's okay," she twittered. "Follow me!"

Quickly Harper and Walt exited the trail, heading through the brush toward a large, circular rock outcrop. "Why would she leave the trail to come out here?" Walt wondered. Walking to the far side, they found Olivia pacing, knotted from panic, with Biscuit in her arms. Meanwhile the other Fae surrounded a large, dark, oval object, grim expressions on their faces.

"Biscuit was off his leash," she confessed. "Normally he stays close to me on the trail, but when he took off barking, I followed him here."

On breaking through their circle, Walt stooped down to examine the object. They watched as he straightened abruptly, his face ashen. Then, with a ferocious screech, he morphed into a great horned owl before taking to the skies without a word, leaving them all far behind.

Startled, Harper bent over the object to get a better look. The lumpen oval mass measured approximately two feet long and nine inches wide. Three large bones protruded at varying angles. Harper guessed them to be ends and segments of femur bones. On turning over the dry odorless mass with her toe, Harper jumped to see what looked like eye sockets, and the teeth of a human skull grinning at her from underneath. And then she noticed a piece of threadbare red plaid flannel hanging from the opposite side, partly buried deep within the ...

She frowned.

With a start, Harper realized she was looking at a hideous, ridiculously large owl pellet. She knew that owls typically cast or expel indigestible bits of the prey they swallow whole, through their beaks. All signs indicated its most recent meal had been human.

Olivia shoved her phone toward her mother. "I've called the police; they should be here soon."

In hearing Olivia's announcement, all the Fae, except for Hawthorne, turned into robins and settled on nearby branches and bushes. The stout hob fixed Harper with a warning gaze. "Please remember occurrences such as this are unnatural in your world. Be careful what you say when law enforcement arrives."

Harper nodded. "Olivia? Do you understand that we need to be careful not to expose our friends? It would do the police little good, and we would likely be labeled mad or worse."

Olivia nodded miserably. "I understand that, Mom. But the police need to see this— someone has died."

At that moment, they heard a siren from the mountainside below. Within minutes, the fluorescent vests of two members of the Whippoorwill Gap police department could be seen climbing toward them through the tree branches. Another siren signaled backup pulling in behind.

"The rescue squad ..." Olivia choked out. "Too late for them."

The robins remained perched on nearby bushes for support. When Olivia showed them the pellet, the officers looked as puzzled as Harper felt. They wore gloves to turn the pellet about while taking notes and photographs from every angle.

After declaring the area a crime scene, they called in for help, then took Olivia aside to question her about the discovery. Olivia, her face mercifully makeup free, began crying again. Though normally self-possessed, the sight of human bones in that black mass had unraveled her composure. Harper heard her tell the police about her experience volunteering at a bird sanctuary in Raleigh where she learned to recognize owl pellets. Except for the size, these looked identical—only much larger. The female police officer nodded, expressionless, as she took notes without comment. They asked Olivia a few more questions, took her contact information, then told her to stay off the trail until she heard from them again.

Harper wrapped her arm around Olivia's shoulder, then took her back down the mountain and followed her to Bright Cloud Adventures. Three of the smaller robins followed, morphing into Alida, Lily, and Piper when they entered the building. In Olivia's office, Harper started the electric kettle to make cups of lavender–chamomile tea to calm everyone's nerves.

Once they settled down with their cups, she asked, "Did anyone notice which way Walt went?"

Piper sipped her tea from where she rested at the edge of her chair. "No, Dearie. But I suspect he's checking about to see what he might learn. I imagine such a sight would be a shock to an owl shifter."

Harper nodded her wholehearted agreement. To her, the heinous sight was tantamount to an ethical affront.

"But what explanation could there possibly be?" Olivia's voice sounded fearful.

"I'm not sure, Dearie. But I do think you should be careful until we find out. And be mindful of young Biscuit. I wouldn't leave him outdoors alone. Do as the police told you. No hiking alone at present. Always make sure you have at least another with you when out of doors." On seeing the alarm in mother and daughter's faces, she quickly added, "Safety in numbers, you know."

Restored by the tea, the Fae flew back to the Robin's Nest. Harper followed Olivia to the small green cottage down the road where Olivia lived. Once her daughter seemed calm, Harper made ready to leave. As she was giving Biscuit a final pat on the head, she overheard Olivia, speaking softly from the kitchen.

"Hi Quinn. Would you mind stopping by my place after you finish up today?"

Relieved that Olivia would have company later, Harper latched the door carefully behind her. While she'd never understand Olivia's friendship with Quinn Ellis, the folklore professor from Sequoyah College, she'd come to accept it. Ever since she'd met him, Quinn had tried Harper's patience with his insistence on helping her with her folklore collection. He'd come across to her as pushy and rude.

From the time he met Olivia, it had been obvious to Harper that Quinn was smitten with her lovely daughter. She'd expected Olivia to send him packing, but instead, they'd become close friends. Harper assigned their relationship to the category "Things I'll Never Understand but Must Accept," and moved on.

For the entire drive to the Robin's Nest, her eyes scoured the sky, in vain, for a great horned owl in flight.

Chapter 2

AFTER SPENDING THE REMAINDER of her afternoon fretting over Walt's dramatic crime scene departure, Harper had been relieved when he'd stopped by that evening. As usual, she'd left her balcony door unlocked for him. With no stairs up to the balcony from the ground below, she had little fear of a break-in, while Walt could swoop onto the balcony with no difficulty. But even if someone with bad intentions attempted to enter, Harper felt they wouldn't stand a chance with F-Troop, as she lovingly referred to the Fae, around to guard her.

Once they'd snuggled up on the sofa, Harper tried to keep things light while still inquiring into his intense reaction to the pellet. When he admitted that similar sights had traumatized him as a child, Harper had been appalled, but also curious. Since she had only discovered her shapeshifting ability in late middle age, she wondered what it had been like to be one as a child. But when she probed for details, he changed the subject, saying that though he'd calmed down, he was still shaken and didn't want to talk about it.

Instead he begged off for the night, saying he had a headache and needed some time to rest. But before he left, he'd asked her over to his treehouse for dinner the following night.

The next afternoon, Harper lingered over preparations for the date, feeling a pleasurable sense of anticipation. Though simple, Walt's meals were tasty, and she loved his secluded treehouse, just over a mile off a hiking trail halfway up Stone Mountain. The house was cleverly built for camouflage, no matter the season. Neither stairs nor ladder led from the base of the tree to the platform on which it sat, seventy feet from the ground. To reach the house, wings were essential.

Walt had finished the structure three decades before with a combination of labor and magic. Before taking her there for the first time, he'd asked her to keep its location secret from everyone. As far as she knew, Harper was the only person in the entire world who knew about it.

If she were to make the trip in her human form, she'd need to drive to the trailhead, park, hike halfway up a mountain, and then hike through thick, off-trail bush. The trek would take an extra hour or longer than soaring with air currents to his nest. And she'd still need to find a way to scale the tree once she got there.

Harper hummed to herself as she slipped a necklace with a carved wooden pendant Walt had made around her neck and dabbed a bit of his favorite vanilla-scented cologne behind her ears. Maybe he would share the story behind the pellet tonight. They had been a couple for nearly seven months now, but she still knew frustratingly little of his past.

She hoped that annoying woman Delaynie had moved on, and that neither she nor Walt would ever see her again. At the thought of Delaynie's haughty face, Harper's blood ran cold. But her heart warmed as she reminded herself that she could trust Walt.

Thirty minutes later, she landed on the railing of the three-foot-wide strip of porch surrounding half the structure, all of it masked by sturdy white oak branches. Without the thick foliage in winter and early spring, the view from up here was spectacular, but today the summer leaves blocked most of the surrounding ridges and valleys from sight. Sometimes wildlife was spotted—mostly racoons and deer, and an occasional bear—but not often. Harper approved. Next to Walt, she loved the privacy and silence most.

Today a gentle breeze rustled the green oak leaves about the porch. Due to the higher altitude, the temperatures here ranged from five to ten degrees cooler than in Whippoorwill Gap below. As Harper touched down on the railing, she frightened an Earth Realm robin, who flew away in a hurry.

After resuming her human form, she took a moment to comb her fingers through her hair, then straightened the clothes that always became disheveled in flight. Today she had worn one of her favorite black muslin skirts with an evergreen-colored linen t-shirt that made the green in her hazel eyes predominate. She hoped Walt would appreciate her efforts.

From the screened-in kitchen window, she heard water splash and pans bang against the stove. Foregoing the knock, she walked into the neat, tidy treehouse with a light step. All the unpleasantness from the past few days dissolved in the joy of being here.

Her elevated spirits rose even higher on entering Walt's home. The interior captured his essence—exuding an understated masculine confidence, both peaceful and self-contained. She stopped on the threshold, smiling to herself as Walt began to whistle in the kitchen. Apparently he hadn't heard her come in. At his first pause, she called out, "Hello! Visitor for Walter Howell, the Part-time Owl!"

His head when it popped through the kitchen door sported a grin, but as their eyes met, his expression changed, revealing unguarded admiration. Her pulse began to race; her stomach tingled like candy moonrocks on the tongue. He jerked his head good-naturedly toward the kitchen.

"Come on back, Harp." He held up his hands, which were studded with dough. "I'm just putting the pizza in the oven."

She followed him through the door, wrapped her arms around his waist from behind, then gave the back of his neck a fond kiss. He closed the oven door and turned to give her a proper welcome, Walt-style. Then, as she expected, he refused her offer to help, weaponizing the dish towel to herd her toward the door.

In the combination living–dining area, a table had been set with stoneware plates and green linen napkins. The kitchen was too small to comfortably hold two people anyway. She came to a stop before a bank of large, open windows, where she reveled in the fresh scent of sunshine and pine.

Early evening light and shade played with one another on the paneled wall. Wooden shelves holding hefty leather-bound tomes and paperbacks lined the other walls. For over two centuries Walt had been an avid book collector. All his sturdy furnishings were handmade, some by himself, others by old friends, including his adopted father, Daniel. Among the few things she knew about his past was that a master carpenter from England named Daniel had taught Walt carpentry skills when he was a child, long ago in the late seventeenth century.

One of the most striking examples of Walt's work stood against the far wall. The pendulum of the massive wind-up grandfather clock provided a steady, cozy accompaniment to the wind blowing through the trees. Today it kept time with Harper's beating heart.

"Here you go, My Tweet!" Walt walked in with a glass of homemade red wine which still tasted of last August's wild foxgrape harvest. "I must admit, I lost track of time while I was cooking. You surprised me when you called."

Harper raised her laughing face to his. “I’m surprised you didn’t hear me land when I got here. As usual, I displayed all the grace of a buzzard settling on its dinner.”

“Not possible, Darling,” he responded, nuzzling her neck. “You have the grace and beauty of a swan.”

She giggled at his gallant fib. “Well, I was a dancer in my youth, you know. What’s on the pizza tonight?”

“Anchovies and mushrooms. We’re also having a fresh bib lettuce salad, and a surprise for dessert.”

Harper’s mouth watered. Before she’d discovered that she had the ability to transform into an owl, she’d never enjoyed the taste of fish. But now she found herself craving it. Anchovies sounded divine.

Once dinner was served, the anchovies proved delightfully salty. The crust, with its satisfying crunch, yielded to a light, yeasty interior. The mozzarella and parmesan tasted fresh, and she guessed Walt had foraged the mushrooms himself. Tangy blasts charged every bite of the salad from the lemon vinaigrette. Why had she thought Walt’s cooking was simple? Clearly he was a master.

After the meal they moved to two comfortable rockers on the porch, with the scant remains in the wine jug on a table between them. The deep purple twilight descended like a stage curtain, ending a perfect day.

Despite her happiness, the thought of the ghastly pellet Olivia found yesterday wormed its way into her brain, disturbing her contentment. “Now that you’ve had time to think about it, what are your thoughts on Olivia’s discovery yesterday? The gang believe it’s Fae. They wished they had arrived before Olivia called the police, but really, what choice did she have?”

When he didn’t respond, she looked directly at him. “It bothered me to see you so upset. Can you fill me in? Do you feel like talking about it?”

Instead of responding right away, Walt reached over to pour the last of the wine into her glass. She was off tomorrow, so she made no effort to stop him. But she maintained her silence, waiting for his answer. Her biggest fear was that an owl shifter might have been the perpetrator.

He sighed, leaning back in his chair. "I'm afraid my thoughts would only bring you down, Harp. A long time ago, when I was a youngster, owl demons lived in this area ... trust me, they were nasty pieces of work." He shook his head. "I thought you'd be better off not to know about them. It seemed they had all deserted this area, so there was no reason to tell you. But after seeing that thing yesterday ... I'm thinking I was wrong. They were sometimes called Tskili'. Have you ever heard of that?"

Harper felt a chill at the word. She wracked her brain to see if she could recall anything about it, then shook her head. She was sure she knew nothing of it.

"They're owl shifters, too, of a sort ... but they're not the same kind as us. Tskili' are evil beings, usually female, who take the form of malevolent giant owls with human faces. They gain energy from the torture and torment they inflict on others. The Cherokee knew about them in centuries past, but with the arrival of the white men, the monsters seemed to have disappeared from this world forever. At least, that's what most of us hoped." He swallowed the last of his wine with a frown.

"And you think that's what produced that ... thing ... we saw in the woods yesterday?"

He appeared uncomfortable as he placed his empty glass gently on the table. "I sincerely hope not. I suppose the pellet could have been created by some sick human trying to imitate an owl. With technology, all sorts of things are possible these days."

They both started as a loud trumpeting sound arose from the forest. Though it sounded familiar, Harper had no idea what it might be.

Walt sat unmoving, a puzzled expression on his face. "That sounds like a swan! I didn't know there were any of those still around these parts. And we're too far from a body of water to hear them anyway." He shrugged. "Maybe they're flying overhead, but out of sight."

Harper began to ask another question, but it fled from her thoughts as Walt stood, holding his hand toward her with a smile. When she placed hers in his, he drew her to her feet and led her back inside.

Much later, Walt accompanied her home, but refused to come in, wishing her goodnight from her balcony. As she stood in the doorway watching him fly away, she realized she knew no more about his childhood than she had before. But it had been a wonderful evening. She smiled. They had years ahead of them in which to talk about it.

Harper padded over the refinished wooden floorboards in her immaculate buttercup-yellow living room. She made her way down the hall to her kitchen, where Piper had left the stove light on. Through the dim light, she spotted a plate of cheese and crackers waiting on the table. Whispering her thanks, Harper moved the plate to the refrigerator. She wasn't hungry after the blackberry pie with fresh cream she and Walt had shared just before they'd left his place.

After washing her face and slipping into a soft cotton nightgown, she went to her bedroom where, as usual after a night like this, she found a small pitcher of ice water beside a glass and a couple of aspirin on a saucer. She smiled. If she called right now, any of her Fae friends would happily pop in for a late-night chat.

But tonight she wanted to be alone. As she turned down the bedcovers, she counted her blessings again. Then she opened one of Walt's novels to read until she was sleepy. At age fifty-eight, she was safe, loved, and cared for. Ever since her grandmother had disappeared when Harper was ten, she'd been sad. But now, with her lonely childhood and loveless marriage over, she had finally found what she'd always wanted. Nothing could be better.

For a moment, she felt a pang, wishing she had her mirror back so she could look within its surface to thank her Grandma Sophie, too. But the mirror was now back in the Faery Realm with her grandmother, where it belonged. No matter—she could still try to reach out, she thought, closing her eyes. "Thank you, Grandma, for everything." Then, instead of opening her novel, she slid down between her sheets and within minutes was sound asleep.

Chapter 3

NEAR CLOSING TIME THE following Friday, Harper hummed as she straightened bookshelves in the shopfront while waiting for Walt to arrive for their Friday night date. Though the cloudy evening threatened rain, she wore a jade green skirt topped with an embroidered flutter-sleeved peasant blouse. Tonight they planned to walk up the street to Take Flight Brewery, where they would sip beers and munch nachos while listening to a local indie band, the WG Oracles, perform their original folk-bluegrass numbers. The day had passed pleasantly, and she looked forward to her evening.

When the entrance bells chimed, just before six, she smiled as she turned, expecting Walt. Instinctively, her body jerked back from the forbidding, tall feminine form that stood unwelcome in the doorway. She fought to keep her face neutral as Delaynie sauntered to the checkout counter, her upper lip hitched into a contemptuous smile.

"Oh, hello. Is Walter not here yet? He and I planned to meet here around closing time. Oh my," she said as she looked at the clock behind Harper. "I suppose I'm a tad early. But that's good. We can get acquainted, you and I."

Harper caught a whiff of an unpleasantly strong, musky, patchouli-based perfume. Her throat closed while her forehead quickly seized with a migraine that strong perfumes always triggered in her. Buying time to formulate a response, she leaned down and placed the duster underneath the counter, deliberately hiding her face for a moment. Then she pulled herself up to her full height and cocked her chin toward the haughty creature before her. "Why don't we start with you?" Harper asked, keeping her gaze level. "What brings you to town?"

Ignoring the question, Delaynie glanced about the shop with evident disdain. "How *do* you keep from going mad while stuck in here all day?"

Harper ignored the barb while laboring to keep her voice light. "It's hard to explain to someone who's never done it. Every day is different. I'm never bored."

Delaynie lobbed a quick dismissal in return. "I can't, for the life of me, understand why anyone would want to read all these tomes. It seems to me that living life is always more interesting than reading about it."

Harper fought back her urge to hurl one of those heavy tomes at Delaynie's self-satisfied face. Instead, she forced a deep breath. Like Quinn, maybe this woman merely lacked social skills. Charity was never wasted, she reminded herself, hiking the corners of her mouth. "Believe me, I have no intention of reading every book in the shop. But I disagree with you about life being more interesting than books. Books enrich life. They help us understand things we may never experience. In fact, to me, learning is what makes life worth living."

She felt proud of her self-control and offered a small smile as a peace offering. But then Delaynie spread her red lips, revealing a mouthful of unnaturally white teeth. Her voice, when she spoke, was dull with boredom. "Do tell? How quaint." She glanced at the clock behind the desk, then flicked her eyes toward Harper's clothes. "You close at six? Walt told you he plans to stop by?"

"I'm not sure he's coming," Harper lied stiffly. "I'll be happy to give him a message if you like." Everything about this woman, from her looks to her superior attitude, made Harper squirm. Who was she, Harper wondered, and what could possibly connect her to Walt?

Delaynie gave a breezy snort as her eyes narrowed. "No. That won't be necessary. We have things to discuss that don't concern you." She cocked an eyebrow. "I'm curious, though. Has Walt told you anything about me?" She leaned across the counter while Harper backed up a step in repulsion.

But before she could respond, the bell rang again. Walt stopped abruptly on the threshold upon seeing Delaynie standing in front of the desk. Surprise and shock seemed to register as color drained from his face.

The door clicked shut behind him. His voice sounded wary and tense. "Delaynie?"

Delaynie chortled as she moved toward him. "Oh Walt! Don't you remember? We have some important matters to settle."

Harper watched Walt's Adam's apple bob. The guarded glance he turned her way left Harper unsure what he might be thinking. Turning his eyes back to Delaynie, he gave a shallow nod to the door. "Let's step outside and discuss it, then."

Delaynie laughed unpleasantly. "I guess that *would* be best. I could tell your friend here all about it, but then I'd have to kill her." She swung a smug face to Harper's. "I'm joking of course."

Harper ignored her, focusing her attention on Walt, who she felt sure would quickly dispatch this irritating woman.

Walt stood still for a moment, then inhaled sharply. He turned to the door. "We'll only be a minute, Harper," he said over his shoulder, then he opened the door and stopped in front of the Robin's Nest's picture windows. Delaynie joined him there, pointedly closing the door behind her.

Walt spoke first, but Harper couldn't hear what he said. She felt queasy as Delaynie threw back her head, allowing audible peals of harsh laughter to escape through her cranberry-colored lips. At this, Harper's stomach clenched along with the temples of her head.

With disbelief, she watched as the woman reached over to take Walt's elbow, and still leaning toward him, led him out of sight toward Puckett's Park. While annoyed, she expected him to return at any second. But the minutes continued their sluggish pace until the mechanical clock behind her chimed six o'clock. The sound stirred her into action.

She walked to the door, key in hand, and craned her neck to catch sight of the handsome couple who should be just out of sight. Her throat constricted painfully at the sight of the empty sidewalk. She couldn't believe Walt had disappeared without a word. After all, they had a date.

For a second, she contemplated walking to the corner to see if they were standing just around the bend. But she forced herself back inside, instead. If they were in sight, she didn't want them to know she was pathetic enough to spy.

She didn't know which of them deserved her irritation most: Delaynie, Walt, or herself. With a jerk, she yanked the door's shade so violently it broke away from its moorings, leaving her holding the whole thing in her hand. Then she let out a curse so loud that Alida and Lily popped into sight, eyes and mouths forming perfect circles. If she hadn't been so angry, she'd have been amused.

Alida placed a small hand on her leg. "Harper! What happened? Are you hurt?"

Harper, unable to speak, looked out the window again through the slanting, early June sunshine. From where she stood, she could only see the sidewalk in front of her shop and the parking lot across the street. Neither Walt nor Delaynie was there. She tapped her foot in agitation. She felt shocked, unable to believe he had walked out like that ... and with that horrible female, of all people.

Freshly incensed, she flung the broken blind in her hand so hard it hit the display of Walt's A.E. Deere books, knocking a few over like bowling pins before it crashed to the floor. Then she stormed behind the checkout counter, slid to the floor, and wrapping her arms around her knees, began rocking miserably. She felt like a jilted high school student. She could feel it. He wasn't coming back. Not tonight.

The two sprites moved to her side as deep shaky breaths heaved from her chest before she finally burst into tears. It was like when her dad ignored her, or her husband cheated on her, all over again. Throughout the whole episode, she could feel four small hands stroking her shoulders and back. Once she'd regained control, she wiped her eyes. "Did you see Walt with another woman anywhere outside?"

The two little beings looked at her, then at one another, clearly puzzled. Alida's head shook with a frown. Lily grasped her hand. "What did the woman look like?"

Harper rubbed her pounding temples. "She's a gorgeous brunette with streaks of gray in her long hair. She dresses like she walked straight off a runway at a fashion show. Her name is Delaynie. Walt says he's known her for years. That's all he would tell me. I met her last week, but thought she'd left town until she walked in this afternoon." She looked up. "So neither of you have seen her?"

Alida stood straight. "I haven't, Harper." She looked quizzically at Lily, who shook her head. "We'll ask the others. Maybe one of them has seen her and knows the story. Why don't you go upstairs and get something to eat? We'll find the others while you rest."

Harper shook her head. "I'll wait down here for a while. If he comes back, I want him to know I waited for him."

Lily objected. "Walt knows you care, Harper. He'll look for you upstairs if you're not here. But I'll bet you anything Walt is waiting on your balcony right now!"

Harper's heart leapt with hope. Maybe he was, at that. They were right; he did know where to find her. Maybe she should just wait on her balcony. She was overreacting. None of this was likely his fault anyway. The minute he could get away from Delaynie, he'd be back. No doubt the whole thing would be a misunderstanding. This time, she would insist he tell her what was going on.

Once upstairs, she rushed to the balcony but found it empty. While clutching the railing, she scanned the tree line across the river and Puckett's Park beside it for signs of either of them. But only a group of young men playing hacky sack were in sight. Her stomach clenched. When Piper appeared at her side to offer tea or something to eat, she refused.

After swallowing a migraine pain reliever, she sobbed herself to sleep while lying on the living room sofa, waiting for the balcony doors to open, and Walt to walk in.

Chapter 4

THREE DAYS PASSED WITH no word from Walt, each embroidered with agonies of doubt for Harper. She'd been grateful they were workdays. Her customers kept her busy and distracted. Without them, Harper felt sure she would have gone mad.

But now, after closing on Monday afternoon, she had seventy-two hours to fill before business hours would claim her attention again. After changing out of her work clothes into knit shorts and a t-shirt, Harper stared listlessly out her balcony door, wondering what to do.

With a twist to her heart, she noticed Walt and Delaynie standing together beside the river just beneath Walt's sycamore tree. Though she was too far away to hear what they said, Walt's arms were flailing about as though he wanted to get an important point across. Delaynie watched him, unmoving.

When they turned to the bench Walt frequented in his human form, Harper stepped back behind the curtain. She saw Walt tip his face in her direction, and she feared they would think she was pathetically spying on them.

"Don't!" she hissed when Earl Grey flickered into sight and peered through the balcony's screen. "I don't want them to think I'm watching."

Earl Grey backed away from the glass and removed his pointed red cap. "I only came to tell you, Lassie, that all of us have gathered in your office. Everyone is waiting for you there now."

Harper felt alarmed at this break from their usual routine, though she felt sure the Fae had mustered only to provide support and keep her busy. They'd been stalwart presences over the past few days when she needed them most. Torn between having her attention ripped from Walt and gratitude at their care, she led the way to her office, beside the kitchen, its windows facing Oak Street and Birdsong Theatre across it. Now she wished she hadn't snapped at Earl Grey. If she'd been kinder, she could ask him to stay behind and watch the couple beside the river, but now it would be awkward to ask.

In the office, her nine friends rested on armchairs, the desktop, shelving, or on the rug. The normally cheerful lilac-colored room now reminded her of a bruise, its atmosphere heavy with her accumulated grief and pain from the last few days. After greeting them, she remembered her manners and thanked them for coming.

Without warning, her emotions overflowed the dam she'd placed around them since Friday. "They're sitting in the park right now! Did you see her? Who is that woman? Whenever she's around, Walt runs like a puppy to its owner. He can't seem to get away from me fast enough. I thought we had a good relationship. I guess I was wrong." Though she felt a little childish, it also felt good to vent her anguish.

Several of her red-vested friends stood, proclaiming their dissent. Hawthorne stepped forward, his expression grave. "I would urge you, Harper, do not be too hasty in your judgement. Things are often different than they seem."

As he backed away, Earl Grey took his place, chest puffed forward, face florid. "Bless you, Lassie, you've got it all wrong! This is our Walt we're talking about. He's been my boon companion for well over a hundred years now. I tell you, the man is not capable of double-dealing!"

Harper stopped pacing to give him an incredulous stare. While until Friday evening, she shared his sentiment, she could no longer afford to believe it. The potential pain and hurt she'd suffer if proven wrong was too great a risk. Her terror hid itself behind anger as she shook her head vigorously from left to right.

"I've been in this situation before," she reminded them, enunciating each word distinctly so there could be no misunderstanding. "I can feel it when I'm about to be abandoned. Repeated experience has taught me the signs. Trust me, I thought Walt was different, too. But this isn't the first time I've been wrong about someone. I'm too old for this now. I'm not willing to just sit by and mope while I'm discarded. If he wants this woman, he can have her. I'm moving on."

Throwing herself into an armchair, she ignored the low gasps around her. Desperation made her obstinate. She needed their support right now, even if she was wrong. Her inflamed thoughts and feelings swept in contradictory directions like wildfires scattered by wind devils. Why couldn't they see she'd been betrayed?

After an uncomfortable silence, Piper stepped up, placing twig-like fingers on Harper's knee. "What do you mean by 'moving on'? What do you plan to do, Dearie? Lock him out? Tell him to go away?" She paused, her deep, dark almond eyes boring into Harper's. "Walt's a good sort. Be patient. Most likely there's a good explanation, we just don't know what it is yet." The others nodded their assent with pained and somber faces.

Harper groaned as she dragged her hands across her forehead in agitation. "If there's such an innocent explanation, why doesn't he just tell me what's going on? He must know how unhappy I am right now. If you're right, and there is a good reason for what he's doing, either he doesn't trust me enough to tell me, or he doesn't care how I feel."

On getting no response, she looked around. "Don't you see? There's no excuse for not letting me know what's happening!" None of them returned her gaze; instead, they stared at the floor or at the sky out the front window. "Do any of you know something about Walt that might help me understand? Have you seen Delaynie? Can any of you tell me anything about her?"

Earl Grey tried again. "We've all at least glimpsed this woman." When the others nodded, he continued. "Does anyone know anything about her?" One by one, they shook their heads.

He continued. "Well then, to my mind, the sensible thing to do is ask him, point blank, who this woman is, and what might be her business. In fact, I will ask him myself, when I next see him out and about ... that will be tonight most likely."

Harper started up in alarm. "Earl Grey! Don't! This is between Walt and me. We need to work it out with no interference."

His nostrils flared as a heavy sigh escaped them. "I'm only trying to help, Lass. Since you're so upset, I thought perhaps a cooler head ..." he spread his hands and shrugged.

As he deflated, Harper left her chair to hug him. If she hadn't known it would hurt his dignity, she'd have placed a finger on his adorable cherry red nose. "I'm sorry, my friend. I know you want to help. But please understand, this is a personal problem. If Walt knew I was discussing it with you, he'd likely be hurt, if not angry. And honestly, I wouldn't blame him. When the time is right to work it out, I will, if he's willing. But right now, all I want is your support."

Earl Grey inclined his head. "As you wish, Lassie."

As he continued to stare morosely at the dark, polished floorboards, she reached over and took his small, gnarled hand. "That doesn't mean you can't remain friends with him, Earl Grey. I wouldn't dream of separating you from a friend." Earl Grey looked back at her with relief in his eyes.

"You can count on us," said Alida, her pale green skin glowing as she flitted forward. "No matter what!"

Harper looked at the windows. The sky over the parking lot had changed from blue to concrete gray. "Thank you, Alida. You have no idea how much I appreciate you. Now, if you all don't mind, I'd like to take a bath and curl up on the couch. And with any luck, Walt might even stop by this evening to convince me I've been upset over nothing."

They perked up at this hopeful speech. With a wan smile, she accepted their goodnight wishes, before one at a time the Fae twinkled from sight.

Later, she sat on her balcony for hours, the smell of bug spray wafting from beneath her summer bathrobe, while she watched in vain for Walt to appear in the empty sycamore tree across the river. She told herself sternly that even if things didn't work out, her life wasn't over. She had options. She still owned the bookshop and loved running it. Fortunately, Olivia lived nearby with sweet Biscuit. And Harper could always get a dog, or a cat, for herself. She had Deanna and Dashawn next door. And it wasn't too late to make new friends, either. Whippoorwill Gap overflowed with interesting people.

But even if Walt had reconnected with an old flame, and seeing them together proved more painful than she could bear, she could always move somewhere else and start again. She could sell the shop and maybe make a profit after all her improvements. There were other towns and folks to meet—all over the world, really. Next time, she'd be more careful with her heart.

But while she stared at the moon, a lump grew in her throat until it threatened to cut off her windpipe. Change was the one thing she hadn't wanted. To distract herself, she considered taking an evening's solo flight down the river, but tonight her arms felt more like anchors than wings. She wished once again that Grandma Sophie were here.

She took to her feet on hearing the same trumpeting call she'd heard during her last night at Walt's. Listening intently, she heard it once again, coming from across the river. The sound reminded her of that perfect night, and the heart-wrenching plaintive call brought tears to her eyes. Blinking them away, she leaned forward on spotting a large white object floating behind the trees. She watched, interested despite herself, until it disappeared upriver toward the dam. Had it been a swan, as Walt seemed to think?

After a moment, she stepped inside her apartment, carefully locking the balcony door behind her with a sharp sense of grief. As she did, the mournful call sounded once again, and a large white bird flew downriver past her building.

Chapter 5

Back at work on Thursday afternoon, the hours dragged on interminably. Harper still hoped to hear from Walt at any minute, but with each glance at the clock, it felt more unlikely. Beauty aside, Delaynie must have something Harper couldn't possibly offer. Harper felt resigned that she was unlikely to ever again enjoy what they had together.

To distract herself from her dismal thoughts, she half-blindly checked shelves, fretted over inventory lists, and absent-mindedly waited on the sporadic customers who walked through the door. Dust proved to be her most constant companion. She noticed it on the shelves, in corners, and even in the air. Apparently, even Tiptoe and Tarryfoot had lost interest in helping. This wouldn't do, she reminded herself. Nothing pushed people away like self pity, but she felt unable to extract herself from its suction. Outside, the sidewalk was nearly deserted. Where were all the summer tourists everyone promised? Harper wondered if opening this shop had been a bad idea.

An hour before closing time, Harper started with surprise when Ivy, of all the Fae, popped into sight. The stately wood nymph had never paid her a solo visit before. While not unfriendly, Ivy was the most forthright and least concerned about Harper's feelings among them. For Ivy to show up like this made Harper uneasy—something important must be afoot.

"Ivy." Harper bowed forward a few inches in acknowledgement. "To what do I owe the pleasure?" She dropped her fingers from the hair she had been twirling off and on, all day, to concentrate on the tightly muscled ebony-skinned being before her.

"Greetings, Harper." Ivy nodded in return with her customary reserve. "As you've likely ascertained, this call is not social. We urge you to remind Olivia of the dangers in the forests at present. Her business requires caution, even in groups. We could tell her ourselves but intuit that, at times, she doesn't take us seriously. We felt it best she hears this from you."

Harper could have retorted that Olivia seldom listened to her, either. But under Ivy's gaze, her mouth went dry, and she began rubbing her hands on her skirt. "Oh? Has something else happened?"

"You remember the preternaturally large pellet that Olivia found?"

"Yes, of course."

"We've just learned that several more have been discovered in the days since. Two of these have been reported to the local authorities. We've become increasingly convinced they have neither the tools nor understanding to deal with this problem."

Harper suddenly felt a chill. "What do you all suspect might be happening?"

"We don't know for certain. But as we told you before, we suspect that they are the work of Fae, not some deranged human trying to mimic an owl." With a face devoid of expression, her next statement caused hairs to rise on the back of Harper's neck. "There are beings from the Otherworld who can and do create such horrors. Though we thought them absent from this country for the past two centuries or more, we fear they have returned."

Remembering Walt telling her about owl demonesses, and dreading the answer, Harper whispered, "Do these creatures have a name?"

"They are called by various names, one of which is Tskili'."

Harper winced. Thanks to Walt, she was familiar with the term.

"They are evil creatures, female in form, who manifest as gigantic owls. They prey on the living: animal, human, and Fae alike. But though they consume flesh, pain and terror are their true sustenance." As she looked at Harper's terror-contorted expression, she softened. "But I stress again, while we are suspicious, we do not know what is happening. But if we are right, your daughter should be aware of what may be stalking the woods. Precaution may save lives."

"Walt mentioned this creature to me, but I didn't really understand. He said they aren't owl shifters like us but are malignant beings of a different kind. I hope I understood that correctly ..."

As though understanding Harper's fear, Ivy shook her head. "No. These are an altogether different class of Fae." She shifted on her feet and changed the subject. "We have a few suggestions for Olivia until this issue is resolved. For instance, it would be best to cancel overnight camping trips in the wilderness. Group hikes should have no fewer than five individuals, and they should stay together, only hike in the daytime, with a weapon available. If, as we suspect, this is a Tskili', they are unlikely to attack in daylight. They are too clever to risk being seen by someone who might get away. We also believe that daylight would be deadly to them in their owlish incarnation."

Her misery forgotten, Harper felt energized with purpose. "Thank you, Ivy. I'll call Olivia now. If I can't get her on the phone, I'll swing by to find her later. I cannot tell you how much ..."

But Ivy disappeared as the entrance bell rang merrily above the door and Bryan Greene, the owner of Whippoorwill Gap Books, her only business competitor, stepped through the doorway. From the first time they'd met in his bookshop, before Harper moved to Whippoorwill Gap, Bryan's intensity had made her uncomfortable. She agreed with her friend Gina that he was a handsome man. But something about the way he looked at her, almost as though he had claims on her, set her on edge. Harper's entire body stiffened with its now habitual reaction to him.

As he came toward the checkout counter, she stopped herself from stepping back. But today, his sky-blue eyes struck her as pleasant. In fact, she wondered that she had ever found them threatening. Maybe she had been unfair to him. Thinking back to the shop's Grand Opening, she remembered Bryan's help. He had even brought carnations afterward to celebrate her success. Perhaps she should lighten up.

"Hello Bryan." She injected more warmth than customary into her tone. "To what do I owe a visit?"

He stopped in front of the counter. "Hi Harper. When I closed shop for the afternoon, it occurred to me that I haven't been by to check on you for a while. I've been wanting to see how the business is faring. Is there anything I can do to help you out?"

Harper shrugged her shoulders, gesturing around the shop. "Business is a bit slow right now. Sometimes I'm super busy, but then I go through dry spells like today. If you have any tips, I'd be happy to hear them."

He smiled. "My store is going through a slow spell, too. Most of the summer tourists come to hike, fish, and kayak. They are not usually here to curl up and read. I don't know how it was for Frank back when he ran your shop, but summer is my slowest season. I tend to do best in the fall. Restaurants, campgrounds, and the family fun industries get a boost during the summer. But I'm positive things will pick up for the two of us in the fall."

She gave him a genuine smile. "Frank left a few records, but I'll be honest with you, I've never gone through them. Same shop, different business model. I'm relieved to hear you think things will pick back up in the fall."

The ice broken, they chatted for a bit, comparing clienteles, which titles were selling well, and which genres were apparently losing steam. When Harper glanced behind her, the clock indicated five minutes to closing time. Bryan, too, looked at the time, then straightened himself from where he'd propped his arms on the counter. Then, he reached into his shorts pocket and pulled out a small object wrapped in tissue paper.

"I know it's time for you to close, so I'll be on my way. But before I forget, I found this at an estate sale. It reminded me of you, so I picked it up. Don't worry," he added as though sensing her wariness. "I got it for a steal, but something about it made me think you might like it. If you don't want it, I'll drop it off at the Bric 'a' Brac. They're always interested in things like this."

He placed the package on the counter between them. On picking it up, Harper found the small package surprisingly heavy. After unwrapping the fabric, she uncovered a small pocket-sized mirror with a fierce-looking swan engraved on the lid, the initials "SC" above them. Harper felt astounded. The mirror was the same size and shape as the one she'd received as a child from her beloved Grandma Sophie.

She gasped. "Oh, Bryan! It's beautiful! Where was this estate sale?"

He seemed both dazed and gratified at her reaction. "My dad passed away recently. The family hired an auction company to sell the contents of his home. They found this in his attic. None of us had ever seen it before, and none of us wanted it. But it reminded me of you, so I bought it at the family discount. If you'd like to have it, it's yours." He looked down as he shuffled his feet, then looked up again, and said in a quiet voice, "It's a gift, free and clear—I don't expect anything in return. I just thought it was too nice to not be appreciated."

As she ran a finger over the raised swan, she said, "It's gorgeous. I have no idea why it would remind you of me, but I love it. And I do appreciate it, really. It reminds me of one I've lost. It was a gift from my grandmother." She stroked it thoughtfully. "Did you have any relatives with the initials 'SC'?"

"No, none that I know of. I suspect it belonged to one of my grandmothers originally, but neither of them had those initials when married or single. Maybe it belonged to a forgotten aunt or someone so far back we don't remember them. Or it could have been picked up at a yard sale at some point. Both my parents were yard sale and flea market enthusiasts." Then he snorted and chuckled. "Honestly, knowing a few of my relatives, it could have been stolen."

Harper smiled. She didn't really care where it came from. The mirror brought a glimmer of happiness for the first time in nearly a week. And that he had thought of her was sweet. When the clock behind her chimed six o'clock, closing time, she was still staring at the mirror in her hand.

"Well, I'll be going so you can get on with your evening." His voice was light. "I'm glad you like the mirror. Give Walt my regards."

And with that, he was out the door and heading uphill toward Main Street. Harper locked the door behind him and pulled down her repaired shade. She watched him thoughtfully through the plate glass until he was out of sight. She nearly turned away but paused to observe a tall, elegant woman with long, straight black hair pass by, following in Bryan's footsteps up the empty street. She was clad in jeans and a white shirt. On her head, she wore an outlandish white cowboy hat that appeared to be covered in long white feathers. Harper had never seen either her or a hat like that before. By this point, she knew most of the locals by sight. She shrugged. The woman must be a tourist.

When she turned back to the shop, she found Piper sitting on the checkout desk, watching her. She walked over to show her the lovely mirror. "Look at this, Piper. Doesn't it remind you of Grandma's mirror?"

Piper's brows knitted in concentration as she examined it closely. "They are similar, it's true. I wonder that Mr. Greene would give you this. Did he ever see you pull out the old one?"

Harper stopped, trying to remember. "I don't know. I suppose it's possible, but I haven't spent a lot of time around him, so I doubt it. He said it reminded him of me, and I have no idea why it would. Really, I'm not sure why he would buy me a present at all." She could feel her cheeks growing warm. "He knows I'm dating Walt. Or at least, that I was."

Piper placed the mirror back on the countertop before jumping to the floor. "It's been a while since we've chatted. Have you seen Walt at all since Monday last, Dearie?"

A dull ache spread through her chest. "Not once, even from a distance. And I haven't heard a word. I don't know what to think." She picked up the mirror and placed it in her skirt pocket, where its weight felt pleasingly familiar, then she headed up the stairs behind her friend. Once they settled into the kitchen with tuna salad, crackers, and fresh vegetables spread on the pink tablecloth, Piper wondered if perhaps Walt would stop by later that evening.

Harper set down the radish she had been about to place in her mouth. "Piper, I'm sorry, but I really don't want to talk about Walt right now. It's easier for me if I expect nothing."

Piper gathered the dirty dishes and changed the subject. "Ivy talked with you earlier today, did she not? We all plan to scout

out Olivia's trails tonight, just to make sure things are clear for her hikes tomorrow."

Harper rose to her feet. "Goodness, Piper! Bryan's visit distracted me. I forgot all about Ivy's warning! Thank you for cleaning up. I think I'll head out to find Olivia now to let her know to be watchful."

Piper nodded. "Good idea, Dearie. Do keep your wits about you while you're out and about. Times like these are not to be taken lightly. Some of us will stay here until you return, to make sure you make it safely back inside."

Harper patted her friend's shoulder, then picked up her keys and her phone. "I will. I'll see you later, Piper."

After glancing around but seeing no sign of Walt, Harper pulled out her phone, then settled into her truck. She did a quick search for Whippoorwill Gap Books, then clicked the call link, not expecting an answer since Bryan, too, was closed for the day.

"Hello, this is Bryan Greene. How may I help you?"

Harper clutched the mirror tightly in her hand. "Hi Bryan. It's Harper. I wanted to thank you again for the mirror ..."

His voice instantly warmed. "Harper! I didn't expect to hear from you. I figured you'd be out with Walt."

Harper closed her eyes. "No. Listen, would you like to meet after work tomorrow for a walk?"

"That sounds like a plan! I take a walk at Gap Park every evening, weather permitting. How about seven o'clock?"

She paused, but ignoring her doubts about the wisdom of this move, plowed ahead. "Okay. I'll see you then."

On clicking off her phone, she put the truck into reverse and headed out to see if she could find Olivia before sunset.

Chapter 6

WHEN HAWTHORNE MATERIALIZED IN front of the kitchen sink early the next morning, Harper spilled half the contents of her coffee mug in surprise. She grabbed a paper towel and wiped the spill while he regarded her with his soulful black eyes. Once she took her seat again, he got directly to the point. "I know you're disturbed at Walter's absence of late, Harper. But do you not think it premature to abandon him for another suitor?"

Harper clacked her mug onto the table before she began to pace the kitchen in agitation. "What makes you think ...? How did you know ...?" She stopped abruptly and stared at him while releasing an audible outbreath. "Really, Hawthorne, I'm surprised at you. Walt and I are not married, you know. He's free to do whatever he wants and so am I. Besides, your assumption that I'm looking for another suitor is a bit of a stretch, don't you think?" She drummed her fingers on the counter as her waist-high friend continued to observe her in unperturbed silence. Despite his lack of height, his solemnity made him a formidable presence.

After an uncomfortable pause, he continued. "As we have stressed to you of late, Walter is a good man. He has a long history among us. Perhaps you are unaware of some of that history's relevant aspects. But even that shouldn't matter. He has been good to you. And since you obviously care for him, perhaps you should grant him the benefit of the doubt."

Harper stared out the kitchen window where the sun's rays spread over Birdsong Theatre across the street. She'd given Bryan little thought and a wide berth before his visit yesterday. But the mirror he brought had seemed to be a sign. He'd been right, she loved it. But now, out of respect for Hawthorne, she stopped to consider her motivations for calling him. Did she wish for a new friend, or did she want to hurt Walt the way he had hurt her? Would he even care if she became friends with Bryan? The thought of Bryan's face as she'd thanked him for the mirror also flashed across her mind's eye. Was it possible he hoped for more than friendship?

Hawthorne moved toward the kitchen entrance. "I only want you to consider the possible consequences of your actions." He stopped talking to nod hello as Earl Grey walked in. Then he turned back to Harper. "As do we all, I wish your happiness. A good day to you." He bowed to her, then Earl Grey, before flickering from sight.

"How are things going, Lassie?" Earl Grey asked in a subdued voice, his pointed red cap in his hands.

Harper pressed her lips tightly together before she answered. "Are you here to chide me as well?" Of the nine Fae in the bookshop's troop, Harper had thought Earl Grey understood her best.

"Hawthorne already warned me about spending time with Bryan. How did you both know? Never mind ... he got the point across. But Earl Grey, Walt and I are not married! We've never even discussed being exclusive. It's just worked out that way."

Earl Grey settled himself on a stool, then placed his hat back on his head. "May I have a grape?" he asked, eyeing the table.

"Yes, of course," Harper flopped into a chair and scooted the bowl of grapes in his direction. Then she buttered a piece of toast and held it out to him. He accepted with simple thanks. As his calm cheerful face soothed her irritated spirits, she topped off her coffee mug.

"I'm sorry for being so crabby, Earl Grey. My nerves are on edge. I haven't seen Walt in over a week."

He continued to eat, pausing only to comment, "Excellent toast and butter, this. Could I trouble you for a bit of jam?"

Harper pulled out a jar of raspberry jam from Great Green Grocer's up the street and passed it over with a spoon.

As he munched, Harper filled the silence. "I'm not trying to make Walt jealous by taking a walk with Bryan Greene, if that's what you're thinking. I just want to make a new friend. I realize now that I've been too dependent on Walt."

The gnome licked the butter and crumbs from his fingers before answering. "I do understand your stance on this issue, Lassie. All will become clear in time. But you know how I feel about Walter. I'm sure he wouldn't be making himself scarce without a good reason ... an honorable reason," he added.

"Is that what Hawthorne was talking to you about?"

Harper's eyebrows shot up. "Oh. You two didn't have a plan before you showed up this morning? I thought you two were tag teaming me."

Without smiling, Earl Grey gave her a stern, pointed look, then shook his head no.

She dropped her eyes to her hands. "Okay, then, I'll confess. I asked Bryan Greene to take a walk this evening. He brought me a thoughtful present yesterday. I assumed you had heard about it."

When he shook his head, she continued. "I decided after he left that it would be good to get to know him better." Harper began pulling lettuce, cucumbers, and red cabbage from her refrigerator. "I'm making a salad for lunch today, since Piper appears to be out. Would you like one?"

"Hum? Oh, yes, Lassie. I'd be delighted. But no dressing for me please. You know how it upsets my tummy."

Harper nodded absently. "Actually, Earl Grey, Hawthorne seemed to disapprove of my seeing Bryan again. Is taking a walk with someone else so terrible?"

Earl Grey's bottom lip thrust forward for a moment. "Why no, Harper, of course it's not terrible. But it is surprising. I thought you didn't care for the Greene Man."

Harper chopped the cucumber with unnecessary force. "Maybe I've been unfair to him. After all, I never got to know him. And even though I've been chilly toward him, he's been polite, and even thoughtful to me. What's wrong with making a new friend?" She picked up the slices and tossed them on beds of lettuce in two bowls.

"Well, nothing. But don't you think it's possible, especially considering the gift he brought you, that Bryan Greene may be interested in more than friendship? How might Walt feel about your new friend?"

Harper rolled her eyes. "Oh, Earl Grey. Don't be so old-fashioned! Walt doesn't own me! That's what Hawthorne hinted at. And it's not fair, you know. How much could I mean to Walt when he hasn't bothered to get in touch with me for over a week? And as for Bryan, trust me, Earl Grey, I know how to keep people at arm's length when I need to."

Earl Grey thoughtfully munched a radish before answering. "All I know, Lassie, is that Walt is a good one through and through. If he's not been about, I'd say there's a reason. Just promise me to be careful. You don't want to ruin your happiness or the happiness of a good man."

"Good grief, Earl Grey! I'm not planning to marry Bryan. I'm just taking a walk with him!"

The gnome polished off his bowl of garden produce and stood on tiptoe to deposit his bowl in the sink. Then he wiped his hands on his pants legs.

"No need to get yer drawers in a knot, Lassie. We care about you, that's all. Be cautious; be aware."

"Rest easy, Earl Grey. I promise I won't elope with Bryan Greene this afternoon."

Earl Grey gave her a wink and a rueful grin, touched the side of his nose, and disappeared.

Harper straightened the kitchen. In her bedroom, she decided to wear a pair of cotton knit navy pants, a loose tan t-shirt, and a pair of sneakers. Then she carefully made up her face.

She missed Walt. She missed his wry sense of humor, his common sense, and the feeling of safety he gave her. Without him, she felt like a sweater-set shell without its cardigan.

She missed those amber eyes, which had pulled her from the first time she'd seem them. She wanted to tilt her head to look up at him. She wanted to admire his strong, wiry build. But most of all, she wanted to experience the feeling that he found answers to the secrets of the universe in her eyes. Perhaps most of all, she missed their romantic late-night flights over the rolling mountains.

Still, no one is perfect, so a few things about him annoyed her, too. His fastidiousness could be trying. While his clothing was casual, he couldn't bear a mess around him. He had a habit of walking along behind her, straightening things as he went. But his secretiveness bothered her most. Harper had told him about her lonely childhood, her hopes, dreams, and fears while growing up. He knew almost as much about her relationship with her deceased husband Tim as she did. It was true that he had listened to her stories with touching attention. He provided sympathy or encouragement as the situation demanded, which was nice.

But he'd shared nothing in return. Other than the fact that he'd lived in the same region for over two hundred years, she knew little about him. For all she knew, Delaynie could be an ex-wife. The fact was, they could be married now. But what hurt her most was the fact that she had no idea.

While his mystery had been part of his allure, it now struck her as selfish, even sneaky. By the time she'd slicked on a coat of light-colored lip gloss, the relationship seemed foolishly one-sided. She'd been too trusting, and at her age, she should have known better.

A new friendship would provide the distraction she needed. And should Walt come back, he'd have to deal with it. After all, he'd abandoned her first.

Back in her bedroom, she lifted the swan mirror from the nightstand. That this mirror had the identical weight as Grandma's struck her as miraculous. Grandma's mirror had been of Fae construction with magical components. Though unlikely, was it possible this one, too, was magical? She looked in the glass. "Grandma? Are you there?" she whispered.

With no response, she slipped it back in her pocket. She was being silly. Wishes counted for little; this mirror held no magic. Though Grandma cared, she wasn't watching from the other side.

Just before Divine Coffee's three o'clock closing time, Harper decided to go grab a cup of tea and say hi to her friend Deanna, the proprietress. It had been a while since she'd been in the coffee shop. While there, she'd ask if Deanna had seen Walt lately.

Harper was happy to see Nate working behind the counter. The blue hair dye he'd used when she first met him had washed out, revealing a light shade of strawberry blonde. It was the summer between his junior and senior year of high school. Harper had missed seeing his sister Abby, who had been such a cheerful presence behind the counter until she'd accepted a job as a nurse, just after graduating college in May.

Nate's friendly greeting lifted her spirits. She liked him, and though she knew he would prefer to work at the bookstore to the coffee shop, she didn't need the extra help. As she studied the chalkboard menu, Deanna popped through the kitchen door. Harper greeted her friend warmly and asked for a glass of iced tea to go.

"Heading back to the bookshop?"

Harper nodded.

Deanna smiled. "Wonderful! Nate can close today. How about I get drinks for both of us, and we take them over to your place? We'll sip and chat. What kind of tea do you want, Harper?"

Harper looked over her friend's shoulder. "Iced green jasmine will be great."

She pulled out her wallet. Deanna waved her hand away. "Oh no, you don't! You head back over to your place, and I'll be over in a few minutes."

Harper nodded and wished Nate a good day before she went back to the Robin's Nest. Within five minutes, Deanna had arrived with two tall iced teas, one green and one brown. Harper sighed at the first sip. "I don't know your secret, Deanna, but everything you make tastes perfect."

Deanna's eyes danced. "I'll tell you the secret, My Friend. It's love. Now, it's been too long since we've had a chat. What's been going on? I understand Olivia has already opened her outdoor adventure business."

Harper nodded. "Her first day was about three weeks ago now. I'm proud of her. But I'm also a little worried." She hesitated before plowing on. "You've heard about the weirdness going on right now, I guess."

"Weirdness?" Deanna looked out the window and nodded to the robins hopping on the shaded sidewalk, one corner of her mouth turned up. "What could possibly be weird in Whippoorwill Gap?"

Harper silently cursed herself. She'd been told to keep the pellets to herself, but she assumed Deanna would know about them. While she tried to think of a good pivot, Deanna solved the difficulty. "You're not referring to those giant pellets that have been turning up around here? Apparently, a tourist stumbled across one over near Old Man Mountain yesterday. And that reminds me of something else that's been bothering me. What's happened to Walt? He hasn't been in the coffee shop in ages." She peered at Harper. "Something going on?"

Harper winced in pain. But she recovered herself and answered in a flat voice, "I don't know, Deanna. I haven't seen Walt in almost a week now myself. To be honest, I was wondering if you had heard anything."

Deanna put her cup down. "I've never had more than a day or two pass without Walt stopping in to see if I need anything. I hate to bring this up, but when I heard about that pellet yesterday, I wondered if the remains inside could belong to him."

Harper's blood froze in her veins as she stared at her friend in horror. "Oh Gosh, Deanna, I never thought of that!"

Deanna reached over and placed a warm brown hand on her shoulder. "Hey, it's okay, Harper. I'm sorry, I shouldn't have been so blunt. Don't worry. It couldn't have been Walt. I heard later the bones belonged to a female." Though they were alone, she spoke in a whisper. "In fact, you know that middle-aged couple that spends most of their days just walking up and down the highways? They've been living in a tent behind Gap Park since last summer. Social Services offered to put them up in the tiny house village on the other side of town, but they refused. Anyway, no one has seen either of them for days. Folks are wondering if they were two of the victims."

Harper knew exactly who she was talking about. It was rare to drive anywhere around town without seeing them, together or apart, often pushing a rusty shopping cart. Suddenly she felt sick. "How did you find out about that, Deanna? Olivia found a pellet days before her business opened. I would have told you, but we were told to keep quiet about it."

Deanna looked at her hands. "Dashawn heard about Olivia's discovery shortly after she found it. I don't know who told him, and I didn't ask. Word gets around. A customer told me about the one they found yesterday. It's safe to assume almost everyone around here knows what's going on by now. I blame that for the business slowdown over the past few weeks."

Harper hadn't known that Deanna's business, too, had been slow. She sat still, thinking. "Do you have any idea how these pellets could be formed, Deanna? I mean, obviously we have a psychopath on the loose, but how are they managing to mimic an owl pellet?"

Deanna shrugged. "I don't know. One of my helpers told me all the Fae around here suspect the Otherworld might have something to do with it. But they aren't positive about that either."

Harper nodded. "That's what F-Troop says. They suspect the perpetrator may be from the Faery Realm, but they have no proof."

"Well, that brings us back to Walt. You don't know where he is or what he's doing? I mean, he didn't say anything?"

Harper took a deep breath. "No, Deanna. The last time I saw Walt, he was in Puckett's Park talking to this woman named Delaynie, who'd been coming in the shop asking for him."

One of Deanna's eyebrows shot up. "Delaynie? Who's that?"

Harper frowned, and she answered in a strained voice. "She first showed up about three weeks ago. She's super tall and I must admit—she's gorgeous. She has long, flowing black hair with white streaks, round, almost black eyes, and a perfect hourglass figure. She asked for Walt first time she came in and he went out to talk to her for a few minutes. Of course, I asked him who she was. He would only say she's someone he used to know. I didn't want to pry and figured that would be the end of it, so I dropped it.

"But then she showed up several days later near closing time to talk to him. He left with her and never came back that night, even though we had a date." Her voice caught and she swallowed to get it working again. "The last time I saw him, he was talking to her in Puckett's Park a few days after that. I haven't seen either one of them since."

"Have you looked for him?"

Harper picked up her empty cup, wiped it with a paper towel, and threw it in the trash. "No, I haven't. He knows where I live. When he's ready to talk with me, I guess he'll stop by."

Deanna folded her lips together and glanced out the window before speaking. "You and Walt have been a couple for over six months now, Harper. I think you have the right to know what's going on."

After clearing her throat a second time, Harper answered tightly, "I did ask him. Since he was evasive and refused to give me a straight answer, I assume he doesn't want me to know what's going on." She took a jerky breath, then began again, her volume rising. She thrust her chin forward. "Anyway, it's okay.

I have other friends. In fact, Bryan Greene and I are going for a walk in Gap Park this evening after closing time."

Deanna leaned back, giving her a keen look. She sighed. "Do tell? Well, under the circumstances, I suppose Walt has no right to be upset. But Harper, I'd move carefully. Walt's ..."

"I know, I know. Walt's a good guy. Everyone keeps reminding me of that. And until this week, I thought so too. But now I'm not so sure. Don't worry, Deanna. I have no intention of starting a romance with Bryan Greene. I just want a new friend, that's all. Besides, he might be a good resource for my business."

"Okay, Harper. I do understand why you're upset, but emotional upheaval can make people vulnerable to bad decisions. I'd hate to see complications crop up where they can be avoided."

"Thanks, Deanna. I'll keep that in mind. But you don't need to be concerned about Bryan. We're colleagues. It benefits us both to be friendly."

The clock behind Harper chimed four and Deanna said her goodbyes. Harper still had a few hours to fill before her walk with Bryan. She wished Biscuit were here. The little beagle mix made such good company. But with Olivia taking him to work, Harper no longer got many chances to dog sit. In fact, he now wore a Bright Cloud Adventures bandana around his neck and earned his keep as the business mascot. It was good for him but did nothing to ease Harper's loneliness. Maybe Bryan would help fill the gap.

Chapter 7

HARPER TURNED HER TRUCK into Gap Park's primary parking lot with five minutes to spare. Though the park was only a mile from her house following a straight line, maneuvering around the intermediate buildings would have made it a thirty-minute walk. She had two reasons for avoiding the extra walk. One, she had no desire to make that trek alone at nightfall with a killer in the vicinity. And besides that, she didn't want to give Bryan an excuse to walk her home.

The evening was sunny and seasonably warm, providing a welcome change from the rain that had hammered the region all spring. Immediately she spotted Bryan sitting on a picnic table underneath the large shelter, watching for her. A leash connected him to one of the most picture-perfect dogs she'd ever seen. Her opinion of him rose immediately. She'd never suspected Bryan was a dog lover.

At seven in the evening, two hours of daylight remained before the sun set. Families dotted a nearby playground; small children buzzed about the equipment with shouts of joy. On the nearest ballfield, a little league baseball game was ready to start. Harper scanned the sizable crowd for familiar faces. She felt gratified on seeing a few.

As she slammed her truck door, she threw up her hand at Bryan, who was making his way over with the slender, long-haired, black and white dog. Harper couldn't help but notice that Bryan's black knit shorts and heather gray t-shirt showed his shoulders and trim waist to good effect, and while he appeared to be in good shape, he was far from muscle-bound. He wore a pair of walking shoes with only a wristwatch for a nod to fashion. He looked good.

But his dog stole the show, with its silky fur waving back and forth as it trotted up to Harper. Settling on its haunches, it looked up at her with a doggy smile as though begging her to rub its long ears. Harper waited to be introduced. Bryan stopped beside the dog, pulling the leash short. "Hi Harper. Meet Leda. Leda, this is Harper."

"She's beautiful." Harper leaned over to stroke the dog's chest. Though the name Leda was familiar to her, she couldn't remember where she'd encountered it.

"She is that—beautiful inside and out," Bryan responded. He stepped back until Harper and Leda finished getting to know one another. "I don't know if you come here often, but there are several trails to choose from. Do you have a preference?"

Gap Park, the largest of the parks in town, wasn't as familiar to Harper as Puckett's Park, near her home. She walked to the welcome sign to study their options. The River Walk was out of the question this afternoon. They wouldn't have time to complete the lengthy trail, and it was too secluded for her liking today. Several bike trails were also available, but she wanted to avoid dodging people on wheels.

"How about the inner loop?" she asked. The two-mile walkway meandered through the park's facilities, in plain sight of everyone.

"Sounds like a plan," he said.

Harper scratched the dog behind her ears for another second. "I like dogs, but I don't know a lot about them. I'm assuming this one's a pure breed."

Bryan smiled down at the dog, obviously pleased. They were standing close enough for Harper to detect that his clothes smelled pleasant, like clean laundry. "You have a good eye," he said. "She's a saluki, one of the oldest dog breeds in the world. I got her a couple of years ago, and she's been wonderful company. Looks like she approves of you, too," he added as Leda began to wag her tail while leaning against Harper's legs.

Harper laughed, genuinely pleased. "What a good girl!"

"There's an enclosed dog park at the far end of the trail." He stuck a hand in one of his pockets and pulled out a tennis ball. "We can throw a ball around for her when we get there. She loves that."

They strolled behind the playground, past the crowded ball field, a Frisbee golf course ahead. As they passed the field, Harper's head jerked upon seeing the woman with copper-colored skin and long dark hair she'd seen on the street yesterday afternoon. Today she wore the large feather-covered white cowboy hat. The brim was enormous. Their eyes made contact for a split second before the woman turned back to the crowd. Harper felt strangely unsettled by the eye contact. Though the feeling wasn't unpleasant, she sensed that woman had read her thoughts.

The park hugged a line of trees that stretched toward the fire department at the top of the hill. Harper noted that the soccer fields, bathed in golden light, were empty this evening except for a small group of teenagers playing an informal game. While she loved Puckett's Park, this offered a nice alternative for evening strolls. Maybe she should come here more often.

She wondered if Bryan had heard about the recent crimes. But when he distracted her by asking if she'd gotten anything interesting for the bookstore lately, she forgot about it. After she described an old copy of an Evans-Wentz book she'd recently chanced upon, he nodded.

"That sounds amazing. I've heard the name, but I'll be honest, Harper, I don't know much about folklore—poetry is more my jam. I've got to admit though; I envy that you can spend time at work trying to find rare and vintage books to resell. I collect old poetry and literary criticism books for myself, but it's a hobby, not something I can do at the store."

She smiled. "You know, it's interesting. When I bought that shop, I expected to sit around reading books for fun all day. But honestly, what I've enjoyed most has been building up the folklore collection. If Frank hadn't already had such an outstanding selection of those books, I'd have probably wound up collecting titles in the performing arts or classic literature or something. But after I read a few folklore books I found in the shop, they hooked me."

She was quiet for a few minutes, thinking. "I hate to admit it, but I might have made a few serious missteps without the help of Quinn Ellis from the college folklore department. Do you know him?"

Bryan rewarded her with a lyrical laugh. "Of course I know Quinn! He's one of my most loyal customers. Anyone who deals in books anywhere within a few hundred miles of here knows him well. But his interest in my shop is likely different from yours. We never talk about folklore when he comes in. Instead, he's always after me to order titles from obscure sci-fi authors, especially in the lost worlds and time travel subgenres. He's an interesting guy. Most of the time, I enjoy talking to him." He looked over at her; his mouth twisted in a wry grin. "But he can be a little too persistent at times."

Harper laughed and readily agreed. "I'm sure this sounds ugly, but I really didn't care for Quinn when I first met him. He's too intense and, well, pushy for my taste. But now that I've gotten to know him, I tolerate him a little better. And I've been really surprised that he and my daughter Olivia have become fast friends."

Bryan looked straight ahead. "When I first met your daughter in your shop this spring, I was shocked at how much she reminded me of you, when you were her age."

Of their own accord, Harper's feet stopped moving. "How do you know what I looked like back then?"

Bryan slowed, then turned back to her. What he said next was startling. "I knew you before you moved here. You don't remember me, do you? Of course, I don't know why you would. The last time we saw each other was decades ago."

Harper's jaw dropped as she stared at him. They had reached a fenced-in vacant field with a sign that said, "Dog Park: Please Help Us Keep the Park Clean" over a dispenser of disposable doggie bags. He opened the gate and leaned down to let Leda off her leash. She stayed close to their legs until he'd closed the gate behind them and pulled the tennis ball from his pocket. Leda watched intently, craning her long slender neck as he pretended to throw it a few times before finally hurling it an impressive distance. He nodded to the panting dog. "Go get it, Girl!" Then she took off with such speed and grace, Harper momentarily forgot everything else.

Leda quickly returned and gracefully dropped the ball at Bryan's feet. "Good Girl," he said, throwing the ball in a different direction.

Harper frowned, then prompted, "You said we've met before?"

He kept his eyes on his dog as he dropped to the ground, crossing his legs to get comfortable. Harper lowered herself to the ground a couple of feet to his side. The curiosity made her antsy. She was about to guess that they had met in college or maybe while she lived in Raleigh. But before she formed the question, he answered.

"I'm from Winterfield too. When we first met, you were a big kid—nine years old. You probably never even noticed me because I was only five then." When Harper knit her brow, straining to remember, he added, "You used to come into my grandfather's hardware store with your grandmother."

He turned his startling marine blue eyes toward hers. She remembered taking trips to Winter-Greene Hardware with Grandma Sophie when she was a child back in the seventies. The store, old-fashioned even then, closed after Harper graduated college. She recalled the smell of old wood, the sound of creaky floors, and the sight of shelves that lined the tall walls with rolling ladders the staff would climb to fetch items Grandma Sophie had requested.

When they'd stopped by the hardware store, Harper usually carried a book from either the library or a bookstore she and Grandma had visited earlier in the day. Impatient to enter the stories, she had read while she waited, paying little attention to either the store's contents or its other occupants.

Now she stared at the grass trying to remember seeing a young boy there. The last time she was in the store, she would have been around nine years old. Once Grandma Sophie disappeared, Harper couldn't remember ever going in there again. Bryan said he was five years old when she was nine. That meant they were only four years apart. She'd thought him much younger than that. Studying his face with surprise, she blurted, "You're fifty-four years old?"

He threw the ball again for Leda, then shrugged. "Like I said, I'm four years younger than you. Before I turned five, Grandpa didn't take me to work much, but I guess I was quiet and manageable enough by then that it was tolerable to have me around. I spent most of my Saturdays there. He found things to keep me busy."

Harper felt completely blindsided. "So you knew my Grandma Sophie?" she asked. Her throat constricted.

He nodded, eyes bright. "Yeah. I liked your grandma a lot. She came in sometimes without you. She always said hello to me and asked me what I was up to. Sometimes she'd slip me a piece of candy or one of the cookies she'd baked. She introduced me to you once, but you didn't seem very interested."

Leda had returned to them, dropping first the ball, then her torso to his feet. Now she sat panting, her front legs daintily crossed before her. After he patted her head, she rested it on his knee and stared at him with adoring deep brown eyes.

Harper compressed her lips while watching the dog. "I'm sorry if I snubbed you back then. But I'll be honest—I never was very social."

Bryan smiled. "It's okay. You always had a book in your hand, even then. Actually, I credit you with my becoming a reader and a bookseller."

"No way. How do you figure that?"

Harper heard metal clanking and turned as a man she recognized from Chamber of Commerce meetings entered the field with two hound dogs. Leda jumped to her feet and trotted over to them as the man raised his hand in hello. Bryan called, "Hi Jim!" The man began briskly pacing the perimeter of the field while the three dogs raced one another toward invisible goal posts.

"That's my tax accountant and bookkeeper, Jim Ottawa. Ever since his heart attack a few years back, you can find him here walking his dogs after work, every day, rain or shine. I'd recommend him if you need an accountant. His business is Early Bird Accounting, up past the library."

Harper shook her head. "I already use the one on Oak Street, just a few doors up from me. I'm happy with them."

She distractedly plucked several blades of grass. "Bryan, why haven't you mentioned that we'd met before?"

His eyes followed Leda. "I guess I wanted to see if you would remember me first. When you didn't, it seemed kind of silly, and a little embarrassing, that I remembered you, but you didn't remember me."

She shook her head. "Well, embarrassment must be contagious. Now I'm embarrassed that I didn't remember you. But I'm happy to have a fellow Winterfieldian for an acquaintance. You said that I influenced you to become a reader and a bookseller. Is that really true? How could I have influenced you so much when we never talked?"

He tilted his head to the side, rubbing his jaw on his shirt. "My family weren't scholars, Harper. They weren't even readers. None of them. I was the youngest kid in a family of five. I had two older sisters and two older brothers. They all took after my parents who were athletic, no-nonsense people. Maybe they were a tad on the wild side. You might know one of my brothers—Greg Greene. He graduated with you."

Harper nodded. Everyone knew Greg. He was a football player who had definitely walked on the wild side.

"My sister Anne was a basketball cheerleader. Our oldest brother Paul dropped out of school in the eleventh grade, as soon as he turned sixteen, to work in one of the furniture factories. My other sister, Regina, dropped out in twelfth grade when she became pregnant. She married her high school sweetheart, and they went on to have two more kids. They're still married, happily it seems."

"I think I do remember Regina, she was a year behind me, I think ..."

He shrugged. "But the point is, none of them read. My granddad, the one who ran the hardware store, read the newspapers every day. But that was it. I'd never set foot in a bookstore or in a library before I started kindergarten. But I watched you, while you read your books, while waiting for your grandmother. You always seemed so smart ... so together. I was dying to know what kept you so interested in those pages. Then, once I learned to read myself, I never looked back. I guess I always felt connected to you, because of that."

"Well, Gee, that's touching, Bryan. I was a lonely kid too. Especially after Grandma disappeared. I was an only child, and I wasn't close to my parents. I was too shy to have many friends."

Through peripheral vision she could see he never took his eyes off her, but she pretended not to notice. Then he spoke again. "I have a confession to make."

Uh, oh, she thought, her stomach fluttering with a mixture of curiosity and dread. "Are you sure you want to tell me?"

"No. But I'm pretty sure I *need* to tell you." His cheeks developed strawberry-colored blotches. "I always had a crush on you. From the first time I saw you. I knew that you didn't even know I was alive, but to me, you were like a fairy-tale princess or something. You were so beautiful, quiet, and poised. You didn't shout for attention like so many other girls. And I guess the fact that you were older made you exotic for me too."

Her nervous grass-plucking ramped up as her chest began to tingle. "Wow. I wasn't expecting that. Really, Bryan, I had no idea."

"How would you have reacted if I'd told you earlier?"

"I'm not sure," she admitted.

"Well, there's your answer. I wasn't either."

She decided to change the subject. "Are you sure you can't remember anything about that mirror you gave me? Why did it remind you of me?"

"Swan Lake."

"Huh?"

"You had the lead role in Swan Lake when you were in high school. I always thought of you and swans as part of a package after that." He shrugged. "What can I say? I was a hopelessly romantic kid. I guess some things never change."

He stood abruptly as the accountant waved goodbye, he and his dogs headed back up the trail.

"I'd planned to walk you home, but I see you drove. I live on Poplar Street, only a few blocks from the park's entrance. I don't want to scare you, but you might want to park close to your door tonight and head in without lingering. Rumor has it there are some weird things going on around town."

Glad for the change of topic, Harper brushed the grass from her seat and followed him through the gate, Leda in the lead, her leash reattached. "Oh? What would that be?"

"You don't know? Everyone says your daughter found the first set of remains."

Harper looked at him, aghast. "You mean that's all over town? One of the policemen must have talked."

He raised an eyebrow. "It's standard procedure to let the public know when something potentially dangerous is going on in their community. Actually, the story has been reported on the AM radio station. Do you ever listen to WAHG?"

Harper shook her head.

"Well, two more sets of remains have shown up in the past few days. A couple of people who were living in a tent near here are missing. They don't know who the other victims were yet. I don't know what kind of sick person would do something like this. But it's strange. In the last two cases, a witness swears they saw a massive great horned owl near the vicinity where the pellets were found."

Harper forced her face to remain impassive. "A great horned owl? Probably just a coincidence."

"Maybe, but it had a distinguishing mark, a large round white patch on its chest. I don't know if you're aware of it yet, but strange things happen in these mountains sometimes. Just be aware. I'd hate for you to get hurt." He paused as they both heard the eerie trumpeting sound she had heard first at Walt's.

"What was that? I mean, I assume a bird of some sort, but do you know what kind?"

Bryan tilted his head to the side. "I'm not positive; it sounded musical, didn't it?"

While it merely sounded like a loud and lonely birdcall to Harper, she nodded as they approached the parking lot. "Well, thanks for the walk, Bryan. I'll keep that in mind."

"Hey, thanks for calling me! I hope I didn't freak you out. I'd like to be friends. Would you be interested in meeting for a walk again sometime?"

"Hum? Oh, sure, Bryan. I'd like us to be friends too. But right now, I need to get home. With the news and all, I'd like to be safe inside before dark."

"Of course," he replied. "Call me if you need anything."

"See you. Goodbye, Leda!"

She patted the dog's head, then slid inside her truck, closing the door firmly behind her. Bryan and Leda stood beside her while she turned the engine. After a quick smile and a flick of her fingers, she put the truck in reverse then pulled away, still stunned at his revelations.

From her rearview mirror, she could see Bryan and Leda watching her from the park entrance until she topped a hill and they fell from view.

While his confession of his childhood crush on her had been disconcerting, she was more disturbed by the great horned owl sighted near the pellets. Worse, the owl had a distinctive large round spot on its chest. She knew an owl with a mark like that—Walt.

Chapter 8

WALT CLOSED HIS EYES, his only defense against the strident voice. "Guess who I saw while I was out and about in town this evening?"

When he remained silent, the speaker modulated her tone, making an effort to sound more pleasant, but as a result, he flinched.

"What's the matter? Aren't you even interested in who it might have been?" The voice switched again, this time mimicking a cartoonish schoolgirl. "But then, there's no reason to be interested. You're having so much fun with me you're no longer concerned about your past life. Right?" She giggled.

He kept his eyes tightly closed while he focused on keeping his breath slow and shallow.

To his ramping dread, the voice changed to that of a petulant child. "Really, Walt? I know you're awake. Open up those handsome eyes so I can see them."

Knowing resistance was futile, he opened his eyes, then forced his stiff body to sit atop his makeshift bed. As he did, Delaynie squealed, throwing her arms wide.

"I *knew* you were faking! Really Darling, there's no need to play coy with me. Anyway, as I was about to tell you, I saw that dreary little woman you hung around with before I arrived. What was her name again?"

She waited a second, but on getting no response, she beamed at him. "Let's see ... Heloise? ... No? ... Helpless? Horrible? No! It's Harper, isn't it? I saw Harper this evening. It was almost dark. Trust me, Darling, you needn't worry about her. She's taken up with a new beau in your absence. That didn't take long, now, did it?"

He closed his eyes again, stifling a groan. "You didn't talk to her, did you?"

Delaynie gave a wild squeal, delighted she'd gotten a response. "Don't worry, My Pet. They were in the town's big park. I kept to the shadows behind the tree line. She never saw me. But yes, as I said, the man she was snuggling up to was rather handsome. Perhaps you know him? Let's see ... curly black hair and, I must say, devastating blue eyes. If I didn't already have you for company, I'd have been tempted to scoop him up myself."

She giggled again. "In fact, I might yet. It would certainly heighten the excitement around here, don't you agree?"

As a wave of nausea washed over Walt, he struggled to keep a straight face.

"Dear Walter." Delaynie came closer, laying an icy hand on his face. "You've grown suddenly pale. Are you feeling alright?"

He swallowed his bile and murmured, "Fine, Delaynie. I'm fine."

She straightened. "Then I'll continue with my report. It was quite clear to me that Pretty Boy is completely smitten with her. If the sentiment isn't mutual yet, I have no doubt it soon will be, her being on the rebound and all. They were accompanied by a lovely dog, one of the more expensive breeds, I think. Perhaps along with the owner, I can bring the dog into our fold. Wouldn't that be marvelous?"

His stomach churned, but he struggled to appear calm. "I don't think that would be wise, Delaynie. Why go looking for trouble?"

She leaned back and smiled. "So sweet of you to worry. You're absolutely right; I should be careful." Then her voice hardened. "But I must tell you, Walter, I'm not fond of that woman. I simply can't understand what you see in her. She obviously cares little for you. If she did, she'd be out searching for you, wouldn't she? And if she really cared, I doubt she'd be out cavorting with another man so soon after you ditched her. Shouldn't she be sitting at home, crying or something?"

Walt could feel sweat forming beads on his back. If only she would end this. But he knew that wish was hopeless. Delaynie whipped out her cell phone and held the screen in front of his face.

"I know you'd never suspect me of lying. But I thought you might suspect I'm exaggerating, so I took a few pictures of the cozy little group."

He forced his eyes to focus on the phone in front of him. First was a picture of Harper and Bryan Greene walking together on a paved trail that he recognized in Gap Park. Delaynie hadn't exaggerated—the dog really was beautiful, but he'd seen it before. He knew it belonged to Bryan. In the next photo, Bryan and Harper sat side by side in a field behind a chain fence, apparently deep in conversation. While he was relieved to see they weren't sitting close enough to touch, he felt shaken at the engrossed look on Harper's face.

Before Harper came to town, he'd never paid much attention to Bryan. Between helping Deanna and Dashawn and keeping an eye on Puckett's Park, he'd had more than enough to keep him busy. And he'd been good friends with Frank Bailies, the previous owner of the Robin's Nest. From there, he got all the reading material he needed to stay occupied when he wasn't building furniture or writing a book himself.

Bryan first drew his attention when Walt surmised that the bookstore owner, like himself, was interested in Harper. After that, he had been vigilant when Bryan was around. But now, he hadn't a hope of keeping them apart. And really, for Harper's sake, he shouldn't wish to. She'd be better off with someone else to lean on.

Delaynie studied him as he looked at the photos. She tutted. "I know how it is to be disappointed in someone." Then her voice took on a dangerous edge. "But believe me, there are ways to deal with these situations." He shrank back as she began to stroke his hair. "Give me enough time and you'll forget all about her."

Chapter 9

HARPER WATCHED AS RAIN dripped incessantly from the awnings in front of the bookshop. Ten days. It had been ten days since she'd lain eyes on Walt. Neither had any of the Fae seen him on their flights around the region. She considered it most likely he had vacated the area and was now off—who knew where—with Delaynie. No other logical explanation presented itself.

But still, Harper was worried. With more daylight hours due to the approaching summer solstice, Harper would have time after work to fly by Walt's house for an aerial view. Maybe that would give her some idea of what might be happening.

As far as Harper knew, no new pellets had been discovered over the past few days. Good news, especially for Whippoorwill Gap businesses. She was relieved for Olivia, who had booked a few group day hikes and a couple of half day kayaking expeditions. But her heart plummeted on remembering Bryan's revelation about the owl seen in the vicinity of the crimes. If it had been Walt, could he be connected to the murders? She shook her head; it didn't bear thinking of. And she remembered how upset he had been on discovering the pellet. If he'd had prior knowledge of it, he'd unlikely have been so distraught.

Business had been brisk for most of the morning, likely due to the rain. Gray, cool days made her customers long for books and coffee. She expected Bryan's shop got a similar weather dependent boost. Unlike her, he didn't have the advantage of a coffee shop next door. But his shop stood two doors down from the winery. She thought that combination might work just as well.

But now in the late afternoon traffic had slowed, and no one new had come through the door for over an hour. She checked the clock behind her; it was nearly five, leaving one more hour to closing time. She heated water to make herself a cup of butterfly pea tea, her latest favorite. After a moment's reflection, she added more water to the hot pot. Should any customers straggle in, they might appreciate a cup as well. The snack bar she'd had for lunch was small, but she wasn't hungry yet, so she decided to forgo a snack and eat a proper meal at closing time. She wondered what Piper might have prepared upstairs.

The entrance bell rang as she poured hot water into her mug. "Welcome to the Robin's Nest," she said, turning to the door. She froze as she saw Delaynie's tall form, stunning in a black silk jumpsuit topped by a white raincoat, standing on the threshold. Without apology, the woman spattered drops of water from her coat's matching umbrella all over the shop entrance.

With no one else around, Harper found no distractions to cover her shock. "Can I help you?" she stammered, placing her untouched mug on the countertop.

The woman's dark red lips turned up in a thin smile below her gathered brows. "Hello to you too. Yes, I'm hoping you can help me with something. Have you seen Walter lately?" Delaynie looked about inquisitively. "Or is he here now, by chance?"

Harper's face relaxed as hope spread through her chest. "No, he isn't. I haven't seen him since ..."

She started to say *last* Monday, the day she saw the two of them in the park together, but she caught herself. She swallowed, amending her response. "The last time I saw Walt, he left here with you. So it's been a while since I've seen him."

Delaynie folded her umbrella loosely, then propped it beside the door. I need to get an umbrella rack, Harper thought with irritation. Today was the first time anyone had ever shaken an umbrella out in her entranceway rather than on the sidewalk.

Delaynie walked to the counter, where she looked down her straight, patrician nose at Harper from a height supplied by nature and the strappy heels on her feet. Her long red nails curved inward, clicking as she rested them on the countertop.

The woman's face contorted into an unpleasant mask: part grimace, part sneer. "We were enjoying a lovely time together until he disappeared a couple of days ago. He's been staying at my rental. I don't know where he lives—silly of me not to ask him to show me his place, wasn't it? But we've been so busy. I thought maybe you'd know where his home is. He'd complained of an upset stomach, so I suspect he's gone home, not wanting to worry me. He's so thoughtful. I want to find him because I hate to think of him lying in bed, alone, and feeling poorly. I could make him a pot of soup, mop his brow, or whatever one does in these situations."

Harper, concerned that Walt might be sick, was on the verge of offering to take Delaynie there herself. But before she spoke, she spied Earl Grey over the woman's shoulder, waving his arms while shaking his head no. His eyes held a warning.

Harper came to her senses, and her chest began to burn as she moved her eyes back to Delaynie. How dare this woman come in here and ask her where Walt lived. If Walt was sick, she'd be the one to check on him—and she'd do it alone. She reigned in her voice with well-practiced control. "Walt is very private. I'm sure he wouldn't appreciate my telling anyone where he lives."

Delaynie took a step back, drawing herself to her full height. Behind her, Harper could see all nine of her friends as they flickered into, then out of sight. Knowing they were there helped fortify her spine.

Delaynie's eyes narrowed as she elevated her upper lip. "Is that so? Well, I suspect his trust in you has diminished now that you're seeing someone else."

Harper's breath fled her lungs, leaving her dizzy. "Excuse me?"

"I was at the park a few days ago for an evening stroll. Walt was feeling poorly that night, so he didn't go with me. I saw you out walking with that handsome black-haired man and a beautiful dog. You all looked very intimate, quite cozy. Walter was surprised when I told him."

She smiled, taking in Harper's frozen face. Then she leaned forward as though revealing a cherished secret. "I thought he ought to know that you're doing fine. He was worried about you, you see. I thought I should relieve his distress."

Harper's face flamed with heat and her heart began to pound. With effort, she held her right hand back from slapping the woman's pale face.

"How dare you?" she spat. "While you were spying on me, you should have paid closer attention. Then you would have noticed that there was absolutely no physical contact between the two of us. That man you saw is a friend of mine. And that's all. Maybe you don't understand friendship. Because if you really cared about Walt, you wouldn't want to hurt him needlessly by telling him about it."

Instead of angry, the woman appeared delighted. "Oh, I've hit a nerve, haven't I? Trust me ... Harper, isn't it? Trust me, Harper, I have known Walter much longer than you have. I think, of the two of us, I understand him better. He's so sweetly naive. But I'm a good judge of character. You'll be fine without him. And I think you can lay off the wronged party routine. If you care so much, why aren't you willing to help him out now?

All you need to do is tell me where he lives. Think about his welfare for a change ..."

Harper walked to the door and picked up Delaynie's umbrella, holding it toward the door. "Closing time. You need to leave." Behind her the door opened, and Harper turned; she was relieved to see Olivia standing there, Biscuit in her arms. The dog stared at Delaynie with a low growl.

Olivia, as usual oblivious to the tension in the air, shushed him. "Hi Mom. Do you have plans for dinner tonight? I have a few ideas I'd like to run by you."

She nodded at Delaynie, who had moved to the doorway, taking her umbrella from Harper's hand. "Don't worry, Harper. I will find him," the woman said stiffly. "And when I do, I'll be sure to let him know you could not care less about his welfare." Then she slammed the door behind her before stepping into the rain and disappearing past Divine Coffee.

The dramatic exit got Olivia's attention. She stared after her, then leaned down to turn Biscuit loose. "What was that about?" After barking at the closed door for a few seconds, the puppy pivoted, running to Harper, wagging his tail. Harper picked him up and buried her face in his fur.

Then she consulted the clock. "Lock the door and pull the shade down, Olivia."

Once upstairs, the Fae joined them in the kitchen where Harper forced herself to calm down. "You all heard what she said down there? If he is sick, it probably didn't help to think I've already moved on. What an evil woman! I can't relax now until I check on him. I think I'll fly over to his place right now. Olivia, if I'm late getting back, I'll call you tomorrow."

Hawthorne moved forward, addressing her calmly. "I advise you to wait, Harper. Since this woman followed you before, she may be baiting you now, hoping you'd head to his house. She could easily follow at a distance and ascertain where Walter lives.

Her story strikes me as peculiar. I've known Walt since he was a young fledgling, and I've never heard him mention this woman. And you are correct. He highly values his privacy, so I think it unwise to take any chances on leading her to his refuge."

Nearly wild with worry and frustration, Harper buried her face in her hands. Lily and Alida led her into the living room, Olivia and Biscuit following, while Piper and the Brownies hustled to get dinner on the table. Harper bounced her feet in agitation while perched on the sofa's edge. "But what if he really is sick? Or hurt? I'd never forgive myself if I could have helped him, but I didn't."

None of them spoke. Harper finally looked up. "And I can't bear that he might think I don't care about him."

Ivy cleared her throat while Olivia patted her mother's shoulder in sympathy. "As usual, I think Hawthorne's advice is sound." She paused while Biscuit jumped on the couch and then scrambled into Harper's lap. "I hesitate to voice our concerns. But there are things about Walt's past that make us fear for him. It may be wise for you to lock your outer doors for the present. Flying alone may also be risky—especially at night."

Harper's voice betrayed her alarm. "What is it that worries you about Walt? You know as well as I do, he would no more harm an insect than I would, despite our owlish traits. And Ivy, you told me yourself that owl shifters aren't evil."

When none of them would return her gaze, Harper felt a chill go up her spine. "Out with it! Do you think he may have had something to do with the murders?"

She scanned their faces. All were clearly miserable. Silence descended in the apartment; even the noises from the kitchen had ceased. She felt an overpowering desire to open the balcony doors and hurl herself into the darkening sky. Instead, she forced herself to breathe and think. "You're asking me to release

Walt to his fate. Okay, for tonight I'll do that. But if you discover anything about him, promise you'll let me know."

"Leave it to us," Ivy said as they all rose. "We'll scout out what we can and be back later."

Piper and Ash moved closer to Harper. "Ash and I will stay here. After dinner, we will fill Harper in on the Swan Clan. She needs to know a little about them." Then Piper addressed Harper. "While we can't answer all your questions, we'll share what we know."

The rest of the Fae nodded before flickering from sight to reappear as robins on the balcony's rail; from there they took flight, heading up the river. Olivia got up and locked the balcony's door, then turned to face her mother. "Okay, Mom. What's going on?"

Harper pulled the swan mirror from her pocket. How could this have anything to do with these crazy events? She looked miserably at Piper, then at Ash. "Dinner can wait. Tell me what you know."

Chapter 10

BRIGHT LIGHT BLAZED INTO Walt's eyeballs, an unwelcome intrusion after untold hours of near darkness. A split second later, the brightness dimmed as Delaynie's shadow fell between him and the light's source. She curled an icy hand over his forehead; the curved nails scraped his skin when she pulled it away.

"There, there. How are we doing?" She helped him into a seated position, then straightened the bedding where he'd been lying. He groaned, leaned against the cool, rough wall, and closed his eyes. Her hand left his head.

"I've been so worried about you." Her voice wrapped him in cotton candy sweetness. "I stopped by to see if your old girlfriend would tell me where you live. Even though I explained why—that you are ill and need help, she refused her aid. I made it clear that I only wished to pick up some supplies to make you more comfortable."

She squeezed his shoulder. "I'm sorry to tell you, My Darling, but she didn't seem concerned in the least. Not only did she refuse to take me there, but when I waited around after I'd left to see if she might check on you, she never left that dismal red brick building." When she paused, Walt, knowing she wanted a reaction, kept his eyes tightly shut.

After two weeks with Delaynie, exhaustion had become a constant companion, making everything more difficult. If only he could figure out a way to leave without making things worse.

"Well, the trip illuminated two things. First, you don't have to worry about interference from her. Second, I'd say your little mouse-girl is quite happy with her new beau. Honestly," she giggled, "I think I'd be happy with him myself."

Her voice took on a less girlish tone. "Unfortunately, I don't have time to waste on side pursuits. We have big plans, don't we, you and I? Before long, we'll flee this boring little hamlet for some truly wild spots. Walter, you don't know what you've been missing. I can't wait to share it all with you."

She moved to his side, muttering. "Damn that woman, I really wanted to visit your home before we left." Then she brightened. "Oh, well. If I can't find out from her, and you won't tell me, I guess we'll just have to leave with the clothes you're wearing. It doesn't really matter, because where we're going, we'll have little need of clothes at all."

She laughed with delight, then paused on seeing Walt looking at her through half-opened eyes. He closed them again at her hate-filled glare. She closed her fist around a handful of his long, tangled hair. "Don't worry, Darling Boy. I know you're feeling poorly, but I've got wonderful news for you. I have something delicious to tempt your appetite."

With a sour taste flooding his mouth, he swallowed painfully. She tutted over him. "I'm so sorry you're still under the weather. But this should put some starch into you."

Walt closed his eyes, shame creeping over him as one tear slid from beneath an eyelid.

"Oh, come now, we'll have none of that," Delaynie coaxed. "It's time to return to your roots, Walter. You're wanted back among our kind. You can't deny your kith and kin, as they say.

But first, of course, we must build up your strength. This snack I brought you should give you a nice boost."

Walt's lips folded tightly together of their own accord.

"Don't be stubborn," Delaynie's oily voice trickled into his ear. "I only want you well again. It's a shame that selfish woman you feel so fond of doesn't share the sentiment."

Walt opened his eyes reluctantly, wondering, despite his revulsion, what Delaynie had brought to tempt him. Potato chips were doubtful. As she reached for her bag, he saw its sides undulate. His stomach threatened to expel bile, these days its only contents.

Delaynie shoved her hand inside. Walt heard a squeal as she pulled out a large, live rat and held it up by its tail. With mighty heaves of its muscular body, it struggled in vain to free itself. Delaynie's grip held firm.

Walt shrank as far away as he could manage while the rat strained to reach her arm to bite her. Revulsion caused Walt to retch.

"No?" She asked sweetly. Walt could smell the fear radiating from the animal only inches from his head. Delaynie smiled. "No wonder you're not well. Who could survive on nasty human food? I promise you'll get no more of that from me. Last chance, My Darling ... Oh well, your loss is my gain."

She hiked the frantic creature above her head, then looked down at Walt with eyebrows raised in a question. "Last chance ..." She lowered it toward her face then lifted it up again, turning to Walt with a grin. Curling himself against the wall, he let out a groan.

Delaynie tilted her face to the rat, then opened her mouth wide and swallowed it whole. Despite his horror, Walt watched her neck grotesquely stretch to allow the entire bulk down her gullet, her powerful neck muscles forcing it down.

Finally, with a guttural ruck, she lowered her head, smiling at him again.

Then she gave a raucous belch. “Exquisite. Give it a try and you’ll be hooked.”

With that, she shook her hair loose from its severe bun and turned to face Walt once again.

Chapter 11

As Harper and Deanna began their second loop around the Puckett's Park trail, Deanna voiced her objections. "While I normally defer to the Fae, I don't agree this time, Harper. Maybe you should check by Walt's house to see if he's okay. Delaynie can't be watching you every minute. You could go in the middle of the day when it's safer."

Deanna's common sense and good humor often saved Harper from her own worst impulses. So now she listened, intently, desperate for a fresh perspective.

"I'm willing to bet good money that if you go over there, you'll find out that Walt hasn't deserted you at all. I'll bet he's hiding out from her. That woman sounds a little crazy to me—following you to see where you're going and who you're meeting. I wouldn't trust anything she says."

"To be honest, Deanna, I'm afraid to go over there. I'm not convinced that Walt is in danger. Knowing Walt, it's more likely he's off having a think or whatever men do when they need a break. He probably doesn't want to see me any more than her at this point."

She felt, rather than saw, Deanna's side-eye. "You really believe that? You think Walt would have a problem choosing between the two of you? 'Cause I don't believe it. I've known Walt a long time and I know he's crazy about you. You're the only woman I've ever seen him act interested in. He's never even talked about another to me or Dashawn. So I don't buy it. Our Walt is loyal, trustworthy, and true. I'd lay my life on that."

Harper sighed. She knew Walt had worked with Dashawn, a local contractor, on building projects for years. While she knew Deanna meant to be reassuring, Harper had little faith in her assessment of the situation.

She tried to explain. "Deanna, you know my backstory with men. First my father took off with that floozy Marie, leaving my mother and me behind. Then Tim had an affair with Melissa, while I was pregnant with Olivia. Nothing from my past convinces me that Walt wouldn't reunite with an old girlfriend. I'm just being realistic. People can fool you. Sometimes they aren't what they seem."

Having picked that sore as much as she could stand, Harper changed the subject. "Have you heard any strange birds or other noises around here lately, Deanna?"

Deanna's face scrunched. Though clearly still annoyed with Harper's obstinacy, she gave the question some thought. "No, I haven't. But then, I'm not outdoors a whole lot, and it's loud in the coffee shop. And I'm a sound sleeper. Dashawn has commented that he thinks a swan or two may have passed through the area, which is unusual. Maybe you've heard them too?"

Harper nodded. "Yeah. Maybe that's it. They're really loud and I've heard them mostly at night. I just wondered if I was the only one." She didn't want to get into the Swan Clan with Deanna just yet. The whole thing felt hazy. After talking to Piper and Ash about them, Harper felt as though one more layer of confusion had been lain atop an already befuddled mess.

"I don't think you're hearing things. Dashawn doesn't have an overactive imagination. If he's heard it, too, I'd say it's real enough."

As they approached their back doors, Deanna slipped through her garden gate. Through the gap, Harper could see neat rows of green tomatoes, squashes, and basil in red clay pots. Deanna turned, care engulfing Harper from her warm, brown eyes. "I need to get inside and whip up some dinner, My Friend. Would you like to join us?"

When Harper declined, she added, "Try to have a little faith; give Walt some time. I think things will work out yet. In the meantime, if there's anything I can do to help, you know where to find me."

With her friend's kindness and support, Harper's spirits felt buoyed. "Thank you for listening, Deanna. That means more to me than anything else could right now."

After squeezing Harper's shoulder, Deanna slipped inside the gate and closed it behind her. Harper looked up at Deanna's balcony, where Deanna's husband Dashawn leaned over the railing. "Hiya, Harper!"

"Hi Dashawn! Pretty evening, isn't it?"

"Couldn't be better!" He held up a book and a glass that apparently held iced green tea. Harper offered a thumbs up before heading back into her own building. Inside, she spotted boxes of books that Walt had helped stack just over a month ago when the flood threatened them. The sight caused her to choke with sadness. Despite the danger and the fear, Walt had been by her side; it now felt like a blessing to have gone through the experience.

Once inside her apartment, she found the balcony door open. The soft, early summer air wafted through the screen, stirring the curtains. She looked out over the river at Walt's empty sycamore tree as tears sprang to her eyes.

Piper called from the kitchen. "Welcome home, Dearie. I've made you a nice mushroom flatbread with a crisp green salad and your favorite lime vinaigrette dressing. Come on in and let me pour you a nice glass of pinot grigio to go with it. And that's not all—I have another surprise for you."

Harper turned to the whip-thin little being who had looked after her for the past year. "Thank you, Piper. What's the surprise?"

Piper took a step back as Olivia and Biscuit appeared from down the hallway. "Surprise!" Olivia said with a smile.

Despite her heavy heart, Harper felt grateful. With her renewed close relationship with her daughter, at least something in her life was working.

She pulled the ponytail elastic from her hair and smoothed it down. "Well, this is a treat! To what do I owe the honor of dinner together for the second night in a row?"

"Dinner last night didn't count, Mom. With everything going on, I never got to talk to you about my new business ideas. Do you feel like talking about that tonight?"

"Olivia brought in mushrooms, and I thought you'd enjoy flatbread, Dearie," Piper announced while placing the food on the table.

"They're local morels, Mom. I picked them up at Evie's."

Harper sat Biscuit back down on the floor after snuggling his tan and white neck against her face. He wriggled happily as she washed her hands.

The food was delicious. Olivia, happy that her business was off to a promising start, turned on the charm, something Harper had witnessed her do with others, but not with herself. As she looked around, she thought: perhaps, rather than focus on Walt, she should look at what was right with her world for a change.

While they ate, Olivia asked Harper what she thought of Olivia offering wilderness survival and kayaking classes in addition to adventures tours. She'd gotten the idea from Quinn, who seemed to need instructions in the most basic skills. Harper agreed it wouldn't hurt to try. Olivia said her next step would be to see what Ida Barker, an older woman and savvy business leader who lived down the street, thought. Ever since Olivia had come to Whippoorwill Gap, Ida had served as a mentor. Her mother felt honored to be consulted first.

Once they finished eating, Olivia patted her stomach. "Piper, that was amazing!"

Harper placed her empty wineglass on the table and nodded. "Piper's meals are always perfect."

Olivia slipped Biscuit a stray mushroom. "Have you heard from Walt?"

With the question, Harper's mood crumpled to the ground like an unsteady kite. She needed a break from the pain. "No, and I don't expect to. In fact, I've been thinking about the whole situation, and I've come to one conclusion, at least."

She hesitated as Piper and Olivia turned attentive faces her way, then began, "My life is my responsibility. I love Walt, but he's free to do as he likes. What he does shouldn't change things for me. Instead of depending on someone else for my happiness, I've decided to rely on myself."

"Okay, that sounds reasonable," Olivia said slowly. "But what does that mean in practice?"

Piper bustled about without comment, setting mugs of steaming hazelnut decaf coffee at every place, then seated herself again.

"It means that I'm going to be open to new ways of spending my time. I plan to sign up for a beginner's Pilates class. And there's Bryan Greene. He's been supportive of the bookshop and ... it turns out, I knew him before I moved here, I just didn't remember him. Did I tell you that?"

Olivia's jaw dropped. "No! You didn't tell me that. Did you know about this?" Piper nodded, her eyes trained on her coffee mug.

Harper filled her daughter in on her conversation with Bryan in the park. She made light of his confession that he'd had a crush on her when he was a child. In truth, she had avoided him since that evening. But the more she thought about it, the more convinced she became that there was nothing wrong with being his friend. They were both adults now. A new friendship would benefit them both.

"And I think I'll get more involved with community activities, like the Chamber of Commerce, maybe. If I'm going to keep busy, I need worthwhile activities, right? I've also considered starting some sort of literacy project, like donating books to local schools or something." She stopped and looked at them with her chin up, ready to face any objections they may have had.

Olivia expressed her enthusiasm by sitting straighter in her chair. Harper thought perhaps she saw a new respect budding in her eyes. "Wow, Mom. All those ideas sound great to me." Then she stood and kissed her mom on the top of her head. "I'm all for it. Heck, I'm glad to hear it!"

But then as she gathered Biscuit's harness before leaving, she hesitated. "But Mom, I'll have to admit, I'm fond of Walt myself. He's been a big help to me, and I'd be lying if I said I didn't like him. If he should show back up, I think you should at least be willing to listen to him."

Piper nodded her approval. "Well said, Olivia!"

Harper nodded. "That's fair, I guess. I should have known you've come to care for Walt too. Okay. If Walt comes back around and wants to talk, I promise to listen."

Olivia rewarded her with one of the blinding smiles for which she'd been famous in her previous life. "Well, it's been a good evening, but Biscuit and I need to get going. Quinn's coming over to play chess tonight."

Why was Harper so startled whenever Olivia announced she was getting together with Quinn? Maybe there was something about Quinn that Harper had completely missed, but for the life of her, she couldn't figure out the glue that would pull her glamourous, athletic daughter and a scholar of an obscure subject together. But she knew better than to let Olivia guess her reservations. Still, she couldn't stop herself from saying, "He is? You two sure have been spending a lot of time together lately …"

Olivia laughed. "You just said it yourself, Mom—a person needs friends. Besides, believe it or not, Quinn is a lot of fun. I think his odd little obsessions are endearing. Thank you for the dinner, Piper. I'll show myself out." With that, she picked up Biscuit and disappeared through the door.

Harper headed to the living room, where she was surprised to find all nine members of F-Troop gathered in the dimming light that filtered through the doors and windows. "A visit from everyone at once? I hope this isn't about something serious. Did you discover anything on your rounds last night?"

Earl Grey began, "Unfortunately, we did not, Lass."

Alida flitted over, her pale green skin glowing in the dusk. "We just thought you might need some company."

But now Harper pulled her swan mirror from her pocket. She wanted to talk about last night. "Piper and Ash told me a few things about the Swan Clan. They said members of the Clan usually show up when some sort of intervention is needed between the Otherworld and this one. And I do think it's odd that Bryan gave me this mirror right about the time I started hearing those swan calls. And I'm not the only one. Deanna said Dashawn had heard them too." She didn't tell them that she suspected Bryan had heard it as well. But she wasn't sure. He'd said it sounded like music to him. He must have heard something else.

They all nodded. "We wonder if Walt's disappearance could be tied to the return of the Swan Clan—if they have, in fact, returned. We nearly all agree that the mirror is of Fae origin. It seems an odd coincidence for Mr. Greene to give it to you just as a member of the Swan Clan seems to have arrived," Hawthorne commented.

Earl Grey cleared his throat. "Perhaps their reappearance is somehow connected to Walter's disappearance."

Harper groaned. "Maybe? I don't see how. This is all so confusing it makes my head spin. The fact is we know nothing other than a killer is on the loose and Walt is missing. But let's not talk about Walt tonight. I'm exploring options to help me carry on without him."

She looked around at their silent faces. "I must, or I'll go crazy," she added with a pang of desperation. Why were her reasonable attempts at self-preservation so hard for them to accept?

Then, as though at some hidden signal, they all stirred at once, like a picture come to life. "Let's share stories," said Hawthorne as they formed a circle. Taking the center, he recited Edmund Spenser's "Prothalamion." While listening to the long poem, Harper caught swan references and something about a wedding.

"Was that directed at me?" Harper asked. Hawthorne rarely did anything unpremeditated.

He tilted his chin toward the swan mirror lying in her lap, his expression unreadable. Her face turned red at the implications.

As though to break the tension, Ash stood briskly, and mercifully shared an old Cherokee legend of the chickadee, hardly a personal subject. From that point on, everyone relaxed. Harper forgot her problems in the joy of sharing stories and poems. Before the evening was done, laughter and jokes flowed freely.

With a new perspective, Harper felt reassured that better times were ahead, no matter what happened.

Later that night, when the last of the Fae winked out of sight, she slipped the mirror into her pocket where she gave it a squeeze. Then she walked to the balcony's door. After a brief hesitation, she locked it tight, then closed the drapes before heading to bed.

Chapter 12

THE FOLLOWING MONDAY EVENING, Harper parked her truck in the driveway of Bryan's remodeled Victorian cottage on Poplar Street. She recognized the sunbeam-yellow house with white trim and Wedgwood blue accents from the months she lived in a rental down the street, while her apartment was remodeled. She'd had no idea this house belonged to Bryan.

She walked toward the front porch clutching a brown paper bag filled with handmade dog treats for Leda from Great Green Grocer's, as a host gift. Each sweet potato–peanut butter flavored biscuit had been cut into squirrel shapes. She hoped the saluki would enjoy them.

She looked around his spacious front porch, decked out for summer in shades of blue, white, and green that coordinated well with the sunny yellow exterior. She had to admire his taste. Before she lifted the ring on the wrought iron door knocker, Bryan swept the door open, inviting her inside.

"Welcome to Chez Greene, Harper! Leda and I are delighted to have you for our guest tonight." Leda wagged her tail with a happy bark. On peeking into the doggie bag, Bryan insisted she give one to Leda right away. The lovely dog took it gently from Harper's hand, then collapsed on her dog bed by the living room entrance, where she began to gnaw it with dainty bites.

Glancing into the room, in which she'd expected to see an abundance of hunter green and brown, Harper was startled to see instead a room painted a delicate shade of mocha rose. Paintings of dancers graced the walls. A couple were framed Degas prints, but several others looked to be original works of art.

As she took it in, Bryan asked if she would rather have a glass of cabernet sauvignon or a stout. Harper chose the cabernet, her favorite type of wine. He placed one glass in her hand while carrying another himself, then led her back out to the porch, with Leda following behind. They settled into white wicker rocking chairs with a small, glass-topped table between them. While sipping the wine and watching the Poplar Street traffic beyond his maple-shaded front lawn, they talked.

"I hope you like Beef Wellington. It's one of the few fancy dinners I've managed to master."

She looked at him in wonder. "It's one of my favorite dishes," she responded. "Did you know that?"

He laughed. "Well, actually, I knew you liked it when you were young. I overheard your grandmother telling my grandfather that you liked it. I don't think you were with her that day, but they both seemed amazed that a young girl would like such a sophisticated dish. It was such an odd thing that it stuck with me. Your grandmother told Grandpop that you were her little soul-buddy ... that the two of you were alike, through and through. Anyway, I'm glad you still like it."

Instantly, Harper was transported to her grandmother's spacious red and white kitchen, which had been built in the late 1930s and remodeled in the '50s. She could see her grandmother pulling a heavenly smelling Beef Wellington from the small, sturdy white oven, while the steamy darkened windows behind Grandma underscored the perfect peace and happiness that a night with her grandmother always conjured for her.

She stared into the leafy green branches of the largest sugar maple tree in the yard. What an odd thing for a kid to remember, she thought. "I'm impressed. Your memory of childhood is keener than mine's ever been."

He laughed. "Not really. I only retained the memories that were important to me." His gaze lingered on her face for a second too long.

"Bryan ..." she began, setting down her nearly empty glass.

Before she could continue, he stood. "Time to check on dinner. We don't want it burned."

She got to her feet and followed him down a long hall, past a wide staircase and several closed doors to the back of the house, where she found a cozy kitchen done up in green, black, and white. It was old-fashioned, yet bold, and to her, held a more masculine air than either the porch or living room. Tucked into one corner was a darling little breakfast nook with a Formica table and green upholstered bench seating reminiscent of an old diner. Leda, she noticed, laid down just outside the kitchen's entrance.

"Oh!" She smiled, running her palm over the swirling tabletop, her earlier concerns forgotten. "Do we get to eat here?"

"Absolutely not! I've got the dining room all set for a fancy dinner for two. But, if it will make you happy, you can warm the nook while I get dinner on the table."

Despite her offers to help, Bryan insisted she relax as he banged the oven door open, then closed, and checked on pots and pans bubbling and sizzling on the stove. "We've got the beef, grilled green beans, mashed garlic potatoes, and yeast rolls. For dessert, I've got a surprise in the icebox. But I thought we'd take a break between dinner and dessert to either chat or play a game ... your choice."

Once he pronounced everything ready, Bryan led her through a tiny hallway, lined with cabinets and shelves, which he called the butler's pantry. From there they entered a small room painted a pleasing shade of leaf green, with a dark polished table and antique-looking chairs with black damask-covered seats. The dinnerware was a black and white toile pattern of swans in pastoral scenes. He had lain hunter green cloth napkins beside the tableware. A phrase that Olivia had often repeated in high school seemed to apply: The room was aesthetically pleasing.

Relaxed from the wine, she smiled as Bryan pulled out a chair for her. Then she nodded as he reached over to fill a fresh wine glass that sat next to a tall glass of ice water. After he seated himself, he raised his glass. "To new friendships!" She raised her own, lightly clinking it against his.

"Hear, hear!" she responded heartily. Really, she thought, who could object to that toast?

The food tasted scrumptious. The beef was perfectly seasoned and cooked exactly the way she liked it—medium well. He claimed to prefer it that way himself. As they sipped the last of the wine, she asked about the intriguing dinnerware pattern. She'd never seen one like it, though it looked vaguely familiar.

"Did this belong to your mother?"

He snorted. "No. My mother didn't own china. Her mother didn't either. They weren't fancy dinnerware types, and I promise you, neither were the rest of my family."

Harper nodded her understanding. "Mine neither. I mean, Grandma Sophie had china but never used it as far as I know. She used sensible brown earthenware dishes. It was nice enough, but not fancy. My mother owned china that she'd gotten for wedding presents, but it just sat behind glass in a dusty display cabinet. My parents never used it. In fact, I grew up eating off tan melamine plates with brown circles around the rims. They were practical, Mom said. Really, I think she just didn't care about homemaking. She was a businesswoman first. Keeping a cozy, beautiful home wasn't a priority."

After a good dinner and nearly half a bottle of wine, a question that had been forming in the back of her mind slid off her tongue without a second thought. "Have you ever been married?"

Bryan turned a guarded gaze her way. "Yes. I have. I mean, we're all encouraged to try it at least once, aren't we?" He shook his head. "Obviously it didn't work out for me. Melanie and I were only together for a couple of years before she took off. Said I was too dreamy for her." He snorted. "I think she meant I'd never make a lot of money."

Harper nodded. "Kids?"

"Nah. I have a niece, Autumn, who comes to stay with me sometimes. Sometimes people around here think she's my daughter. She's nine now. She likes to read and she's a good kid. We get along."

Bryan drained his glass and got up to clear the table. Harper helped carry dishes into the kitchen, where he loaded them into the dishwasher. Since he didn't offer to open another bottle of wine, Harper asked for a glass of water, which he gave her iced, with a slice of lemon. Through his back window, the sunlight slanted over a slate-covered patio, creating a pretty scene.

"How long have you lived in this house, Bryan?"

He paused, eyes to the ceiling. "Let's see. I bought it after my grandfather, my mother's dad, passed away, leaving me a nice chunk of change, for which I was grateful. My siblings were jealous, but they were never as close to him as I was. This was back in the early nineties and property values were just starting to inch up in Whippoorwill Gap. So, I bought it thirty years ago, give or take. I got it for a steal because it was in rough shape. I spent the first few years with iron in my water and paint peeling from the ceiling.

"But after the bookstore started making a profit, I gradually restored it. I did a lot of the work myself but what I couldn't do,

I paid a contractor to coordinate. I finished with the upstairs last year. I'd offer to take you up there, but that's one area I didn't have time to clean before you arrived."

Harper shook her head. "No need."

Once he'd cleaned the kitchen, the music, piped through house speakers, changed from cool jazz to classical. To that backdrop, they toured the main floor. Seeing no bedrooms, she assumed he slept on the second floor. She'd already availed herself of the half bath outside the kitchen and inspected the living room and the tiny parlor across the hall, which Bryan had decorated in true Victorian style, complete with authentic antiques.

One doorway remained unopened. Bryan placed a hand on the doorknob. "Of all the rooms in the entire house, this is my favorite." He whistled to Leda, who joined them from the living room, her tail wagging.

He threw open the heavy, dark-stained oak door, his eyes trained on her. The first thing Harper noticed was that clutter filled the room. Unlike the rest of the house, where everything else felt perfectly staged, as though for a set, this room felt lived-in. She felt he spent a lot of time in here.

Instead of bright, overhead lighting, wall sconces threw dim pools of light up and down the burgundy walls. A large wooden desk stood before the windowless interior wall. Bryan walked over and pulled a chain on an old-fashioned desk lamp, then lit lamps on tables scattered around the space. From the desk's chair, Bryan would be able to see through the wide, latticed window, which looked out onto the detached garage. The small building stood in shadow beside a massive oak tree now lit by the setting sun.

The remaining walls contained floor to ceiling bookshelves. While most had books crammed into every space, some held odds and ends that Harper had yet to explore. A well-stuffed black velvet sofa was separated by a coffee table from matching armchairs beneath the latticed window with an end table between them. Archival notebooks obliterated the surface of the long low coffee table.

She was distracted by Bryan, who appeared nervous as he took a seat on the sofa, setting his water glass on the coffee table. Then with ramrod straight posture, he gestured with twitchy motions around the room. He took a deep breath. "Please. Take your time. Look around."

With her curiosity aroused, Harper began by exploring the shelves to her left, intending to make an orderly sweep of the room. The books that greeted her were deluxe editions of classic novels. Nice, she thought. No surprises there. But on glancing back at his desk, she stopped short. There, looking into an upper corner of the room, stood a small replica of a bronze Edgar Degas ballerina sculpture. Debussy's "Clare De Lune" began to play softly through the speakers. It all seemed surreal. From the time she was a small child, she had been obsessed with that exact statue ... and that musical composition.

Her eyes wandered to the walls behind the desk, which were covered in handsomely framed paintings of more dancers. Harper knew enough about art to know that these had not been cheap. She bit her lip, then asked, without turning to face him, "Are you a fan of ballet or Degas?"

Bryan's voice was so soft, she could barely hear. "I've always been a fan of a particular dancer."

Harper's heart burned. She tried to pinpoint exactly what she was feeling; dread was part, but so was electricity. She turned to him. "Oh? Sounds like there's a story there."

He studied her face, then allowed his eyes to travel down her torso to her legs before finally laying them to rest at his own feet. "My grandpop told me you were a ballerina. I was so young I didn't even know what that meant, so he had to explain it.

I begged him to take me to see you dance, so we went to one of your recitals after your grandmother passed away. Even then, you took my breath away. I thought you were the most beautiful creature I had ever seen. I asked him to take me to all your performances until you went away to college at Wake Forest. Then, after I got my license, I drove myself to see you dance."

As Harper's eyes sped around the room, she saw that dancers weren't the only motif. There were also swans ... sculptured, painted, and embroidered on pillows.

On one set of shelves, she scanned the spines of lovely volumes of vintage poetry. As she moved closer to see those, she was distracted by the shelf beneath it. She stiffened on seeing a framed photograph of Grandma Sophie. Harper studied the picture. It was one she had never seen before. Oddly, the frame reminded her of the faery mirror that Grandma had given Harper for her tenth birthday, just before she disappeared. Still staring at it, she asked, "Where did you get this picture? And the frame?"

Bryan cleared his throat before answering. "I found it in my grandfather's house after he died. My grandmother died when I was a baby. I assumed your grandmother gave it to him."

"It's a lovely photo." From the clothing and hairstyle, she guessed it was taken when Grandma was in her forties, a decade or so before Harper was born. She and Mr. Greene must have been close friends for her to give him this. A shocking new thought occurred to her. "Do you think your grandfather and my grandmother could have been sweethearts?"

He cleared his throat. "I don't know. They seemed to like each other a lot. I know he was upset when she passed, so I wouldn't be surprised."

Though shocked, Harper forced herself to continue her investigation of the overcrowded room's contents. She came to a collection of books on Dante Alighieri, along with his works, in Italian and in translation. Harper knew very little about the Italian poet and philosopher.

She came to a couple of shelves of memorabilia he had collected. But instead of being from Bryan's life, she was confronted with relics of her own high school career. There were framed pictures of clubs in which she had participated, and her class's silk flower under glass. She shivered as the air-conditioning switched on.

As though in a place of honor, her senior year photograph, nicely framed with ornately engraved silver, sat on a shelf of its own. She swallowed. Not knowing whether to be flattered or threatened, she merely gaped at him. He patted the seat beside him. "Please. I have one last thing to show you."

Harper perched on the edge of the sofa, leaving room between them and poised to bolt should he do anything threatening.

Though he'd seemed nervous before, Bryan now seemed oblivious to her reaction. He picked up one of four acid-free photo albums stacked on the table in front of them. An archival box lay on the floor. He had spared no expense to preserve all this stuff. "Normally, I keep these in the closet, but I thought you'd like to see them."

Harper's heart began to pound. Bryan stood. "Can I get you another glass of wine? You can look through the pictures while I go get it."

"No, thank you."

"Oh. Well, how about a small glass of brandy? Or would you prefer a cup of decaf coffee?"

"Decaf," she murmured distractedly.

He left the room and Harper picked up the top album. When she opened it, baby pictures of herself, newspaper clippings from pageants her mother had forced her to compete in, and even dance pictures from her preschool years displayed themselves in neat rows. Where had he gotten all this stuff?

On laying it aside, she grabbed the next book, similarly filled with her elementary school memorabilia. She threw it to the couch beside her, picking up the next, where, without surprise, she found middle and high school photographs, programs, and other materials—all about her.

Nerves taut, she picked up the last album. Inside were her college, engagement, wedding, and birth announcements. There were also pictures of Tim and Olivia through the years.

Unable to focus on the photos in front of her, she sat still. What sort of person would cling to a childhood crush to this extent? And where had he gotten all these photos? Could he be some sort of psycho? Her eyes scanned the room for something to use as a weapon, just in case.

He walked back into the room with two mugs of steaming coffee, Leda padding in behind him. "You like it with cream, no sugar, right?"

That was the last straw. She stood, attempting to make her voice steely through her trembling lips. "What's this all about, Bryan?"

His shoulders gave an almost imperceptible slump. "I guess it must seem weird. Give me a chance to explain."

At his contrite expression, she softened her tone. "Oh, you're right about that. It seems beyond weird. How did you get all this stuff? I mean, where did you get my baby pictures? And why?" Her hand strayed to her pocket. As her fingers closed around the mirror, she felt it work its magic, flooding her with confidence and washing anxiety away. Instead of fear, she felt powerful.

"There's a term for this sort of thing, Bryan. It's called stalking." Later, she wondered what would have happened if Leda hadn't moved to her feet and looked up at her with soulful brown eyes, whining softly. But now, no longer afraid, she began to stroke Leda's long, silky coat.

Bryan released a heavy sigh. "My wife was right, you know. I've always been a dreamer. I told you I had a crush on you. But that really simplifies it too much; it makes it sound too simple, too juvenile." His eyes held a plea for her to listen.

"I remember the very first time I looked at you. I literally couldn't move. Really, Harper, I think you were the first truly beautiful thing I'd ever seen. I decided early on that I wanted to be worthy of you, to live a life as beautiful as you were. I understood, even then, that you would never want me in your life, but I could make you a part of mine, forever. You've been my inspiration. I'd never want to cause you harm or pain. If you hadn't walked into my bookstore on the day of the Whippoorwill Gap Christmas Parade, I'd have never contacted you."

She gestured to the albums scattered on the table, managing to keep her voice steady. "Where did you get these?"

"After you married, I visited your mother one day. I told her we were old friends and that I remembered her mother—at least that last part was true. She must have been lonely because she invited me in. We talked and she showed me all these things of yours that she had saved. She struck me as sad. You know, her health wasn't good. She let me borrow these pictures."

Vermillion splotches sprang to his cheeks. "I told her I needed them for a project at the high school. Now that I think about it, it's odd she did that. Maybe she just wanted to give me an excuse to return and visit again. Okay, I guess maybe I took advantage of her. But I spent some of my savings having them reproduced. As for the newspaper articles, I've collected them from the family newspapers since I was eight or nine years old. No one in my family ever noticed the missing articles. Later on I was on the high school yearbook staff. I had access to old photos of you from their archives. I did the same—I'd borrow them, have them reproduced, and then return the originals."

Harper sighed. She didn't feel bad for her mother. No doubt, her mom had never pulled out those pictures to look at them before the day Bryan showed up. She felt disappointed with her and irritated with Bryan. "I should go now."

His face contorted with pain. "I'm sorry, Harper. I hoped you'd understand." His hands stayed on one of the albums while he turned pain-filled blue eyes to meet hers. "I only want to be friends, but I do need for you to understand the truth. I'm not very good at hiding my feelings; it would all come out eventually anyway. Maybe I shouldn't have let you see it all at once. It was too much. I'm sorry."

She swallowed. "You think, from all this stuff, that you know me. But you don't know me, Bryan. Not really." She picked up a swan sculpture from a side table. "You think the parts I played in ballets represented me and how I felt. But it was all performance. I've never been serene ... or graceful. And if I was ever beautiful, which I doubt"—she inhaled a shaky breath—"I'm not beautiful now."

"I disagree," he muttered, his eyes glued to the statue in her hands. "Look, I messed up. And even if I got it all wrong, I still want to get to know you. Can we start over? Please?"

Leda moved to Harper's feet and placed a paw on her knee. Expelling a long, slow breath, while looking the saluki in the eye, Harper began to relax. Bryan obviously had an artistic soul. She knew what it was like to feel lonely and different. But when she'd had crushes on boys in the past, she had always gotten over them.

He stood. "Listen. I made French silk pie for dessert. I want you to have it. Can I wrap it up so you can take it with you?"

This wasn't the way she wanted the evening to end. She admitted to herself that she'd always been hard on people. "It's okay, Bryan. I'll give this more thought tomorrow. But right now, let's enjoy our coffee and a piece of pie. Then I'll be on my way."

Chapter 13

BEFORE SHE OPENED HER eyes, Harper wistfully longed to be a child again at Grandma Sophie's. Back then, she'd wake up to the smell of pancakes and bacon wafting up the stairs, undergirded by perked coffee. She'd snuggle happily into the white cotton sheets of her bed until Grandma called her downstairs.

While enjoying their delicious breakfast, she and Grandma would plan their day's quiet adventures. Sometimes they would go to the town's old red brick library with its green-tiled floors to check out books. Other times they would drive to nearby Greensboro for lunch and a movie, or perhaps they would visit a bookstore there. If they opted for the latter, Grandma always allowed Harper to pick one book to buy. Then, if the weather was nice, they might take a walk or stop for a picnic lunch.

Nothing they did was flashy or expensive. The much-anticipated yearly trip to see The Nutcracker performance by the North Carolina School of the Arts in Winston-Salem was the only exception. But no matter what the day held, Harper basked in love and safety. She didn't have to suffer through her parents' sour silences, or worse, their heated yelling. She didn't have to worry about creepy, hungover strangers she sometimes encountered lighting cigarettes in her parents' living room. Instead, she enjoyed fresh air, good food, and wonderful stories, all burnished with Grandma's beautiful smiles.

She decided that after enduring weeks of despair and confusion, she needed a day to recapture those feelings of security and comfort. Though Grandma, off in the Faery Realm, was no longer here with her, she had the Fae. And she had herself.

Her chest felt heavy as she remembered Grandma's picture and all the other fragments of her past life collected in Bryan's office the night before. Maybe she should be more worried about it, but she only felt sad. The man must have an obsessive personality disorder of some type. Nevertheless, the fact that he had known her grandmother as a child made him seem less scary, and more like a long-lost cousin or something.

As she thought it over, she realized Bryan now seemed surprisingly similar to Quinn. Ever since she'd met Dr. Ellis, she'd considered his compulsion to control her book collection as vaguely threatening. Yet Olivia found Quinn charming. Though disturbed by Bryan's obsession with her, she decided he wasn't a danger.

She threw the bedcovers back and looked up her music streaming service. After typing in "Swan Lake" and hitting play, she was calmed by the opening bars of Tchaikovsky's ballet. She'd performed the lead role of Odette and Odile in her senior year recital. She thought back over Bryan's revelation that he and his grandfather had sat in the front row during the production's opening night. He'd thought she was brilliant.

She smiled to herself as she went through warm-up exercises, surprised her aging body could still assume the positions. But she knew sentimentality had gilded Bryan's memory of the performance. Her major memories consisted of missed cues and adjusting Terry Macmillan's clumsy performance as Prince Siegfried.

Padding into the bathroom, she looked at her reflection in the mirror. As she leaned in to examine the laugh lines around her eyes and the frown lines in between, she stopped herself and backed away. No more of that, she promised her reflection.

She dressed for the day in a flowing skirt and light tee before heading for the kitchen. Piper wasn't there, but she had left a loaf of carrot–cinnamon bread and a tub of creamed cheese softening on the table. Harper pulled a container of fruit salad from the fridge and spread the white, creamy cheese across a slice of bread while examining her sweet little kitchen. Through the windows, she could see the tops of the red brick buildings across the street, and the bright blue summer sky above them, reminding her that she had an entire day to spend as she wished.

Before she started seeing Walt, her early days in Whippoorwill Gap had been good ones. But then, she'd been busy getting the shop and her apartment ready. Perhaps if she rededicated herself to the bookshop, she could recapture the joy she had felt then. Even better, she no longer felt spooked by odd happenings in the building, with the additional benefit of knowing her faery co-inhabitants.

Downstairs, she attempted to examine the Robin's Nest through fresh eyes. Over the past nine months, it had become overly familiar. First, she'd find her next book to read. She'd been making her way through all of Walt's A.E. Deere novels, but thought it wise to switch to something different now. A book called *Nine Lives: The Folklore of Cats* by Katharine Briggs caught her eye, and she placed it behind the counter to read later.

Next, she headed up the street to explore the tea selection at the health food store. Evie updated her stock every month. Later, instead of sitting on the balcony, she planned to read in her cozy office with a cup of tea beside her. On her outing, she purchased an eight-ounce sack of loose-leaf sencha tea to use.

Back in her apartment, while waiting for the kettle to boil, she picked up the phone and called an old friend and co-worker,

Gina, who still lived in Raleigh. The time had come to invite her for a visit, and Gina was delighted to hear from her. If it hadn't been for Gina, Harper would still be in Raleigh. She'd only visited Whippoorwill Gap at her friend's invitation over the Thanksgiving holidays over a year past. So much had changed since then.

"Oh, Harper, I'd love to come for a visit. But Jim and I have planned a trip to Italy during July. We'll be gone for three weeks."

Though initially disappointed, Harper was happy for her friend. She secured a promise for a raincheck, then Harper rang off, pleased to have something to look forward to at summer's end. Gina had always been up for anything. Besides that, she was easy to talk to. They looked at things from completely different points of view, and Harper wanted Gina's perspective on Walt and ... on Bryan.

It had been a while since she'd taken a physical fitness class. Since tomorrow was another day off, she decided to head over to Yo' Chicks, a studio across town, to sign up for a qigong class.

Though she'd planned to read, she found it impossible to settle down and concentrate. Casting about for something else to occupy her attention, she reminded herself she had been neglecting her spiritual health of late. She rummaged through a kitchen drawer to pull out two pillar candles, then lit them before settling on her bedroom rug to meditate. After a minute or two she popped back to her feet. As always, the promised serenity wanted no part of her. Even though naturally quiet and reserved, Harper found it impossible to sit still with nothing to occupy her attention. Maybe, starting tomorrow, she'd try again—for five minutes, tops—and repeat the ritual every day until she could manage.

To work out a little excess energy, she went to the park and made three solo trips around the park's trail. Later, after dinner,

Harper was relieved when the sprites, Alida and Lily, stopped by for conversation. Piper and Harper sat on the couch, watching as the smaller Fae zoomed about the room, sharing bits of gossip they'd picked up from the nearby lakes and rivers.

The next morning, Harper headed back down to the shop a couple of hours before it opened to see if inspiration for any improvements might strike. The first thing she noticed was the display of A.E. Deere books standing prominently near the doorway. The novels, based on local lore, attracted positive attention from newcomers.

But now pain clawed her chest as she remembered Walt's help the previous October during her Grand Opening. She refused to allow sadness a chance to pry its way into her consciousness. The time had come, she decided, for a refresh. The A.E. Deere books could go back in the folklore room out of sight. She'd think of a replacement display this afternoon.

Then the cookbooks caught her attention. She pulled a random one from the shelf. On flipping through the vintage 1960s entertainment guide, she wondered if she should invite Deanna and Dashawn over for dinner. Olivia was too busy to come over for dinner now that her business was picking up. Besides, it had been nearly a year since she'd had her next-door neighbors over for dinner.

But after pondering for a moment, she decided that instead, next Monday night, she would host the Fae to thank them for brightening her days and lightening her loads. Though they were outside much of the time during the summer and early fall, she could gather some of their favorite dishes, make oatmeal cookies, and pair everything with generous helpings of nuts and berries. They'd wash it all down with beer, wine, lemonade, and cream, each to their preference. It would be gratifying to concentrate on making them happy for a change. And her friends, never boring, would no doubt lift her spirits, too. She'd get to work on it that evening.

That evening, after she'd distributed the rag paper invitations that she had purchased from Evie, she threw herself into finding recipes and creating decorations for the event. All weekend her spare time went toward party preparations. For after dinner entertainment, they would play crowd-pleasing games like crack-the-whip until everyone was tired out. The game was so much more fun with her friends, who could literally sail around the room once they were flung from the tail end of the line. Once they were worn out, they could take turns telling a tale or reciting a poem, one of their favorite activities. Harper chose to read "Queen Mab" by Percy Shelley, feeling sure it would be a hit.

On the night of the soirée, her guests arrived in full regalia. Hawthorne had obviously washed his white ruff and cuffs in bluing, making them blindingly white. His leather boots were spotless, and a new turkey feather graced his hat band. Lily and Alida arrived with extra sparkles on their tutu dresses. Ivy wore a choker of green acorns, which set off her dark skin beautifully. Piper and Ash wore deer skins and linens so fine they resembled velvet. Earl Grey had his hair and beard curled and styled for the occasion. Even the brownies, Tiptoe and Tarryfoot, had worn breeches, blouses, and vests that looked newly made. Gone were the patches that had always adorned their clothing. Instead, fine embroidery work set off the hems of their bright red vests.

The evening went well. Though she knew they were still disturbed by Walt's absence, none of them mentioned him. And they quickly got into the spirit of the evening. They were Fae after all. They laughed, sang, and celebrated their bonds until well past midnight.

Just before two in the morning, Harper prepared for bed convinced that she'd turned a corner. She absolutely could create a joyful life for herself. Without another thought, she locked the balcony door carefully behind her and shut the drapes against the night. Once in bed, as she drifted into sleep, she told herself she no longer even missed Walt.

On arising late the next morning, Harper parted the balcony's curtains. Black clouds had moved in during the night, bringing the threat of heavy rain with distant thunder rolling in from the west. She opened the balcony door to savor the rain-scrubbed air sweeping down the mountainside.

As she stepped onto the balcony, she felt a tickle beneath her bare foot. Looking down, she saw a single large feather lying before the threshold. Picking it up, her chest seized in a spasm of anguish as she recognized Walt's feather pattern. She quickly scanned the park, hoping to catch sight of his form, either perched on his customary sycamore branch or sitting on his bench in faded jeans and a t-shirt. But both were vacant. Then, clutching the feather to her cheek, she bent over double as a heartbroken cry tore itself from her throat.

Chapter 14

A WEEK WENT BY while Harper, reeling, processed the fact that Walt had, in fact, come by her apartment ... and found himself locked out. There was no one save herself to blame. She'd flown by and around his treehouse since, several times. Once, she'd even landed on the porch. But finding no sounds or signs of life within, she had left without trying to enter.

As the week passed by without another sign, Harper's mood had slipped from sad to morose. When Bryan called the following Monday morning, Harper had accepted his invitation for a walk with him and Leda around the Poplar Street neighborhood. At this point, she felt anything would be better than crying in front of the Fae, or worse, alone in her apartment.

After a nice stroll through Bryan's neighborhood, they'd left Leda lying on her living room dog bed with a rawhide stick while they walked to the brewery for a pint. As though sensing Harper's mood, Bryan steered the conversation to book selling, keeping their conversation cordial and comfortable. After one pint apiece, Bryan walked her home, saying a quick goodbye at the door.

With the next day being Tuesday, the only day of the week she and Olivia were both closed for business, they had agreed to take a hike together. For Olivia, it was a chance to check on a trail's condition. For Harper, it was a chance to scope out the periphery of Walt's treehouse.

Though the flybys had turned up nothing, she was determined to investigate at the ground level to see if she could find any clues to what he might be up to. They didn't need to go within sight of his place, but she hoped she might find something. And while she could have gone alone, the thought made her uneasy, though the daylight hours should be safe.

The fact that Harper wanted to strike out off trail only increased Olivia's enthusiasm. But Harper had declined Olivia's request to invite Quinn along. Another day, she'd promised her daughter, but today she wanted to visit with Olivia alone.

Before she left her building, she knocked on the small door that led to a little room underneath the basement stairs. Then she asked Tiptoe and Tarryfoot, who'd just finished their night's work, to ask the others to keep an eye on the shop and around the park while she was gone. She didn't mention Walt, but she knew they would understand, and that if anyone saw anything related to him, they would let her know.

Tarryfoot gave her a tiny thumbs up while Tiptoe responded, "We'll tell all the others!" Then they wished her a good day before winking out of sight. She left, secure in the knowledge that the others would watch while the two brownies caught up on sleep on their cushions underneath the stairs.

In the parking lot and on the drive to Olivia's, she kept an eye out for tall women with a gray streak in their long dark hair. Since she'd discovered that Delaynie was prone to spy on her, she didn't want to chance being followed. But both tall women and cars seemed to be avoiding her that morning, and she breathed a sigh of relief on pulling into Olivia's drive.

Inside the cottage, Olivia packed a quick picnic of cheese, olives, crackers, and fruit. Then she added Biscuit's travel bowl and some water bottles to their backpacks. They rode in Olivia's

SUV to a trailhead, upriver, just below the dam. Parts of the area had been damaged in the flooding a few months back, but they were confident they could get around any rough spots.

About a mile and a half up the trail, they would need to strike out to the right, before beginning a steep ascent toward the summit. Harper estimated it would take a little over three hours to complete the hike, including a wide sweep of the area around Walt's treehouse. Along the way, she hoped to catch up with her daughter and enjoy Biscuit's company. But most of all, she desperately hoped to catch sight of Walt or gather any clue as to his whereabouts.

The morning air was warm when they parked the vehicle and began climbing the banked steps through the thick tree cover to where the trail began. Once there, the trail, which looped around the mountainside, could be traveled in one of two directions. Olivia hesitated. "Okay, Mom, which way do you want to go?"

Harper consulted a line-drawn map of the trail she had printed the day before. "Let's go right." They walked the relatively flat terrain for a few hundred yards before the path veered left and began to climb steeply past a small bench. Harper found herself struggling for breath as the grade grew steeper, so they talked little. Once they neared the top, where the trail meandered once again to the left, Harper kept her tone casual. "Let's explore here. I'd like to see if there is a decent view from the top of the ridge."

Olivia cheerfully consented, reaching down to unhook Biscuit's harness. "Do you think that's wise?" Harper began. The thought of losing sweet little Biscuit truly scared her. He was only a puppy.

"Oh, Mom, he'll be fine. Biscuit and I have taken lots of hikes together off trail. The only time he's ever left me behind was that day I got stuck in the bog. And he was a hero then. Weren't you, Boy?" She rubbed his back, then stood as Biscuit zipped to a nearby bush to mark his territory. Olivia began walking, assuming, like most wilderness guides, that Harper would follow.

"Let me lead, Olivia. I have a specific spot I want to see up ahead." Olivia's glance was quizzical, but she stopped, waiting for her mom to pass. Harper headed further uphill, keeping her eyes peeled for signs of Walt. She estimated his treehouse to be a quarter to half a mile away.

"Are you looking for something in particular?" Olivia asked. "We might not want to go too far. You know, they're still finding those pellets occasionally."

For nearly a month, the Fae had been keeping both Harper and Olivia apprised of the mounting pellets. "Don't worry, I told the others we were heading out. They'll come looking for us if I'm late." She didn't add that she hadn't told them exactly where she was heading. Still, whatever was making those pellets seemed to target lone individuals at night.

"Oh, I'm not worried," came Olivia's confident voice. "Quinn and I have tracking apps on our phones so if anything should happen to me, I can be found in a jiff."

Harper halted and turned to her daughter with astonishment. "You sure are spending a lot of time with Quinn, Olivia. And the two of you are about as compatible as winter and summer. What is it about him that you enjoy his company so much?"

Did Olivia's face turn slightly red? As Harper looked at her more closely, Olivia became engrossed in something from the opposite direction. After a moment, she turned her back to her mother with characteristic cool. "You need to give Quinn a chance, Mom. He's caring and interesting. Okay, maybe he was a little overly enthusiastic when you first met him, but can't you forgive him for that? Folklore is his life's work, and he knew you had a good collection. Passionate interests aren't crimes, you know."

Harper nodded without comment. Olivia was right, she realized. Quinn had rubbed her the wrong way from the start, and she really had no idea why. And of course, that didn't mean he was a bad person. Olivia tended to be a better judge of character than Harper. But none of this mattered anyway. Her daughter was turning twenty-nine next week, making it a bit too late for Harper to pick her companions.

She hesitated as they neared the vicinity of Walt's treehouse, though the structure was well hidden by the summer foliage. Harper had always suspected Walt also had it under enchantment so humans wouldn't spot it. But Olivia had Fae sight now, which made Harper nervous. She glanced at Olivia's feet and saw them encased in the lady slipper sneakers that had been given to her only a few weeks ago, by a mother of the forest. Wearing them today had probably been a wise decision with a murderer on the loose. But wearing them also meant that if Olivia saw the structure, she would see it clearly.

As if reading her thoughts, Olivia said, "I hate to bring it up again, Mom. But have you heard from Walt lately?"

Harper sighed as they drew nearer to his treehouse. The air was cooler up here, and a light breeze rustled the tree branches overhead. Biscuit headed straight toward it. To stop him, Harper picked him up and turned him in a different direction. Then she began to trace a path around his place, carefully remaining out of sight.

She sighed. "No, Olivia. I haven't heard from him. But I'm assuming that he's no longer interested in a relationship with me. I'd be lying if I said I wasn't sad, but I insist I do need to move on. I have no choice." That she was searching for him now didn't bother her. Her public stance was that she had moved on. No one need know how much she missed him.

From behind her, Olivia said, "I know it's none of my business, but what about Bryan Greene? He's certainly handsome enough, for an old man."

Her feet stopped so fast that Olivia ran into her. "Olivia!" she gasped. "He's not that old! He's only fifty-four!"

Olivia laughed. "Oh ... sorry. I know ... one day I'll be there myself. But the fifties have always seemed old to me. Anyway, what about him? Have you seen him recently? What's his story?"

"How did you know?" Harper began. She stopped herself with a shake of her head. "As you said, Olivia, that's a personal matter. I need to get along with him, since he's the only other bookseller in the community. In any event, it would be wise. He knows more about the business than I do, and he's been helpful. Besides, aren't you the one who's always insisted I need to be more social?"

She stopped, spotting an old feather lying on the ground. It was small and probably didn't belong to Walt. "I agree that Bryan is handsome, but he's not my type."

"Oh? What is your type?"

Harper's chest burned. "Walt, Olivia. Walt is my type." She swallowed before continuing. "Let's not talk about this right now."

"Okay, we won't talk about that. You definitely shouldn't get involved with anyone else when you're still hung up on Walt."

Harper started to protest, but Olivia stopped her. "You don't have to pretend with me, Mom. I have eyes. But I am worried about you. You're starting to lose weight again. And while I ribbed you about it when I first came here, the extra pounds looked good on you. You looked healthier. But honestly? I just want you to be happy and I wish there were some way I could help."

Harper, genuinely touched, glanced over at her daughter. They were nearing the end of the circle around Walt's property. To her disappointment, nothing unusual had presented itself. "That's sweet of you, Honey, but I will ..."

She trailed off as she heard the loud trumpeting sound once again. Turning her head frantically from side to side, she saw a flash of white that appeared to float about six feet from the ground through the tree trunks, between them and the treehouse. Her stomach lurched. Could it be Delaynie?

She stopped and waited, watching intently as the white patch disappeared. "Did you hear or see anything?" she whispered.

"What? Where?" Olivia asked, her head swiveling about. Harper craned her neck, but whatever she had seen had disappeared, as though it melted into the forest. Though she couldn't be positive, she felt sure it had not been Delaynie, but instead, the tall woman with copper-colored skin and long dark hair she'd spotted around town. For one thing, she couldn't imagine Delaynie wearing a feathered cowboy hat, and her bleached skin held no tones of brown. The pain in her heart moved up to her throat. Was it possible Walt had more than one girlfriend hanging about his place?

Then a stab of fear pierced her heart. What if the woman had seen her? Maybe she would go back to Walt with the news that Harper had brought someone else to his place. She turned and quickly stumbled back in the direction of the trail head. Once there, she headed down it with a speed that surprised her. Biscuit, thinking it was all a game, ran ahead, then back, while barking with delight.

"Mom?" Olivia had picked up the pace and quickly caught up to her on her long legs. "Is something wrong?"

By the time they made it to the trail's parking lot below, Harper's skin was covered in cold, slick sweat. She slid into the

SUV panting. "Olivia, are you sure you didn't see anyone up there? Wearing a large white hat?"

Olivia took Biscuit from his harness, then got inside. In her hand, she held a large, silky white feather. "No, Mom. I didn't see anyone. But look at this! Isn't it beautiful? What kind of bird has feathers like this?"

Harper took a ragged breath and tried to relax. Ignoring the feather in Olivia's hand, she asked, "Would you mind terribly, Olivia, if instead of having a picnic, we went back to your place for our lunch?"

Olivia didn't skip a beat. "Sure, Mom. Let's go."

Back at Olivia's small home, they spread a blanket underneath a large elm tree in the backyard. To calm herself, Harper sipped her water and focused on the sounds of the birds and the cars passing on the highway. Biscuit waited patiently beside the blanket for Olivia to notice his good manners and reward him with a treat of his own. Harper regarded him fondly. Olivia was doing a wonderful job training him.

She wondered idly if perhaps they should introduce Biscuit and Leda, the saluki. Olivia interrupted her thoughts. "So what are your plans, Mom? I hope you're not thinking of moving somewhere else, because I like it here, and I was hoping we could stay close together."

The statement startled Harper upright. "What makes you think I might leave?"

Olivia gave Biscuit a dog treat, then began packing the remains of the picnic. Her voice stayed neutral. "I pay attention. Believe it or not, I've watched you all my life, Mom. When the going gets rough, you withdraw."

Harper wiped her brow. "I stick it out when I need to, Honey. But to be fair, I had considered moving to a different town, but not too seriously. I've thought about doing a lot of things. But for the near future, I think I'll stay put and play it by ear. If I decide to do anything rash, I promise you'll be the first to know. But really, how could I bear to leave Biscuit?"

Olivia laughed. "What about me? Wouldn't it be hard to leave me?"

Harper reached over and squeezed her daughter's shoulder. "You, most of all."

Later, while driving home, she wondered if she had really seen the woman in the white hat through the trees. She was certain she'd seen something white, and it looked to be sitting atop a woman with copper skin and long black hair. But might her imagination have been playing tricks? She decided to go home and rest for a while. Maybe after a nap, she'd run her thoughts by the Fae to see what they thought.

But on arriving at the Robin's Nest, she found all nine of the Fae gathered in her living room. All sat silent and still. Though alarmed, she forced herself to sound cheerful. "What's up, Guys?"

"We have disturbing news, Lassie," said Earl Grey as he removed his hat.

Chapter 15

HARPER'S HEART LEAPT TO her throat. Her eyes landed on Ash, the reliably thoughtful, serene Fae who was so adept at calming her frazzled nerves. But he refused to return her gaze, staring straight ahead, brow furrowed. To his left, little Alida rocked side to side, while Lily bit her lip and stood on one foot, with toes curled beneath.

"What's the matter?" Harper whispered.

"Why don't you sit on the couch, Dearie?" Piper patted the seat beside her.

Once she was settled, they all arranged themselves loosely, either at her side or along the semi-circle of the rug before her. Now seated, they proceeded to contemplate the floor until Harper could no longer stand the suspense. "Why are you all here?" She turned to Earl Grey. "What happened?"

His red hat snapped upright as he cleared his throat. "Well, Lassie, we kept an eye out around the shop and park as you asked us to ..."

"Yes?" she prompted. "Go ahead. Please, out with it! What's wrong?"

Hawthorne stood and took a step toward her. "We discovered fresh pellets directly across the river," he said. "Two of them were hidden in the bullrushes just behind the back parking lot."

"Looked like giant Easter eggs," piped Tarryfoot. The sprites shushed him severely, and chagrined, he dropped his eyes to his lap.

"Two in one place?" Apprehension squelched Harper's ability to form a coherent thought. "That means ..."

Ivy spelled it out. "While not conclusive, it suggests two killers. Of course, the pellets could have been expelled by the same creature, but on different days."

Harper's blood froze as she thought of all the people who walked alone in Puckett's Park, Deanna for example. This new information also meant the killer had been at their back door. But then her brow wrinkled. "You said 'creature.' So, you don't think whatever is responsible is human?"

"We weren't sure in the beginning," Ivy continued. "And we hoped it was a deranged human because law enforcement would be able to stop a human eventually."

Hawthorne now picked up the conversational thread. "But now we are convinced this is the work of Others from the Faery Realm."

"But ... which of the Others would be capable of producing a giant owl pellet?" Dread seized Harper. She looked to Piper and Ash. "But you told me the Swan Clan only comes to help ..." Her muscles tensed as she waited for their response, as though a blow were imminent.

Before either could answer, a distressed Earl Grey jumped in. "How much has Walter told you about his past, Lassie?"

Calm down, she ordered herself. "Not much. To be honest, it always bothered me that he wouldn't confide in me. I told him all about my childhood, even about my relationship with Tim, hoping he would confide something." Her throat constricted. "But he never did."

"Self-preservation," Hawthorne responded. "Unfortunate souls such as Walter are often exposed to harsh judgement, without understanding or merit. He was likely afraid of losing your esteem."

Harper managed to choke out, "What do you mean by 'unfortunate souls,' Hawthorne?"

"We're not one hundred percent certain of Walt's background ourselves. And while we loathe to share information without his permission, it's crucial for your safety to understand. Therefore, we will tell you what we know.

"Back in the days before this country was the United States, when North Carolina was not yet a distinct colony, let alone a state, Piper and Ash found a young boy wandering alone in the forest. He was pitifully thin and bleeding from lacerations to his head, arms, and torso. He couldn't speak—at least, he couldn't speak English or in any of the indigenous tongues with which we were familiar. He could, however, screech and chirp like a great horned owl. In addition, he uttered other, more dreaded, vocalizations." Hawthorne's grim expression made her shudder.

Harper interrupted. "Walt."

Piper patted her hand. "Yes, Dearie. It was our own Walter. Because he appeared to be a young boy, we brought him to some humans we knew—a young Cherokee named Degataga and his wife, an English immigrant named Alice. The two of them lived in a cabin just up the mountain across the river, near Alice's father, an English carpenter named Daniel. The humans nursed him back to health. With patient instruction, he learned to speak English in time."

Her heart ached to think of any child, let alone Walt, suffering so. "He was an orphan, then? What had caused his injuries?"

Hawthorne, Piper, and Ash exchanged uncomfortable glances before Piper answered. "We're not positive, Dearie. But with proper food and good care, the boy grew into our Walt. And before he died, Daniel, who had been a master carpenter in the old country, taught him everything he knew about carpentry which, trust us, was a lot. In time, Ash here taught him to read." She nodded to the quiet Fae beside her. "Walt elected to stay in this area even after Alice and Degataga were buried. Until now, we can't recall him ever leaving this area for more than a day or two at a time."

Harper struggled to absorb this information. Why hadn't he told her this? There was no shame in being an orphan. While she pondered, Piper continued.

"He's always been secretive, even with us. Since growing mature enough to take care of himself, he has never invited any of us to visit his home. Though, as you know yourself, Dearie, he's a friend to all, always willing to lend a helping hand."

Harper nodded. She had personal knowledge of both his helpfulness and his secretiveness. That he'd had enough confidence in her to show her where he lived now struck her as a sacred trust. "Okay, but I don't understand what this has to do with the pellets you found. We already know he's an owl shifter, just like me. No secret there." She suddenly became still, looking at them with shock. "You guys aren't saying Walt is responsible for the murders, are you?"

Hawthorne pinned her to the sofa with his fathomless gaze. "Owl shifters hold little worry for us. But for millennia, another creature haunted these ancient valleys. Called the Tskili', a large owl demoness—feared by the Cherokee—for good reason. I encountered it myself once." He shuddered. "I wouldn't wish that experience on anyone. I'd have never escaped without the help of some excellent friends."

Piper and Ash bowed their heads. "It is the nature of the Dogwood Clan to offer assistance where needed."

"If I didn't thank you adequately at the time, I do so now, my friends." Hawthorne turned back to Harper. "We thought the monster left with the coming of the white settlers, as had the

Nunnehi and many of the Yunwi Tsunsdi'." His voice became grim. "But now we suspect we were wrong. Either it never really left, or it has returned ..."

"And you think Walt has joined with it ..." Harper added miserably.

The gathered group shifted uncomfortably.

Hawthorne began again. "Though we consider it unlikely, we can't rule out the possibility. Since he's lived among us, we've never seen a single sign that this evil might be a part of his makeup. And we are puzzled by something else. Owl shifters such as yourself, while not abundant, are still around. We are unaware of any of them ever savaging humans. Most, as you know, have no instincts to hunt wild animals at all."

Earl Grey, still squirming uncomfortably, finally leapt to his feet. "I simply cannot believe that my friend Walter would be capable of ..." He stopped with a catch in his voice, incapable of continuing.

None of this added up for Harper. If they didn't think Walt was responsible for the murders, she could relax a bit. "I admit, it's disturbing that this creature has been so close to my apartment, but we've known for weeks that it was around. Maybe two of them have crossed over to attack our realm for whatever reason. Don't worry about me, I've been keeping the balcony door locked whenever I'm alone. I'm relieved you don't think it was Walt."

Then she became silent, remembering Walt's feather waiting on the balcony only a week before.

Clearing her throat, she added, "I promise to be more careful when I'm out. Some of you can stay in with me at night if you want. In fact, under the circumstances, I'd appreciate it."

Harper's words died as Ash tossed a burlap sack to the floor at her feet. "We found these near those pellets this morning."

On looking inside, Harper found two of Walt's distinctive feathers on top of the light blue, nearly threadbare t-shirt he was wearing the last time she saw him. When she pulled it from the sack, it still carried Walt's scent of fresh air and pine.

"But that doesn't really mean anything. He could have been kidnapped by the creature, couldn't he? Maybe this Swan Clan has something to do with it."

When none of them responded, she pulled out the white feather she had taken from Olivia's SUV before heading back to Whippoorwill Gap. "I found this today, myself," she confessed. "It was in the woods, near Walt's house."

Long after Harper closed her curtains against the dark and retired to her bedroom for a sleepless night, Earl Grey and Ash stayed awake, keeping vigil in the living room. Piper had bunked down in the kitchen, while the other Fae guarded the building's entrances, inside and out.

As a wail rose from the nearby river, Harper bolted upright in bed. Slipping into her bathrobe, she padded to the living room and pulled the curtain aside an inch and placed an eye to the opening, Piper, Ash, and Earl Grey by her side. From there, under the light of a full moon, she watched as the tall woman with long dark hair who, even now, wore a large white cowboy hat, glided to a stop at the riverside.

Piper, who had slipped between Harper and the window to watch through the curtain's gap, gasped. "That's the spot where we found the newest pellets." Stepping aside, she allowed Ash to look. He nodded.

As they watched, the woman tilted her long, graceful neck to the skies and opened her mouth. A melancholy keening arose, then faded. She took to her feet. Harper and the faeries strained to track her as she faded away, into the forest.

Chapter 16

THE SHADOWS IN HER head had obscured her common sense. She knew Bryan liked beer, for goodness' sake. Why hadn't she chosen to serve that instead of pinot noir? Why did she consistently fail to consider the consequences of her actions?

But when her friends hinted at Walt's dark past, she'd come loosened from the pillars that held her psyche steady. Then came the eerie spectacle with the woman in the white hat across the river the very same night; she'd become completely unmoored.

Desperate for a link to her former sanity, she'd invited Bryan over for dinner. His connection to her childhood memory of Grandma Sophie made his company more attractive. She'd also hoped he would remember more about the origin of the mirror he had given her. Learning all she could about the Swan Clan now seemed urgent.

Regarding her over her pale green kitchen tabletop, Bryan raised his glass with sparkling eyes. "This place is even more charming than I'd expected. To you, Harper. To the return of the muse!"

In return she winced and, reaching into her skirt pocket, gave the mirror he had given her a squeeze.

Blind to her reaction, he continued. "Did you know today is my birthday, or was your invitation to dinner just a happy coincidence?"

Harper's eyebrows shot up. "No, Bryan. Sad to say, I had no idea it's your birthday." She raised her glass. "A Happy Birthday to you!"

He clinked his glass against hers and they both downed a sip. With all the drama, she'd failed to celebrate her own birthday, just a few days before. "Actually ..."

"I know." He interrupted with a smile. "Your birthday was a few days ago. I didn't get in touch because you seemed so freaked out at my house the other night. I was afraid of upsetting you. But yes, I knew last Tuesday was your birthday. We're both Cancers. You know, in astrology? We share the same sun sign."

Harper stared at him while shaking her head slowly. The fact that they shared a sun sign meant nothing to her. Besides, she had no wish for him to turn intense on her again. "Bryan, about our conversation at your house the night you had me over to dinner ... I've been thinking ..." She faltered at the inscrutable expression in his startling deep blue eyes and failed to pinpoint exactly what she'd wanted to say.

To cover her confusion, she bent over to scratch Leda behind the ears, then presented her with a dog treat. Something about the regal but affectionate dog calmed her spirit. Looking into those big brown eyes, she felt they understood one another perfectly. And if Leda was happy with Bryan, Harper felt he must be okay underneath his unnerving surface.

She turned to the hostess gift Bryan had brought her—a just-released coffee table book about swans and swan lore. While she looked, Bryan picked up the conversation again. "Of course, you're free to consider that a birthday gift. Did you know that each sign of the Zodiac has a bird attached to it? Our sign, Cancer, is represented by the swan."

Harper's mouth dropped open. "You're making that up!"

He laughed. "I promise you I'm not. Look it up. I've seen some sources say other birds, like owls, are connected to our sign too. But I prefer to think of the swan as the correct one."

This couldn't be real, and she'd definitely do her research later, but ... owls?!

The muggy early July air forced her to close all the windows. She'd turned on the air-conditioning to cool off the apartment earlier that afternoon. But she'd drawn the curtains back, letting in the light through the balcony door and the dramatic nine-foot windows to either side. Bryan appeared suitably impressed as she led him into the living room. Several members of F-Troop perched outside on the balcony's railing. They'd made it clear they weren't comfortable with Bryan around, and Earl Grey in particular seemed offended.

She ignored them all. Once dinner was ready, they'd return to the kitchen. With tomorrow a workday for them both, Bryan would likely leave shortly after the meal. Surveil all you want, she told them silently, there's nothing to see here.

Harper had prepared a simple but delicious dish of cold spaghetti studded with fresh tomato, basil, and parmesan cheese that she'd discovered in her days of apartment living during her senior year of college. Back then, she'd practically lived on it. Though she knew pasta was frowned on by the health food community these days, she'd replaced the regular spaghetti with a sourdough, gluten-free version. To go with it, she had a loaf of Piper's day-old sourdough bread topped with butter and garlic, ready to be popped under the broiler for five minutes before they ate. In the refrigerator, she'd stashed a Mediterranean salad of green leaf lettuce, olives, and assorted veggies she'd picked up that morning at the farmers' market in Gap Park. She'd used one of the few recipes her mom had left her to make the Greek vinaigrette dressing. And for dessert, decaf coffee and lemon cream pie were standing at the ready.

She sat on the couch, placing her glass of wine on the table and the coffee table book in her lap. Bryan settled on the cushion next to her, close enough for him to see the pages but not so close as to be alarming. She regarded the robins outside again. It might be fun to give you something to tweet about, she thought with a stifled grin. But that wouldn't be fair to Bryan. She noted that Leda had gone to the door and was observing the birds with friendly curiosity. Bryan didn't seem to notice, and Leda settled down on the floor, her head resting on her front paws.

"Okay, tell me. What do swans have to do with Cancer?"

She was unprepared for the litany of similarities between the sign and swan lore. "To begin, Cancers, like swans, are placid on the surface, but struggle mightily underneath. We're sensitive and thin-skinned, so we are easily hurt, but try to hide it. We think too much about our pasts. We love our home but like to travel too. We like to work and we're moody, but loyal. All these traits are also attributed to swans. Shall I go on?"

Her eyes opened wide. Laid out like that, the similarities were uncanny. She didn't like where this was headed. "Bryan, we need to talk."

A dramatic sigh flew from his mouth. "Uh, oh. The dreaded phrase that no man ever wants to hear, especially when he's just bared his soul." He moved to the sofa's edge, eyes wreathed with tension. "But please, continue."

Once again, she reached in her skirt pocket to clutch the mirror he had given her, the raised swan pressing against her palm. She cast about for a diplomatic way to broach the topic, but unfortunately, she'd never been graced with tact. "All that stuff you had in your study—the pictures and mementos of my life ... I must admit, it made me uncomfortable."

He cocked his head to the side. "Yeah, I got that. And I'm really sorry it bothered you. But honest, I didn't mean to be creepy. I thought you'd be flattered."

Could he be serious? How could he not know that he had come across as a stalker? She decided the best approach was the direct one. He needed to understand.

"It was just a lot, Bryan. Think about it. I didn't even know who you were two years ago. Then we meet and have a business relationship, which was fine."

"Glad to hear that wasn't too upsetting for you." He gave a small smile.

"But then I find out you've been following me ... going to my mother's house and collecting things about me ... for most of my life. Would you feel comfortable if some woman you didn't know well told you she'd been doing that to you?"

His brow wrinkled as he stared at his wine glass. "I guess I never thought about it like that." He gave an audible exhale, then a rueful smile. "Believe me. No woman has ever told me anything like that. Although I have had a few make themselves too available."

She looked away out the windows, unsure how to deal with that comment.

He straightened and moved to the sofa's edge. "Okay, Harper. What you say makes sense. The last thing I wanted was to come across as creepy or to make you uncomfortable. But honestly, you don't need to be freaked out. I don't expect anything of you. And I'm not trying to pressure you into a relationship you don't want."

When she didn't respond, he looked up at the ceiling, as though for help. "It's just ... I've always been a poet, deep down inside. For my whole life, you've been my best, most reliable inspiration. I just want to get to know you as a person, no pressure, I promise."

She sat quietly while she thought. Did she really believe him? "Bryan, I'm not fourteen years old. I've been around enough men in my life to know that getting to know my mind won't be enough for long."

He frowned. "This may come across as clichéd, but I'm not most men, Harper. I had hoped that would be obvious to you, but I guess it's not."

This wasn't going well. "Don't be mad. I just wanted to clarify my position. All that stuff at your apartment ... that was a lot to take in. We really don't know each other very well yet."

At that, he closed his eyes. When he opened them again, he said, "That's my point, exactly. Look ... you're my Beatrice. I just want to get to know you better and add depth to my inspiration. I'll never pressure you to do anything that makes you uncomfortable. In fact, if you'd like, Leda and I can leave now."

He stopped speaking, waiting for any indication she wished him gone. If any came, she had no doubt he'd head for the door. Was that what she wanted? To eat her dinner alone? She glanced onto the balcony. The robins had flown away.

She found herself trembling. "No, Bryan. I don't want you to leave. Who would help me eat all that food? I just wanted to clear the air. I want to be friends with you, but I'm not ready for a romantic relationship." Her voice quivered, feeling weak. "To be honest, I'm not over Walt yet."

He reached over to squeeze her tensely balled fist. His gaze, though intense, was sincere. "Harper, I only want to make you happy. If being friends would make you happy, then that's what I want to do. If jumping off your balcony would make you happy ..." he stood.

Leaving the couch, she put a hand on his arm, laughing as she pulled him to sit again. "Stop it!" she said. The pressure relieved, they both chuckled.

"Who's Beatrice?" Harper asked.

"You know. The Italian poet, Dante? He's the greatest poet of all time, in my opinion. The Divine Comedy?! Surely you've heard of that."

"I've heard of it, but I've never read it."

He leaned back on the sofa, clearly warming to a well-worn topic, and swirled his wine. "Well, Dante was a late thirteenth- and early fourteenth-century poet. He first saw Beatrice when she was eight and he was nine." His voice grew wistful. "They met at a party in May. He fell in love with her and loved her his whole life through. Apparently, his attraction was unrequited, but she inspired his poetry until he died, even though she married another and died much earlier than he did."

"What a sad story."

He looked at her as though he had temporarily forgotten she was there. "Do you really think so? Because I don't. To him, she represented love and beauty. In fact, in The Divine Comedy, she led him to Paradise. Just seeing you in my grandpop's shop when I was a kid opened a whole world of possibility to a sad kid like me. Watching you made me feel things I'd never felt before. So that's what you've been for me—an ideal to capture and emulate through my work."

Harper sat quietly, letting this soak in. She'd never imagined such a thing.

She cast about for a change of subject. "So our both being Cancers was why you chose to bring the swan book? Or is there another story behind that, too?"

He arched his brows. "Well, that and Swan Lake, remember? I told you I was sitting center stage on the front row when you danced it at your senior recital. I was fourteen at the time. That's another reason I've always been taken with you. I could see from your performances that you had an artist's soul, like me."

How had she forgotten he'd mentioned that? And she took exception to his description of her dancing. "It was a horrible production ..." she began.

"Which you saved with your graceful performance. You took my breath away. Besides that, there's the swan mirror I found at Grandpop's. That all adds up to a lot of swan symbolism. Poets thrive on this stuff."

She could feel the mirror's weight in her pocket. He downed the last of his wine. His voice sounded newly energized. "So like it or not, you're my inspiration, Harper. Much of my poetry, while not about you on the surface, tries to capture what you mean to me in spirit." He stood and held out his hand. "Should I fetch us both another glass of wine?"

She stood as well, thinking of opening the shop the next morning. "Let's go ahead and eat dinner. I don't want to get too loopy."

"Expecting a busy day?"

She smiled. "Not really."

He looked at Leda, who had stood. "Stay." The dog promptly sat back down.

Harper's hands shook as she put the bowl of pasta on the table along with the bread from the oven. The salad was waiting on the table with the dressing in its cruet. She didn't own china anymore, so her recently purchased pink and white stoneware comprised the settings.

In some ways, what he'd revealed tonight had been more overwhelming than what she'd discovered at his house. How could she possibly live up to being a muse? Nothing in her past had prepared her for this sort of thing. If she did something gauche, would he lose his inspiration? But she had to admit to herself that the idea was flattering. It was probably a good thing she hadn't known about it earlier in life or she'd have gotten a swelled head.

Fortunately, while they ate, Bryan lost his sentimentality. All those grand notions were apparently everyday fare in his world, nothing to be embarrassed about. He ate her food with gusto and complimented every course. They could have been discussing baseball before dinner for all the effect the conversation had on him. In contrast, Harper's discomfort with the intensity of the conversation prompted her to down first a second, then a third glass of wine. She'd pay for it in the morning, but for now, it seemed to be the antidote to her anxiety.

By the time they'd finished the lemon cream pie with coffee, it was dark outside. As she tried to think of a polite way to usher him out, he began stacking the dishes in the sink. "Should we wash these by hand, or do you prefer using the dishwasher?"

"I'll put them in the dishwasher later, Bryan. Thanks."

He straightened and gave a short whistle. Leda appeared from the living room. "It was a lovely dinner, Harper. Thank you. I hope you're willing to be friends. I'm harmless. And now, it's time for me and Miss Leda to head home."

Her shoulders dropped with relief. Until then, she hadn't realized she'd been holding them aloft. When she walked them to the front door, he reached over and gave her a quick side hug. "I'm not sure I want to be anyone's muse," she mumbled.

"I'll not speak of it again." He smiled. "We're just two humble booksellers working in the same small town."

She locked the door behind him and watched as the man and his dog walked to the parking lot across the street, where Leda jumped into the back seat of his red Audi.

Back in her apartment, she expected to find the Fae waiting. Instead, the dishes waited untouched on the countertop where Bryan had left them.

After cleaning up, she went to the living room and closed the blinds. She noticed the book Bryan had given her had been left open. She sat down to look at it. It was open to a page about a third from the front. At the top of the right-hand page was a poem. She gasped on seeing the title, "Leda and the Swan."

As she read it, the vision of rape created by W.B. Yeats horrified her. She had no memory of leaving the book open, so how had it come to be turned to this page? Flipping through its pages, she found photographs, paintings, sketches, legends, poems, and prose about swans. She circled back to "Leda and the Swan."

"This isn't my idea of a joke, you guys. Who opened the book to this page?" she asked aloud. Only the ticking wall clock responded.

Chapter 17

WALT GROANED WEAKLY AS he took in the foul condition of his surroundings. Wall sconces burned a noxious-smelling oil of unknown origin, releasing thick black smoke that reeked of decay and marred the stone walls with a greasy residue. Not wanting to see what else may lurk in the shadows about him, Walt kept his eyes trained straight ahead.

Since he'd first arrived weeks ago, he had lost his appetite, regained it, and lost it again many times over. Starvation had become his constant companion. Maybe Delaynie would ignore the signs long enough that one merciful day, it would take him away from this hell. The thirst proved harder to bear and brought a higher level of agony. He drank the revolting, metallic-tasting liquid he was offered despite himself. But now his body mutinied against even this necessity.

Time had become a rocky, meaningless river of pain. One night, weeks ago, before he had weakened to his current state of helpless disability, Delaynie had released him. Though he knew that she'd never allow him to remain free, in desperation he'd flown straight to Harper's. Landing on her balcony, he'd pulled at her door, finding it locked tight. The closed curtains blocked the interior from his sight, though he could see no light.

As he scratched and clawed at the door's handle, he beat against the glass, calling as loudly as he dared, first in his human voice. Then, exhausted, he commenced the gravelly hoot of his owl form. Either Harper wasn't home, she couldn't hear him, or she didn't want to see him. This last possibility left him weak with despair. He'd finally closed his eyes and slumped by the balcony door.

Before long, Delaynie swooped in and grabbed him, clutching in her claws as her powerful wings lifted them both into the night. He was outsized, and much too weak to fight her. As they flew over the river, he watched Whippoorwill Gap grow smaller the higher they climbed. He wondered where the Fae had been. Usually some of them spent the night patrolling the shop and the nearby park. But on that night, none of them had shown themselves.

The next day, Delaynie had treated him to the contents of a restaurant's dumpster she raided a day or two before. At the time, having not yet given up on the idea of escape, Walt had consumed all he could hold. The garbage proved more palatable than the rats, moles, and stray cats she had been expecting him to consume. She was wrong about him. He wasn't like her at all. But after several half-consumed dinner rolls and some leather-like pizza slices, his stomach rebelled and he was forced to lie back in his corner, swallowing hard to keep any remaining food down.

Gradually, after numerous failed attempts, he had given up on his dream of freedom. Growing weaker by the day, he now merely lay in a corner of the cage in which she had imprisoned him. Even if she opened his cage and left him alone, what could he do? Too stunned and weak to fly, he gave himself over to wasting away atop a pile of thin, filthy blankets.

At some point during this long nightmare, Delaynie had begun to bring human victims back to the cave, making him watch as she devoured them. Most were young people, either indigent or solo backpackers camping in the mountains. He recognized one man, a war veteran, who had lived in an abandoned cargo box off Route 19. While Walt had never talked with the man, he had swooped over him many times. The unfortunate fellow's screams had been heart-rending. Though horrified, a part of Walt envied him. At least the man was now released to a better place than this one.

From his position in the cage's corner, Walt could see the cave's opening twenty yards away. Though he couldn't be certain, it now appeared to be night. Likely Delaynie was out hunting. As miserable as it was when she brought back her prey, it was nearly as bad for Walt when she returned alone. On those nights, she relieved her frustration by viciously tormenting him.

More than once, he had wished she would snatch him from the cage, throw him down her gullet, and be done with it. If she'd truly wished to corrupt him, as she'd said in the beginning, she'd have tired of him by now. The prospect was obviously hopeless. In fact, the weaker he grew, the less attention she paid him. Did she have an endgame, or was torture the one and only point?

Finally, her tall form thudded just outside the cave's entrance. Slinking inside, she stopped on finding his eyes were open. Her lip curled in a sneer and Walt involuntarily grimaced. Apparently she'd found no victims tonight, which promised an agonizing evening. If he got lucky, she'd go too far.

With a hideous grin, her head morphed in size, her eyes taking on the dimensions of bagels in her contorted face. Her transformations had begun. By the time it was complete, her eyes would resemble glowing circular sawblades. She groaned with pleasure as feathers sprouted from her torso and two tufted horns appeared on her head. Within seconds, she had reached her full height of nearly eight feet. The rocky cave ceiling cleared the top of her head by mere inches.

He shrank to the corner of the cage as she preened for a moment before turning back to him, the mouth beneath her massive beak curved into a grotesque smile.

After expelling a large pellet, she weaved toward his cage so unsteadily she appeared drunk. Just outside the bars, she resumed her tall shapely female human form. He never understood why she didn't just pick a form and stay there. Was she trying to scare him with her transformations? The time for that trick had ended long ago.

"What a pity I couldn't find fresh prey tonight. I had to make do with a rotting large bull in a nearby field. I've had my eye on him for a while, saving him for a night like this. I considered sharing him with you, My Pet, but he was simply too scrumptious." Her breath reeked of decaying blood and entrails. Walt held his breath and closed his eyes. He shuddered as he heard the cage door open with a screech.

Delaynie walked in, towering above him.

"Sit up."

When he remained motionless, she kicked him, hard, in his stomach. He retched with pain, his eyes blurry with tears. "Sit up and look at me when I'm talking to you!"

Then her voice softened to her nauseating girlish simper. "Really Walter, your rudeness is trying. Especially after all the effort I've exerted to feed and care for you." She snorted. "Ungrateful wretch! You'd be dead without my attention, you know."

As she heaved his head up by his hair, terror focused his sight on her hostile eyes.

"I could kill you now. You'd like that, wouldn't you? Death would be a relief for you. No, not yet; I plan to make you suffer much more before the end. You see, Little Brother, I've anticipated this for far too long to let it end so quickly. Before

I'm done with you, you will pay dearly for what you did to our mother."

Chapter 18

Columns of light streamed down from the windows near the twenty-foot ceiling. As Harper and Bryan traversed the creaky wooden floor below, they scrutinized tabletops and shelving in an old warehouse in Asheville, North Carolina. Today was opening day of the second annual Asheville Rare and Vintage Books Festival, and they had joined the antique book lovers and dealers who had come from all over the South to attend.

They alternated between hunting together and splitting up, each pursuing different treasures. Harper had recently created a page on her website devoted to rare folklore books. She hoped to find collectible titles today, in first editions if she was lucky. Bryan also had an interest in amassing items for his store's small rare books section, which featured general fiction titles, but his primary goal was adding vintage poetry volumes for his personal collection.

She'd looked up Beatrice, which had calmed her fears. If she were a muse, it wasn't really her at all that he was attracted to, was it? Though she didn't completely understand his feelings for her, she now considered him less a creep and more an artistic, sensitive soul who needed tolerance.

Besides, he was interesting to talk to, and his company distracted her from Walt's absence and the feelings of abandonment and hopelessness she lived with every day. On the hour-long journey to the big city, they'd had a reassuring conversation about the poem "Leda and the Swan." Like Harper, Bryan remembered the book lying closed on the sofa when they left to go into the kitchen. She knew he hadn't gone back to the living room. So someone else had opened the book. And, to her relief, he agreed with her that the poem was disturbing.

"Just ignore that one if it bothers you, Harper. Heck, tear it out and throw it away, if it would make you feel better. Everything else in it is more cheerful. One of the reasons I brought it was that you might find it uplifting."

Though the book fair opened its doors at ten that morning, she and Bryan had arrived at half past eight, taking their place in a line that snaked hundreds of yards down the street. Because she still had much to learn about the rare book market, Quinn had given her a list of titles and authors to scout out, for which she'd been grateful.

The morning had been discouraging, however. At one in the afternoon, she only had two books in her basket. But later, on rounding the final row of vendor displays, she found a copy of John Fox, Jr.'s *The Trail of the Lonesome Pine*. While not on Quinn's list, the title sounded familiar, it was based in Appalachia, and it was old. She hoped it would fetch a good price. With the book in acceptable condition for a low asking price, she concluded it was a safe bet.

For most of the day, the two booksellers wandered about alone. Harper had little interest in poetry, while Bryan cared nothing for folklore reference sources. Fortunately, both found plenty to keep them engrossed. By the time they jointly entered the queue to pay for their purchases, it was ten past four in the afternoon. Bryan jiggled on his toes while waiting. His zeal for books made her smile. He reminded her of a boy soon to be handed an ice cream cone.

The day's only dicey spot came as they passed an A.E. Deere display on the way out. Bryan had wanted to stop and check it out, confessing he was a fan. The fact that the author was rumored to be local, though anonymous, intrigued him. "We could head back inside and buy some of these if you'd like."

She turned away, feeling a fresh blow at the sight of the familiar covers. "No, thanks. Didn't you notice my display? I've got all his novels, some in multiple copies, back at my shop. You can come in and take all you want if you're interested."

He shot her a puzzled look. "You can always use more, can't you, Harper? They're collectibles. Eventually you'll sell out. I think, except for *The River's Call,* they're out of print. People sometimes ask me where they can find them."

To reveal that Walt had written those books was out of the question. Harper opted to deflect his attention. "It's been a long day, and my feet hurt. We've been walking around for eight hours, and I'm ready to eat."

He placed the book back on the display rack and turned to her, looking contrite. "You're right. I get carried away and forget everything else when I'm around books. Why don't you go wait by the entrance, and I'll pull the car around to pick you up? After we collect our purchases at the loading dock, we can find something to eat."

Harper agreed, then waited for him to pull around while she thought of Walt. It had now been over a month since she'd seen him. She considered flying back to his house, possibly tomorrow morning before her shop opened. At this point, it didn't matter if he thought she was spying. Desperation was making her reckless.

Once she and Bryan were at the loading dock, Harper helped place their boxes of books into the back of his SUV. She had bought ten books in total. Some were for the shop while a few were to keep for herself. She wanted to read *Mules and Men* by

Zora Neale Hurston and *The Heroine with 1,001 Faces* by Maria Tatar. Once she'd read those two, she might sell them in the shop—but if she really enjoyed them, she'd probably squirrel them away in her office.

She felt ready to go home, slip into her pajamas, and curl up on the sofa, a cup of tea at her side. She was tired and she wanted to think about Walt. But unlike Harper, Bryan was in no hurry to get home. He'd left Leda with an employee at the shop and had promised to pay extra if she'd take the saluki for an evening walk. He planned to pick Leda up from the shop when he got back.

Once they'd loaded the books into the back of his SUV, they drove to a restaurant a few blocks away called Ye Olde American Chestnut for an early dinner. Inside, they settled into a booth, grateful to be off their feet. Bryan insisted they order celebratory drinks. Harper got the house take on a gin and tonic, flavored with bergamot, while he ordered a whiskey concoction with orange bitters and elderberry syrup. Halfway through her drink, Harper began to relax, thinking that she and Bryan were well suited for a friendly relationship. And at some point, the pain of losing Walt might even begin to fade.

Reclaimed teak paneling lent the restaurant a cozy air, while the smells of sizzling steak, garlic, and onions made Harper's mouth water. It was nice they had arrived early. With few people about, the noise level was tolerable. Only soft bluegrass fiddle music played in the background.

They discussed their finds while sipping their drinks, until a group of women were seated in the booth behind Harper. Though she couldn't see their faces, they made no effort to modulate their volume, and she could hear everything they said.

Apparently, after a day of shopping, they were ready to hash over the details of a horrifying discovery that morning, near one of the city's parks on the French Broad River. In a high-pitched voice, one showed the others a picture she'd just spotted on her IG feed. A giant pellet had been analyzed and found to contain the remains of a Great Dane. Another woman, in the rough voice of a longtime smoker, claimed to have a neighbor whose Great Dane, Rex, was missing. The others gasped at the implication.

They continued talking about the recent spate of missing people and speculated that a serial killer must be on the loose. One of them wondered if that bizarre pellet could be connected to the missing people. Others asserted that for a killer to go to the trouble of making pellets would be bizarre, to say the least. What kind of sicko would do something like that? Whatever was going on, they all agreed they wouldn't be going on walks around their neighborhoods alone until the authorities resolved the mystery.

As Harper listened, gloom smothered her budding feelings of hopefulness. Whatever was making those pellets had made its way all the way to Asheville. Tremors caused the ice in her glass to rattle, so she placed it on the table and shoved her hands beneath her legs. To kill a family pet ... could Walt possibly be that craven? It was crazy, she knew, to be more horrified over a pet than a human, but animals were more helpless, weren't they? No matter what, the insanity of the situation distressed her.

By the time the server came to take their dinner orders, Harper's appetite had fled. As she examined the menu uneasily, Bryan ordered a filet mignon. Then he and the server turned to her expectantly. She had considered the shrimp and grits but rethought that choice, doubtful she could hold down anything containing sausage and cheese. Instead she opted for dinner from the appetizer section, ordering a plate of fried brussels sprouts and a cheese and olive spread with crackers.

Bryan peered at her over his drink. "That's not much. Didn't you say you were hungry?"

Harper grimaced, tilted her head back toward the women behind her, then leaned forward and whispered, "Not so much after overhearing them. Have you been listening?"

He nodded. "Not really good conversation for mealtime," he agreed, "but it's hard to blame them. The whole thing really is disturbing." He pulled back and studied her face with concern. "Do you want to cancel the dinner and head home?"

Harper shook her head. It would be selfish to ruin his dinner, too.

Bryan took another sip of his drink, then smiled. "I propose we talk about something else."

"I'm game. You pick the first topic."

"Okay. Let's talk poetry."

She shrugged, then took a gulp from her water glass. "We can talk about poetry if you like, but I have to confess, even though I taught writing, I'm shockingly ignorant about it." But the tactic worked. Harper forgot about the women behind her as she focused on steering the conversation to one small aspect of poetry she could understand, because if he started talking about anything related to dactyl or trochee, she'd be in trouble. She kept it broad. "Do you have a favorite poet?"

"John Keats is my all-time favorite. You know him, right? 'La Belle Dame sans Merci' and 'Ode to a Grecian Urn.'"

"Oh, yeah. 'Ode to a Grecian Urn.' That sounds familiar. I think we studied that in college. But I'm afraid I don't remember much about it."

"Yeah, it's likely you did. It's a masterpiece. Beauty and time are its primary themes. But that's not my favorite of his. My favorites are the ones about magic and fairies."

Harper choked on the last sip of her drink. Once she stopped coughing, she took a drink of her fresh mint-laced water. "He wrote about fairies?"

"Well, that's basically what 'La Belle Dame sans Merci' and 'The Eve of St. Agnes' are both about. 'Song of Four Fairies' is another favorite of mine." He grinned. "Does the idea of fairies disturb you? I figured a ballerina would be all about them."

She cleared her throat. "You clearly aren't acquainted with many dancers. But, no, the idea of fairies doesn't bother me ... I'm just surprised you're interested in them."

He frowned. "Why?"

The server brought their dinners. Harper was hoping the interruption would give her an opportunity to change the subject, but after requesting a glass of wine and more water for them both, Bryan brought it up again. "Why would you be surprised I like to read about fairies?"

Harper picked at a charred brussels sprout. She considered how to answer his question without offending him. She quickly took a sip of the cabernet when the server brought it. "Oh my gosh, this wine is delicious."

Instead of responding, he continued to look at her expectantly, so she answered with reluctance. "I've just never met a man who was interested in the Good Folk."

His head tilted. "Really? I think you'd be surprised, Harper, at the interests we men can have. Not all of us are into football and hunting. At least, I never have been."

Chagrined, she waved a verbal white flag. "I'm sorry, Bryan. I guess that sounded judgmental. You're right, just because I haven't had a man tell me he's interested in faeries doesn't mean none of them are. And it absolutely doesn't mean they shouldn't be. But I am intrigued. Where or when did you become interested in them?"

"Well, for starters, the poems of Keats and Yeats." His lips curved into a teasing grin. "Both of them were men, by the way." She gave a rueful smile. "And from watching ballet. A Midsummer Night's Dream is one of my favorites. So while I've never thought much about it, I guess, in a way, that's another obsession you helped spark."

Her face froze; she had no wish to discuss that right now.

"My childhood obsession," he amended. He shifted in his seat.

She changed the topic back to swans, which seemed a safe bet. "All this talk about swans reminds me of a stranger I've been seeing around town. I wonder if you've seen her too." Harper described the beautiful, tall, copper-skinned brunette in the white-feathered cowboy hat. "I only thought of it because her hat is so striking. It kind of reminds me of a swan."

"Hum. Sounds intriguing, but if I've seen her, I don't remember it." He didn't sound interested, so Harper gave up the topic.

Suddenly her energy deserted her and Harper only wanted to be home. It was too much ... the exhaustion ... the murders ... Walt's possible involvement ... and now Bryan's unfortunate obsessions. She needed to decompress.

For the rest of the meal, she steered the conversation toward business. After the meal, they skipped dessert and split the bill.

Both were quiet on the drive back to Whippoorwill Gap. Harper found herself preoccupied with a new, disturbing line of thought. If Walt had become a monster, was it possible for a latent monster to be hiding in her as well? Did owl shifters sometimes do this? Like a werewolf at a full moon, was an appetite for fresh meat something that "took you over" at a certain point? Knowing little about beings like herself, she thought it prudent to learn what she could, thus avoiding any triggers that might turn her into a blood-thirsty beast.

As Bryan jockeyed for position with other vehicles on I-40, she resolved to research everything she could find about owls and their lore. Maybe she could somehow locate Walt himself and question him. One thing was certain; it was past time to conquer her fears and get to the bottom of what was going on.

Chapter 19

After oversleeping the next morning, Harper didn't have time for a flyby over Walt's before opening the Robin's Nest. Instead, she climbed the hill to Main Street to Whippoorwill Gap Books.

On arriving in her apartment the night before, Harper had discovered that one of Bryan's book fair purchases, *The Lady of the Lake* by Sir Walter Scott, had gotten mixed in with her books somehow. It was a Thursday, and while Harper opened at noon, Bryan opened at nine. She hoped to find him at his bookstore, saving her a trip to his house. While the walk to Poplar Street might be good for her health, on a morning as steamy as this she'd need another shower before opening her shop. The cloudless deep blue sky this mid-July morning promised a scorching day.

As Harper entered Whippoorwill Gap Books, the frigid, air-conditioned air hit her with force. She breathed a sigh of relief on seeing Bryan behind the counter, his back to her while he examined the books on the shelf behind him. When he turned to see her standing there, he made a barely perceptible jump and his face flushed a shade brighter.

"Harper! What a nice surprise!"

She held the book out. "Hi, Bryan. One of your books was in my box. Here you go." She hesitated. "I also wanted to apologize."

"Apologize? For what?" His brows knit as he stared at the book in his hand as though he'd never seen it before.

"For being such poor company last night on the ride home. That was selfish of me. I didn't mean to spoil the fun. But all the talk about nasty pellets made me nervous."

When he looked up, the look he gave her would have been more suited to someone pulling her close for a dance. "It's okay, Harper. I completely understand. I was just happy to spend time with you. I wish I could put a stop to the craziness going on around here." He pulled his gaze away, glancing around his store. "Everyone is nervous, and if they don't figure out what's happening soon, it's going to impact the town's tourist dollars."

This pronouncement gave her pause. Compared to the death of innocent people, it was a small point, but it mattered to the people who depended on tourist dollars for their livelihood. "You're right. I hadn't thought of that."

"Yes, if it's spread as far as Asheville, it's only a matter of time before it hits state or even national news. Something like that could really set our economy back."

She nodded, and having nothing to add, soberly turned to go.

"Would it be okay if Leda and I met you at Puckett's Park for a short walk after work today?"

While she didn't really want to see him again this evening, she could think of no graceful way to say no. So Harper reluctantly agreed.

With the remaining time before her own shop opened at noon, she planned to research anything she could find on owls and owl shifter folklore. But on arrival, she found all the Fae waiting for her in the living room. Ever since Walt left, coming home to a somber welcoming committee had rarely boded well.

"Hey guys. What's going on?" she asked, trying to sound cheerful to hide her nervousness.

Earl Grey stood and removed his hat to scratch his gray head before speaking. "We won't beat around the bush, Lass. While you were out cavorting with Mr. Greene yesterday, we split up and combed the area both here and in the Fae Realm for signs of Walter. Sad to say, we found not a trace. To be honest, Harper, we are becoming increasingly perturbed. He's never once been gone this long. We fear for his safety." Earl Grey paced as he spoke, only stopping to gauge her reaction when done.

She looked at him in exasperation. "I wasn't 'cavorting with Mr. Greene,' as you put it. We were on a business trip. And that you couldn't find Walt is surely not surprising at this point. Look, I'm as alarmed about Walt as the rest of you. I've been more than worried ... I've been heartbroken ... for quite a while. And you'll be happy to know that I've decided to do some digging to see what I can find. Once I'm armed with more information, I plan to go out searching for Walt myself. I'm even willing to risk a visit to the Fae Realm to ask for an audience with Grandma Sophie. Of course"—she hesitated—"if I do that, I'll need some of you to escort me."

While she often yearned to visit her grandmother, the Faery Queen, she knew doing so always involved risk. Grandma herself had discouraged Harper from making unnecessary trips through the tunnel beneath the riverbank that led to the Faery Realm. And a visit to Walt's treehouse might endanger her as well. But she had no choice other than going alone, having promised not to reveal its location. And the thought of what she might find there terrified her.

Hawthorne's eyes burrowed into hers. He had removed his hat, twirling it between his fingers before him, a sure sign of high emotion. "As with many things involving the Fae Folk, Harper, there are things about Walter of which you remain unaware."

"So I gather," she answered, suddenly frustrated beyond restraint. "Then, for goodness' sake! Stop beating around the bush! Just tell me what I need to know! Is it something to do with owl shapeshifters? Does something turn us into crazed killers against our will? Is that what you think is going on with Walt? Because if that's the case, we've got to do something to stop him!" At this outburst, they all stared at her, motionless, with eyes wide.

She waited. When no one answered, she continued in a strained voice. "And how does the Swan Clan figure into this whole picture? You tell me they only show up in times of need. Well, if ever there was a time we need help, it's now. Does the woman in the white cowboy hat have anything to do with what's going on? Why can't you guys just tell me what you know." She paused for a ragged breath, finding herself near tears.

Hawthorne, hat still in his hands, answered gravely. "With your permission, Harper, I will continue."

Harper nodded, sniffling.

"We believe a deep dive into owls and owl shifter lore may be wasted time. I told you earlier that Walt came to us as a young lad, beat up and bleeding. As he grew older, he did tell us that as a nestling, he was held captive by a creature long thought to be gone from these parts called the Tskili'. Do you remember that discussion?"

Harper nodded as a chill swept up her spine.

"This creature is an owl demoness who once ruled the nights, haunting dark hollows in this land. Her reign of terror lasted for eons. Though rare, she occasionally spawned offspring to take her place when she sensed her end was near.

"We've kept this information from you, not wanting to worry you unnecessarily. The Tskili' in this area was rumored to have produced two offspring—one male and one female. Though we never learned what transpired, none of the Tskili' have been seen since we discovered young Walter, bruised and bleeding, in the forest." He paused, searching for the right words. "Some of us have lately wondered if Walt could have been the rumored male offspring. Before now, we had never considered the possibility. It makes little sense. As you know yourself, Walt is too kind to be descended from such a monstrous creature."

Taking in Harper's horrified expression, he held up his hand. "All this is speculation, of course. Walter never spoke to any of us about it, even as a child. The humans who took him in raised him as their own. His habits are more human than owl."

He hesitated before continuing. "But we have wondered if he spent any time with the Tskili'. Is it possible he was somehow raised by the beast? If so, he could have picked up its unsavory tendencies. Perhaps something caused an unconscious regression ..."

Harper shook her head in dismay. "I know Walt is not a monster," she began, her voice wavering. "I will never believe that. You said there may have been two offspring ..."

"None of us can verify any of this. But around the time Walt was found, both the creature and any offspring disappeared. We've neither seen nor heard rumor of one in the intervening years. That is all we know."

Harper groaned, wondering briefly why they had chosen this morning to bring her this vague but disturbing information. What had they hoped to accomplish by telling her this?

"Okay. Thank you for letting me know, but I don't see how this helps me out. While the Tskili' may be responsible for the murders, Delaynie was the last person I saw Walt with, so isn't it possible that you're overlooking the obvious? He may simply have chosen to be with her instead of me. Most likely he's already started a new life somewhere else, and he's forgotten all about the pellet Olivia found."

For a moment none of them moved. Hawthorne nodded morosely, took his seat and replaced the hat upon his head.

Harper stared at her hands. "Believe me, all this breaks my heart. But I'd rather believe Walt is off living a new life with someone else than the alternative you're suggesting."

Ivy stood, her linen tunic gleaming in the morning light against her midnight skin. "Time may prove you right. But you should also consider that the disturbing and unexplained recent events indicate the killer is somehow related to an owlish being. But you are correct—right now, all remains unclear. Still, if you try to discover what is happening with Walt, it may provide valuable clues that would help to catch the killer."

Harper pulled out her swan mirror and examined it while they looked on. "But what about that being we watched across the river a few weeks ago? Do you agree that she may be part of the Swan Clan?" The memory of the eerie trumpeting cry that came from near the pellets across the river that night still gave her gooseflesh. She felt a small stirring as little green-faced Alida settled onto the sofa beside her.

Ivy shrugged. "While that sounds like a reasonable assertion, we do not know. Neither do any of our sources have definitive information. We guess the Swan Clan may have returned to deal with the murderous being in our midst. But that mysterious Clan operates according to their own rules. They may be here for another, but equally compelling reason."

"So are you saying that it is futile to try to learn more about the Swan Clan? You think their presence here is merely coincidental?"

"We believe it would be a waste of time to try to discover their purposes. And Walter's safety is our primary concern."

Hawthorne stood again. "Unfortunately, Walter presents a unique quandary for us. As you know, our moral code does not allow interfering with another's destiny. Unless Walter directly asks for our help, we are not free to give it. We urge you to begin your investigations. But perhaps you would be wise to begin your search with the Tskili', and not with owl shifters."

Despite internal protestations that their news had done little to help, Harper felt a sense of dread she hadn't known before. She looked at the wall clock. The shop needed to open in ten minutes. She needed to think. "Well, I thank you for sharing your thoughts. Unfortunately, it's almost time to open the shop. If you discover anything helpful ..."

They all piped up together, "We will let you know!"

Harper was surprised and touched as one by one, they came over and laid a hand atop hers. Once they were all connected through touch, she felt love rush through her body, strengthening her spirit, before their lights flickered out, leaving her feeling stronger than she had felt in days.

After grabbing the wrapped sandwich Piper had left on the counter and pulling a water bottle from the refrigerator, Harper headed downstairs. Once she'd unlocked the front doors and pulled up the shades, she sat behind the counter, staring into space until her first customer arrived.

As the hours ticked by, she settled on two plans of action. First, she would research the Tskili' and its history at the Sequoyah College library, and if needed, at the public library. If nothing useful was available in either place, she might take a trip to nearby Cherokee to see if she could learn anything there. Second, on her next afternoon off, she would visit Walt's treehouse, alone, and go inside to discover what she could.

✦·✦

In a quick online search later that afternoon, Harper uncovered two terms that likely applied to what the Fae had described: a demonic owl, called a Tskili'. While the Cherokee respected owls as representatives of a great spirit who watched the world at night, a medicine man was required to distinguish between a real owl and the evil witch being. Beyond that, she found a few interesting stories to keep her entertained, though none were especially helpful.

Later that afternoon, to her surprise, Quinn stopped by. With all the time he'd been lavishing on Olivia, it had been weeks since she'd last seen him. Unlike the pushy man she had met the year before, this Quinn looked both confident and fit. A tan had replaced the pallor and dark circles he'd previously sported beneath his brown eyes.

He approached the counter. "Hi Harper. Olivia told me that you and Bryan went to the rare books festival in Asheville yesterday. I wanted to go myself, but I'd promised Olivia I'd help organize her supply room. I couldn't let her down. But I've been curious about what you might have found. Would you mind showing me?"

He looked hopefully around her desk for stacks of fresh books to peruse. Unfortunately she had left them in her office upstairs. And for now, that's where they'd stay. Harper wanted to look through them herself before anyone else did.

But she smiled at his eager face, after reminding herself that he'd been helping her daughter. "I haven't looked through them myself yet, Quinn, so they're upstairs. But I don't think any of them would be of particular use to you. I got one by Zora Neale Hurston that you probably already know about. Most of the others weren't local, they were global reference works. But I did pick up a copy of *The Trail of the Lonesome Pine* and Jesse Stuart's *The Thread that Runs so True.*"

He shook his head. "No, you're right, I'm not interested in those. They don't really have a lot to do with folklore."

She shrugged. "I guess not. I picked them up for the Appalachian culture connection."

"Maybe. But you know neither is about North Carolina, don't you?"

Her sigh, when it came, was mercifully imperceptible. This was the pugnacious Quinn she knew. "Yes, Quinn. I do know that. But both are set in the mountains, not that far away."

Remembering her research plan, she changed course, interrupting as he started to speak. "Quinn, I plan to go by and visit the Sequoyah College library on Monday afternoon. I know you're on summer scheduling right now. But is the library open on Mondays, and are you available to help me do some research?"

"Yes, to the first. But, unfortunately, no to the second. I have a doctor's appointment in Asheville Monday afternoon. But if you'd tell me what you're searching for, I'll see what I can find, then bring you a report with references. I can drop it by here Monday morning on my way out of town, if that's okay."

Her mood instantly improved. "Okay? Quinn, that would be amazing!" She jumped up. "In fact, to pay you back for all the time you'll be saving me, I'll run upstairs right now and get that stack of books for you to look through."

Quinn promised to keep an eye on the checkout counter while she ran up the stairs to get the small stack of books for him. After she'd removed the Kentucky-based books he'd eschewed, there were only a few to bring.

Back downstairs, she checked out an older woman and a small child, who purchased a cozy mystery and several reprints of Lyle the Crocodile titles, while Quinn flipped through the books. Seeing the woman and child brought Harper a stab of nostalgia—they reminded her of herself and Grandma Sophie all those years ago. The fact that grandmas still brought children to bookshops cheered her.

After they left, Quinn scooted the books across the counter to her. "You're right, Harper. None of these interest me. When the bookfair comes back around next year, I'll ride there with you guys." Harper forced her lips together, squelching the retort that of course he could go with them—if he was invited.

As he walked whistling out the door, she felt renewed astonishment at the strange relationship between this humorless scholar and her glamorous, athletic daughter. What could possibly be the glue holding their friendship together, she wondered.

But, as promised on the following Monday morning, Quinn dropped off a typed twenty-page, single-spaced report, with footnotes and references, bound together in a smart pressboard binder. From then until closing time, she studied its interesting, though maddeningly vague contents. As she read, she highlighted a few unfamiliar terms to explore further.

At her one o'clock closing time, she tucked the binder into her messenger bag before heading up the hill to the Whippoorwill Gap Public Library. Once there, she went straight to the reference room, looking for Greta, the reference librarian who had helped her with local history questions in the past. She spotted the blonde, middle-aged woman helping another patron with an online database.

Once Greta turned a warm smile her way, Harper explained that she was searching for information on a creature called the Tskili'. Greta looked at her over her reading glasses. "Would this have anything to do with the large pellets that have been found around here this summer?"

Harper froze. It hadn't occurred to her that anyone would think twice about her request. Were legends of these creatures commonly known to the people who grew up around here? She played along. "Yes, Greta. You're on to me. Hearing about the possible connection has me curious, so I decided to dig into the lore just to see what I can find."

Greta thought for a minute. "Well, they were mythical creatures, so we don't need to worry that one of them is out flying around here at night. But it is possible some deranged person decided to emulate them. I assume the police have considered that angle."

"I'm not sure," Harper replied uneasily. "But if I find anything that may be helpful, I'll let them know."

Greta showed her how to log in to a scholarly database with folklore information and brought her a small stack of pertinent reference books. She promised to check on Harper later, then turned her attention to a man who had a question about prehistoric weaponry.

After several frustrating searches, Harper found little that wasn't already in Quinn's report.

Next, she went to the local history shelves and pulled Walt's book, *Hootin' in the Holler: A History of Whippoorwill Gap.* In the index, she looked for the terms "Tskili'" and "Skili," but with disappointment, found nothing.

She reluctantly laid the history aside after gently swiping a finger across Walt's name, then turned to the first folklore book Greta had brought her, *Myths and Legends of the Cherokee* by Branwen Smith. Published in 1994, the book promised a near comprehensive covering of Cherokee lore. Glancing through the book, Harper was surprised at the variety of creatures she found. She already knew that Piper and Ash were Yunwi Tsunsdi', also called "the Cherokee Little People." There were a lot of stories about them and information about the different clans. She made a note of the name of the book and promised to track a copy down for herself. Ash would enjoy reading it, if no one else did. But that would wait for another day.

She went to the card catalog and found a book Greta had missed: *Monsters of the Appalachians* by Curtis Crowe, which contained an entire short but informative chapter on the Tskili'. The description of the pitiless monster sucked all warmth from Harper's body, leaving behind a tight dense knot of fear.

While Harper knew that folklore wasn't literal history, she also knew it often held a kernel of truth. For centuries past, there had been stories of a demon, usually regarded as an evil female or witch, with an ugly disposition augmented by demonic powers, whose only purpose for existence was to torture and devour. But according to Crowe, the creature could be defeated with a combination of distraction, purity of intention, and luck. Harper stared out the window at the garden behind the building. What did he mean by "purity of intention"? More unsettled than comforted, she closed the book.

Time slipped away as she sat beneath the cold, dark swirling fog of her thoughts. Could the suspicions Hawthorne and the others shared have merit? Was Walt somehow connected to, or even worse, descended from such a beast?

But the more she pondered, the more determined she felt. She'd survived harrowing circumstances in the past, hadn't she? As a young adult, she'd supported her emotionally needy mother after her father deserted them. She'd nursed her husband until his death from cancer. She'd raised her uniquely headstrong daughter Olivia. And only months ago, against unlikely odds, she had helped rescue her beloved Grandmother and the Fae when they were in danger.

An unaccustomed sense of confidence blew through her, and with it, a sense of determination. Somehow she would figure out what was going on. She looked over the aging books on the shelves. Like Amelia Earhart, whom she'd admired as a child, she would head out—come what may. Harper paused briefly, considering Earhart's last flight, when she disappeared forever. Sobered, she reflected that the same fate could await her as well. She straightened her backbone. Yes, she thought, I absolutely will.

For a moment, she considered a quick search for the Swan Clan as well. But on recalling Ivy's assertion that the Clan may not be connected to the pellets at all, she decided to look into that later. She did, however, promise herself that the next time she spied the woman in the white hat, she'd chase her down for answers.

No. Her next move would be to locate Walt. She had no idea where he might be unless, for whatever reason, he was hiding out in his treehouse. Whether he was there or not, it was the most logical place to begin. If he wasn't there, maybe she would find clues to his whereabouts. Why had she waited so long? But in her heart, she knew the answer. She was afraid he no longer wanted her.

On checking her watch, she stood. It was only three in the afternoon. She had been sitting for most of the day. It was time to go for a stroll around town. If she got lucky, perhaps she'd run into Delaynie or the woman in the white hat.

While the thought of talking with Delaynie was distasteful, perhaps she could pick up some information from her. Maybe, with luck, Delaynie would let slip something and reveal what was going on. Then too, she thought reluctantly, if Delaynie was still seeing Walt, she'd need to be warned about the potential danger he posed. Despite her aversion to the woman, Harper had no wish for an innocent death on her conscience.

Chapter 20

AFTER HIKING AROUND TOWN for an hour, she only encountered one striking, tall woman, Evie Adams, who was sweeping the stoop in front of Great Green Grocer's. Tired out, Harper headed back to her apartment. She had agreed to another evening walk with Bryan and Leda at Puckett's Park this evening, so she ate a bowl of rice with stir fried tofu and vegetables, then chatted with Piper until the appointed time. She speculated that Delaynie may have left the area, possibly accompanied by Walt, as she'd seen no sign of her for the past two weeks.

The walk through the park provided a nice diversion. She and Bryan had taken turns throwing the ball for Leda in the park's small open field before taking the side path to the river to let her splash about in the water. As she'd gotten to know the saluki better, she'd come to appreciate how consistently calm and affectionate she proved to be.

The sun was dipping behind the trees when Bryan announced it was time for them to head home. They strolled up the drive from the park, past the coffee shop to Oak Street, where they parted ways. Bryan and Leda took a shortcut across the Birdsong Theatre parking lot before making the trek back to Poplar Street. After a busy day, Harper was ready to retire. She looked forward to settling down in her little nest upstairs.

But before they reached Oak Street, Harper spied a familiar woman, her black hair pulled back in a severe bun, her tall figure clad in a white sundress with black sandals, walking away toward Main Street. With a sudden burst of energy, she wished Bryan and his dog a hurried goodbye before she zipped across the empty road to catch the woman before she disappeared around the corner.

When she drew near enough to touch her, Harper raised her voice. "Excuse me!" After the woman stopped and turned, she felt a chill on looking directly into Delaynie's cold, black eyes.

"Oh, it's you." The woman's red-lipstick-lacquered upper lip curled slightly as her eyebrows raised. "Tell me you're not still out looking for Walt. How sad for you, if you are. I can assure you, he's quite well. In fact, you'll be happy to know he's enjoying his escape from this boring little hamlet."

Harper forced down the humiliation and rage arising in her throat at the woman's demeanor and tone. She suddenly wondered why, if Walt was so happy with this woman, he wasn't out walking with her right now.

"Oh?" she began coldly. "If memory serves, last time I saw you, you were asking me where he lives. If he's so happy with you, where is he now?"

The woman took a step back, looking puzzled. Harper hesitated. For all she knew, Delaynie and Walt had reconciled the day Delaynie had tried to find out where he lived. If that was the case, Harper had no hope of enlisting her help to track him down. Then, with a sinking heart, she reminded herself she still had a duty to warn this arrogant shrew that she was possibly in danger. She swallowed her bile. "But actually, no. I wasn't looking for Walt. I was looking for you. I have something to tell you."

The black eyebrows stretched up as the red lips took a downturn. Delaynie glanced down at the expensive wristwatch on her arm. "Fine. I can spare a few minutes." She waited expectantly.

Harper didn't want to discuss the situation on the street. As they reached the corner, she asked, "Do you have time for a beer or a glass of wine? I'll buy."

Delaynie sighed and resumed walking toward Take Flight Brewery. "I suppose I could go with you, if you need one. I'll stick with water."

Harper bristled, responding with a sharp, "I don't care what you get, Delaynie. This won't take long."

Harper led the way into Take Flight. On Monday nights, the atmosphere inside the brewery stayed quiet and lowkey. Harper asked for a half pint of porter and a glass of water for Delaynie. Chase said, "Coming right up, Harper." Once she'd paid, the women claimed a corner table in front. The sight of Deanna and Dashawn waving to her from a table near the back where they were eating dinner bolstered her confidence.

While Delaynie waited across the table with unconcealed irritation, Harper cast about for a suitable way to broach the topic. Only now did it occur to her that her efforts to warn Delaynie about Walt would likely be perceived as a jilted woman's desperate attempt to scare off her opponent. She studied Delaynie's beautiful but cold face, running through her options.

"You wanted to tell me something? I'm listening."

Harper instantly decided bluntness would serve as well as any other approach. "I assume you've heard about the human remains that have been turning up and about the missing people in the region."

Delaynie's aggressive demeanor switched to one of surprise. "Of course I have. It's been all over the news and social media. Walt and I overhear talk about it when we're out and about. Why?"

Harper took a deep breath. "I don't know what's going on. But I've been researching."

"Really?" The woman hooted unpleasantly. "My, my. So you're an investigator, too? There are no end to your talents! I guess that should make us all feel better, just knowing you're on the case." Her eyebrows knit together and she leaned forward. "Ms. Wood, unless this has something to do with me, I really do need to be going."

Harper blinked, surprised that Delaynie knew her last name. She started to ask where she'd learned it but brushed it off as unimportant. Walt likely told her, she thought, a stab piercing her gut. She cleared her throat, throwing caution out the door. At worst, Delaynie would share Harper's concerns with Walt later, and they would have a laugh at her expense.

She looked Delaynie directly in the eye. "Look. This will sound crazy to you no matter how I put it. But you're a human being and I don't want you to get hurt." She took a deep breath. "I think it's possible Walt may be involved in the killings."

Delaynie, who had been leaning forward, relaxed back into her chair with an open snicker. She reached in her shoulder bag and removed a tissue to swipe beneath her eyes. "Oh, Ms. Wood, really. You are too funny. What an imagination! Goodness ... you should be writing fantasy, not selling it! I know Walt well, and trust me, he's not capable of such savagery. Besides." She leaned forward as though to share a confidence, and Harper moved back, surprised that her breath held a hint of rot, which Harper attributed to overzealous dieting. "He's been much too busy for that."

Harper winced. She should have expected the dig. She worked to hold her voice steady. "All I can say is, be careful. There may be more to Walt than you think."

Delaynie stared at the ceiling for a moment, her tongue planted firmly in her protruding cheek, as though reconsidering. When she looked down again, her tone, no longer mocking, had become businesslike. "Okay, Harper. I'll watch him closely. While I think your assertion is, oh, insane, I do appreciate your concern for my welfare. But I'm curious. What is it about Walter that makes you think he could be capable of such villainy? Is he some sort of evil chemical mastermind with the lab equipment and know-how to turn human remains into pellets, or is there something else I need to know about him?"

Harper's muscles tensed. She refused to allow this woman to bait her. Her motives had been genuine. She'd done nothing of which to be ashamed.

"You'll just have to trust that I have my reasons for telling you this. I don't want to get too specific. And of course, I could be wrong. You wouldn't believe me if I explained them to you anyway." She lifted her chin. "And I know Walt just as well, if not better, than you do. Just be mindful of your own safety. That's all I'm asking."

Delaynie took her first sip of water, then sat the glass delicately on the pale blue napkin that served as a coaster. Harper felt relieved that she had said her piece, despite the woman's derision. No matter what happened, she had performed her responsibility.

While replacing her bag's strap on her shoulder, Delaynie said stiffly, "Thank you for sharing your concerns, Ms. Wood. It must be painful for you to talk to me."

Then her tone became laced with stevia: too sweet and with a bitter aftertaste. "But you must believe me when I say that Walt is happy. We're staying at a place I've taken up in the mountains. We've been reveling in our time together again. Our relationship goes way back; you could say it's been an off-again, on-again affair." She leaned forward as she stood, whispering in Harper's ear, "And right now, it's definitely on." She straightened. "Au revoir, Mon Cherie."

Harper sat speechless. Soon after the woman had swept out the door into the humid late July evening, Deanna walked over while Dashawn paid their dinner bill. “I hate to be nosy, Harper, but who was that woman?”

When Harper didn’t answer, Deanna took Delaynie’s vacated seat. “What’s the matter?”

Harper choked out, “She’s the woman Walt left me for, Deanna!”

“Oh my Lord! Why were you talking to her?” She leaned back while staring at her friend. Then she shook her head. “But I’m sorry, Harper, I still don’t buy that. I’ve known Walt for years. Believe me when I say that woman is not his type.”

“He has a type?” Harper snuffled. “How many of us have there been?”

Deanna placed a warm brown hand on Harper’s arm. “You are the only one I know of. You are his type.”

Dashawn approached the table and began a cheerful greeting, which he cut short on seeing their faces. “I’ll let you ladies talk while I head to the gentlemen’s room. I’ll be back in a few.”

Once he was out of earshot, Deanna continued. “Walt is a good man, Harper. What makes you think he’s seeing that woman?”

Harper reminded her that the last time anyone had seen him had been in mid-June, when she’d seen him walking in Puckett’s Park with Delaynie. “She just told me they’re staying up at a place she’s renting up the mountains!”

Deanna shook her head. “Nuh, uh. That does not sound right to me. I don’t think Walt is staying with that woman. Think, Harper. You know Walt! You know what a kind and gentle soul he is. I can’t believe he would be so callous with your feelings! And her bad attitude radiated all the way to the back of the room. He’d never take up with such a cockatrice.”

Harper noticed Dashawn was now talking with a man at the bar.

"Why would she lie to me? Besides, there's more to the story." Harper filled her friend in on the information she had found about the Tskili' and her Fae friends' concerns. "What if something turns owl shifters into monsters? Or what if Walt is actually descended from this monster? Is there a better explanation for these pellets?"

Dashawn looked over at them with a question in his eye. When she smiled weakly at him, he clapped the man he'd been talking to on the shoulder and turned toward them. Deanna quickly said, "Harper, I know things look bad, but don't be so quick to judge Walt. I've known him for over twenty years, and I just feel it in my bones. He's not capable of being so loathsome."

Dashawn's solid, reassuring bulk approached the table. "Can we walk you home, Harper?" She nodded with gratitude, glad to have company in the fading light. While the conversation had been trying, at least she had done the right thing. If Delaynie's bones were found next, Harper had no reason to feel guilty. Standing, she ignored the untouched porter on the table.

She had little hope of sleeping well tonight. Tomorrow, she planned to visit Walt's treehouse, alone. The thought terrified her. There was no telling what she might find.

"I SAW YOUR LITTLE songbird today. What was her name again?" Despite his lack of response, she continued chattering as though filling him in on a day at the office. "Oh, yes, Harpy

Wood!" He continued to lie motionless as possible. "Well, aren't you curious about how your little friend is getting along?"

Only minutes before Delaynie's noisome entrance, Walt's mind had been soaring, as he'd escaped to his memories. In it, he and Harper sailed through the air above the river on their first ecstatic flight together, the night she'd discovered her Fae gift. They had lightly touched wingtips, then woven a path, over and above one another, in the light of a full hunter's moon.

But now Delaynie's nauseating artificially sweetened voice continued, "Apparently she's quite well. She was playing in the park with her new beau before I caught up with her. Yes, she looks quite satisfied with life now."

He slowed his breathing, aiming to become as still as possible. He always clung to the hope she would grow bored with him and turn her attention to something, anything, else.

But instead, she grew a notch louder, never a good sign. "Really, Walt, it's rude of you to ignore someone when they're talking to you. Sit up and look at me."

Hinges squealed as the door to his cage was thrown wide. He felt, rather than saw her towering over him. She waited a minute, but when he continued to lie motionless, she reached down, grabbed his hair, and jerked him upright. He opened his eyes then and whispered, "Hello, Delaynie."

She tightened her grip on the hair wound in her fist, causing his scalp to throb. "Really, Walt, you should know better than to try my patience. Well? What do you have to say about your darling Harper? We're getting to be quite chummy, she and I."

The thought of Delaynie talking to Harper caused his insides to freeze, but he carefully kept his expression neutral.

"Our little tête-à-tête was quite sweet, really. It seems your sweetheart is worried about my welfare. Now why do you suppose that would be? Care to take a guess?"

Walt's chest began to ache as the fetid air from her breath slunk into his lungs. His body stiffened of its own accord, as though to ward off a blow. Delaynie observed his reaction with glee. Still gripping his hair, she thrust her face only inches from his. "I confess, I wondered myself. But it appears she suspects you may be involved in the murders."

Though he knew she was likely lying, he flinched all the same.

"She cautioned me to be careful around you. But don't worry, Darling. I promised her to be very, very careful where you are concerned." With that, she flung his head to the stone floor with a thud that jarred his skull, bringing with it a fresh wave of nausea.

Though he knew she watched him, he was powerless to stop a tear that worked its way loose from beneath a lash before it made its wet way down his dry, dusty cheek.

Chapter 21

PIPER'S ALMOND EYES SHOT sparks of agitation. "Do you think it wise, Dearie, to go on such a venture alone?"

"I don't see how it matters, Piper. I promised Walt I'd never reveal where he lived to anyone. And until I know what is going on, I don't want to betray his confidence. If I don't return before nightfall, you can head toward the dam and scout the wilderness between here and there. That's all I can tell you."

When Piper began clutching at her linen tunic, Harper took to her knees so she could look the stalwart faery in the eyes. "I promise I'll be careful. With any luck, Walt has a new girlfriend and he's happy. We can all live with that. But if he's in trouble, I need to do what I can to help him."

"I don't like it," Piper sniffed. "You're taking an awful chance, Dearie."

Harper understood the danger. Even if she avoided physical injury, the emotional harm she'd endure might be worse. But she had to try. If Walt had chosen to leave her, she'd be hurt, but also relieved. And she'd never visit his home again. But if he was in any sort of peril, either from others or from himself, she must do what she could to help.

Leaving a distressed Piper behind, she headed to the park and took a little path down to the river. On looking this way and that for familiar robins, Fae figures, or worse Delaynie, and seeing no one, she forded the rushing water at a shallow spot and climbed the bank on the other side. She continued, stopping occasionally to make sure she was still alone, until she reached a massive mountain laurel. She made her way underneath its thick leafy foliage, then transformed herself into a great horned owl.

Ten minutes later, Harper landed on Walt's lofty wooden balcony and resumed her human form. She reached into her pants pocket and clutched Bryan's mirror for reassurance. She reminded herself that she'd take her owl form and flee should she encounter anything hostile.

Clinging to the mirror until she felt sufficiently calm, she paused to survey the porch. A rocking chair had been turned askew; otherwise, it was exactly as it had been the last time she'd seen it. There weren't even any leaves lying out of place. Either Walt or the wind had swept the floorboards clean.

The entire scenario felt surreal. Was she really breaking into Walt's cottage, scared of what she might find inside?

Her last visit here seemed impossibly long ago. At the time, she'd felt secure in their relationship. Though she knew about Delaynie, she felt no qualms about her. The first pellet had been found, which was disturbing, but she'd been convinced that this matter would be cleared up quickly as well. Never in her wildest imaginings had she thought Walt would soon vanish so abruptly from her life.

As she touched the chair Walt had occupied that evening, pain pierced her heart. Lowering herself into its seat, she tried to feel Walt's presence. He'd been right here beside her, sipping a glass of wine. She closed her eyes for a second, hearing only cool mountain air rustling the tree limbs around her. Searching her memories of that night, she could find no hints that Walt was dissatisfied with either her or his life. She could almost smell the pizza wafting from the oven. But when she reopened her eyes, the shutters on the windows were closed. Neither sounds nor smells emanated from the kitchen. The treehouse felt abandoned.

Their relationship, so full of joy and promise, had literally swept her to new heights. But now she crashed in despair. It's time, she told herself as she left the chair behind.

The closed door stood before her. Though she knew it had no lock, everything about turning the sturdy brass knob felt wrong. What if Walt was inside but didn't want to see her? Or worse, what if Delaynie was with him? Her stomach turned, while the sensation that this was all a sick hallucination amplified. Her heart toppled. What if their relationship had been the mirage, and this, instead, was the reality? Maybe she'd been lying to herself all along. With a sense of dread, she twisted the knob. As usual, the door gave a soft sigh upon swinging inside.

On the threshold, she stood alert, poised to change form and fly if need be. But inside the house all was still and heavy. The air carried only the scent of stale dust. Walt's magnificent wall clock had stopped ticking, which struck Harper as an ominous sign. "Walt?" She waited in tense silence before adding, "It's Harper."

Her hoarse whisper dropped to the floor as the dense silence greeted her in return. As her eyes adjusted to the dim light, she noted the thick layer of dust coating the table next to the doorway. Walt, always fastidious about cleaning, likely hadn't been inside recently. His clock rested at one minute shy of twelve o'clock; whether to midnight or noon, there was no way to tell.

The sound of a faint noise coming from the bedroom nearly ripped her heart from her throat. Get a grip! she told herself sternly. "Hello? Is anyone here?"

But as the noise continued, she hesitated, then tiptoed to the closed bedroom door and knocked softly. "It's Harper," she said again, not knowing what else to say. The noise stopped, but when she got no other response, she eased the door open, holding the mirror in her free hand to use as a weapon. Adrenaline careened wildly through her veins.

Through the shifting shadows, she glimpsed Walt's unmade bed, a pile of clothes on the floor, and others partially hanging from the chest of drawers. The sight disturbed her. Walt would never have left such a mess—at least, not the Walt she knew. Once more, the noise distracted her. Now she could tell it came from behind his closet door. Steeling herself, she padded over, then jerked the door wide. Inside, a tiny brown-gray mouse huddled beside one of Walt's shoes. It stopped gnawing on the desiccated acorn in its paws, frozen, its black eyes bulging in terror.

Harper took a shaky breath, then softly closed the closet door and leaned against it, allowing the icy tension to ebb from her limbs. Once sufficiently calm, she inspected the room more closely. Obviously, no one had been here in weeks.

With no need to stay quiet, she began her search in earnest. First, she opened the dresser drawers but found they contained nothing except for clothing. On top, a dusty hand mirror and hairbrush lay forsaken. She picked up the brush and spent a few seconds running her fingers over the few black, white, and brown hairs clinging to its bristles. After setting it down, she picked up one of the t-shirts hanging from a drawer and held it to her face. It still held traces of his scent.

Tears sprang to her eyes. Stop, she told herself sternly. Turning her attention to the floor, she saw a shoe, much too small for Walt, peeking from beneath it. Her heart pounding, she reached down and pulled it out. As she'd suspected, it was a woman's shoe but not one of her own. It looked old, and much too small to fit Delaynie. She held the cracked leather close. It appeared to be a leather slipper, like one someone would have worn hundreds of years ago. The uppers were an aged and discolored ivory with a thick grayed satin ribbon for a lace. She looked about for its mate but found nothing. Harper had no idea to whom it might belong.

She wished yet again that Walt hadn't been so reluctant to speak of his past. As she carefully placed the shoe exactly where she'd found it, she concluded the bedroom would yield no more clues. As she left, she pulled the door closed behind her.

Pausing at the archway to his study, she moved on. She'd save that for last.

Compared to the bedroom, the kitchen was orderly. On the floor, a glass lay on its side as though it had been dropped but not broken. A dark, sticky stain spread around it. She guessed it had been filled with juice or perhaps sweet tea. With the bedroom in disarray and now this spilled glass, she surmised Walt left in a hurry. Only a significant event would have prompted him to leave his bed unmade, much less a spilled glass on the floor. She placed the glass in his sink and turned the tap, but no water issued forth. Then she remembered that Walt's running water and power came from magic, not electricity. In his absence, the magic must have disappeared as well.

In the living room, she found everything dusty, though tidy and in its place. Since the wide picture window in this room opened onto his balcony, she decided to open the shutters, allowing in more light. Even if someone knew the house was here, it was unlikely they would be able to spot the open window. With her eyes adjusted to the dim interior, the stark noonday sunshine almost blinded her. She turned back to the living room, purple spots before her eyes.

After a few minutes, her vision cleared. But since a search through every drawer and shelf here revealed nothing unusual, she turned her attention to the small study. If she were going to find any hints at what had become of Walt, she felt sure they would be here, among his beloved papers and books.

Glancing around the golden oak-paneled room, dappled with light and shadow from the living room window, she decided to risk opening the shuttered window above his desk. No longer afraid of being discovered, she began with the bookshelves lining the walls. Many of Walt's books were heavy, leather-bound tomes ... some centuries old. The topics covered varied, but history, furniture, plants, animals, and copies of Walt's own works predominated. But after working through one entire wall and finding nothing, she decided to move to his desk.

Through the window, the sun dipped closer to the treetops. Time was precious and the desk would most likely yield information as to what Walt had been thinking and doing leading up to his disappearance. That's where she would begin.

She settled into the old-fashioned chestnut swivel chair that matched his old-fashioned schoolteacher-style desk. He'd been so proud that the set was built from the sturdy but now unavailable hardwood. The chair was comfortable and practical; she marveled again at Walt's construction skills. It was so like him, she reflected, to perfect such a useful and functional craft, turning everyday objects into practical yet beautiful works of art.

Inside the desk's top central drawer, she found troves of rubber bands, paperclips, and pristine writing paper. There were also a bottle of ink and a fountain pen. Once again her heart twisted. Everything about Walt was uncompromisingly analog. Crestfallen, she grappled with despair at losing this cherished quaint man.

Three drawers were stacked along the desk's right-hand side. In the first, she found ledgers. A quick flip through showed all contained records of his books—how many had sold through the years, dating from the 1960s to this past May, providing more proof that he had not been here since she'd last seen him in June.

After carefully replacing the ledgers, she closed the top drawer and moved to the one beneath it. Here she found files filled with research, probably for his next book. But on opening the top folder, her heart nearly stopped as "owl shifters," "Skili," and "Tskili'" studded the top page. Apparently he had been researching them too. These notes were written on ivory paper which looked new, unlike the ledgers, many of which were time-browned around the edges. She skimmed as quickly as she could until her eyes began to water and she could no longer focus. Cursing herself, she realized she'd forgotten to bring a pair of reading glasses.

She stopped short on finding that the last page contained scribbled notes about the Swan Clan. Her mind went back to the sound of trumpeting that night. Walt had seemed on the alert at hearing it. She felt sure the sound had been connected to the woman in the white cowboy hat and that the whole thing must have had meaning for him. The question was, what?

Giving the notes the attention they deserved would take time. She quickly decided to leave the piles of notes stacked on the desktop. Early tomorrow morning, she would drive over and hike to the treehouse and haul these notes back to her apartment in a backpack. A glance out the window made the need to finish even more pressing; the sun's golden rays came from below the treetops. She felt a renewed sense of urgency knowing dusk would descend shortly.

On opening the final drawer, she gasped. Underneath a stack of empty notebooks, she found one half-filled with dated entries, in Walt's meticulous, cursive handwriting—his journal.

Regretting the time she'd spent reading through the notes, she quickly flipped to the last entry, dated June 7. While she felt a little guilty at reading his journal, she needed to discover what had happened. Now she desperately wished she possessed a photographic memory. That not being the case, she forced her breath to slow. Only when she felt calm did she begin to read the final entry.

Remorse arose palpably from the page. He hinted at some horrible deed from his past, long hidden, that had returned to annihilate him. She flipped back to the earlier pages where the penmanship was fastidious. The contrast to the last pages proved stark. The writing here was difficult to read, as though Walt frantically struggled to get his thoughts down with a shaking hand. "There is no escape ..." And then the final line. "How can I bear to lose Harper?"

She sat back, stunned. His final words, his last thoughts were about her. Absently, her hand reached into her pocket where she grasped the swan mirror that Bryan had given her for comfort. At the exact moment she closed her fist around the metal, a loud trumpeting came from the skies beyond the foliage outside the window. Her eyes darted out the pane of glass, where she caught the sight of something white moving through the distant trees near the forest floor.

She quickly placed the journal on top of Walt's research, craning forward to see the white object, now out of sight. Leaving the study behind, she raced out the door to the porch and resumed her owl form. Whoever or whatever that was, it wouldn't get away from her this time.

After taking flight, she glided around the property to no avail. She knew she hadn't imagined it. Convinced it had been the tall woman in the white-feathered cowboy hat, Harper landed in a tree near the spot where she had seen it, swiveling her head, first in one direction, then another. Finally she spied something glittering through the fading light, not far from the creek below.

"Wait!" she shrieked, then sailed down. Landing near the spot, she resumed her human shape. At sensing movement through the trees, she began the chase on foot, but her toes caught on something large and solid. Pitching forward, she landed face down in the undergrowth.

After catching her breath, she sat up, expecting to see a rock or a log that had been responsible for her fall. Instead, what she saw by her feet caused her to scurry back in horror. An eyeless human skull grinned at her from the side of a monstrous pellet. And beside it lay one of Walt's tennis shoes.

A scream for help tore from her lips as she ran blindly down the mountain, but before she'd covered more than ten yards, she became dimly aware that the branches of a large mountain laurel began to shake. It then unbelievably stretched out to pull her underneath the murky, ground-hugging canopy into the darkness beneath.

Chapter 22

LIGHT, THE COLOR OF bleeding hearts, bathed the world around Harper in a soothing glow when she next opened her eyes. From her prone vantage point, she marveled at the enormous mountain laurel branches hanging above, forming a natural cathedral about her. As she struggled to sit, she inhaled sharply at the pain jackknifing through her left hip.

A familiar, beloved voice spoke from behind her. "It's not broken, only bruised. You'll be fine, Darling."

The pain forgotten, she sprang to her feet. Grandma Sophie beamed at her from an upholstered armchair that appeared to be constructed entirely of branches and evergreen-hued moss. Harper saw she had been lying on a couch cushioned with the same spongy material. Dizziness descended, forcing her to sit again. "Am I in the Faery Realm?" she asked, passing her hand across her eyes.

Grandma sounded amused, answering with a riddle. "Where, exactly, is the Faery Realm, My Sweet?"

Harper tried to clear her head. "I thought you had to go through a tunnel on the riverbank ..." she began. On hearing another chuckle, she gave up with relief, "... it doesn't matter! Grandma! I'm so happy to see you!"

She refrained from her impulse to run to her grandmother for a hug, after carefully surveying the wrinkle-free face, topped by a delicate pearl-strewn cobweb crown nestled in her wavy auburn hair. This rendition of Grandma was similar, yet also formidably different, from the one she remembered from her childhood. The eerie change reminded her that though this being was still Grandma Sophie to her, in reality, she now served as Queen Sophia of the Faery Realm, and as such, was due proper pomp and respect. Harper hung back, uncertain how to approach her.

Seeing her hesitation, Grandma came to the rescue. Rising to her feet, she approached the couch, where Harper joyfully rose to meet her. "It's okay, Sweetheart. We're alone now. In this place, I'm merely Grandma. Here, does this help?"

Everything about the figure before her became momentarily fuzzy, as though Harper were observing it through moving water. Once Grandma returned to focus, she looked just as she had when she had been sixty-three, and Harper, eight.

She had the same Doris Day haircut, sandy-blonde and close-cropped, with predominately gray eyes sprinkled with arresting flecks of violet. Wrinkles punctuated her face, while age spots dotted the arms that emerged from the short sleeves of a lilac-colored pant suit. The crown was gone, and Harper felt like a child again, safe and loved in Grandma's presence. The tears sprang to her eyes unbidden.

Grandma lowered herself to the sofa at Harper's side and hugged her tight. "There, there, Darling. I haven't changed for you. Since it's just the two of us here, you can talk to me as you used to."

Only the fact that they looked at one another eye-to-eye reminded Harper she was now an adult. Nevertheless, dropping her pretense of strength felt wonderful. She wiped her tears with the handkerchief Grandma handed her—the woman had always carried an endless supply. It seemed to be one thing that would never change.

To enhance the illusion, Grandma's voice had also regained the shaky quality it had when Harper was a child. "Now, tell me, Harper. What's the trouble?"

Harper blinked in confusion. She couldn't remember exactly what was happening or why she was here. Her last memory was of running through the forest after the woman in the white cowboy hat. Then she remembered tripping, the hideous skull, and the panic she'd felt as she was dragged underneath the mountain laurel.

She frowned. "How did you find me, Grandma? How did you know I was in trouble?"

Grandma pushed Harper's wild hair back from her forehead. "You called me. The need was great enough that I heard all the way from the Faery Realm."

"I don't remember calling you."

Grandma reached over, squeezing her hand. "You yelled for help. If the need hadn't been dire, I wouldn't have heard it." She stopped smiling. "Would you like to tell me why you're out in a forest so distant from your home, alone?"

Harper groaned. It all came back in a rush. She related how Delaynie's appearance in town had preceded Walt's subsequent disappearance. She described the horrifying pellets, and how the other Fae thought perhaps they were connected to Walt, a notion Harper found inconceivable. Then she moved on to her research and plans to help Walt any way she could, which was why she had gone to his home to find clues.

Though embarrassed, she admitted to reading some of his journal. But then she blurted, "It seems he still loves me. Or at least he did, up until he disappeared over a month ago. My Fae friends suspect this may be the work of some of the Others. Do you have any idea what might be going on?"

Her grandmother lifted her eyes to the branches above, then closed them. When her lids lifted a moment or two later, Harper was startled to see they had changed from gray to bright purple beneath their crinkled lids.

But when Grandma spoke, her voice sounded the same, though troubled. "Unfortunately, Walt is hidden from my sight at present. My connection with the owl folk in this area is weak. You did not inherit your owl shifting ability from me, although it could have come through other of our ancestors. But the Tskili' you've investigated is a different creature altogether. I cannot believe Walt has the same blood running in his veins." The volume in her voice trailed off, as though she were speaking to herself. "Most unsettling."

Harper's shoulders slumped as the fact that Grandma didn't hold the answers sank in. Without thinking, she pulled the swan mirror from her pocket. Holding it out she said, "Do you know anything about the tall woman in the white cowboy hat? My Fae friends think she and the mirror may be connected to the Swan Clan. Have you heard of them?"

Without answering, Grandma leaned in to examine the mirror.

"That's a lovely mirror, Darling. Where did you get it? May I have a closer look?"

Harper held it out silently. After scrutinizing it from every angle, Grandma handed it back. She was now sitting erect on the edge of the couch, head tilted inquisitively. "Harper? Where did you get this?"

"Bryan Greene—he's the man who owns the other bookstore in town. He gave it to me."

Grandma's eyebrows raised perceptibly. "Bryan Greene," she breathed. "That name sounds familiar. Do I know him?"

"Maybe. He says he met you when he was a boy. Bryan grew up in Winterfield. His grandfather ran the hardware store, Winter-Greene Hardware, remember that? And he said when he was a little kid, you used to give him candy."

Then Harper remembered something else he'd said that puzzled her. "He said he was always struck by your violet eyes—that you were the only person he'd ever met with eyes like that. But your eyes weren't violet back then, they were gray ..."

The mirror dropped into Grandma's lap.

"Grandma?"

Grandma Sophie took a shaky breath. "Yes. I did know his grandfather—very well, in fact. I didn't tell you because your happiness was precarious, and I didn't want to upset you. Bryan's grandfather and I dated one another for a short time before I got word to return to the Faery Realm. I had nearly forgotten."

Her voice took on a wistful tone. "I was quite fond of his grandfather Austin. And little Bryan ... such a quiet, sweet boy." Looking up from the mirror, her eyes pierced Harper's with laser beam intensity. "Is he still quiet and sweet?"

Harper picked up the mirror, her face growing hot. "Yes, he's still ... quiet, anyway." She felt as though she had been caught cheating at cards. She had been honest with Bryan, and they weren't romantically involved. So why did she feel so guilty? "We're just friends. He showed up unexpectantly one day to give me this. He told me it reminded him of me. But I don't really understand why it would."

Without comment, Grandma's attention drifted back to the mirror. "Did he tell where he'd gotten this?"

"In his father's attic. It's possible his grandfather owned it originally. He said the swan on it reminded him of watching me perform the lead in Swan Lake when he was a kid." She paused, then added, "I really hate that you missed that."

Grandma placed the mirror back in Harper's hands and wrapped her gnarled fingers around Harper's fist. "Well, I'm sorry too, Sweetheart. Believe me, I struggled over leaving, but I felt I had no choice. I'd keep this with me, Darling. I suspect it might be helpful to you somewhere along the line."

"But what about the Swan Clan? See, the letters *SC* are also on the cover. The workmanship looks similar to the mirror you left me before. Hawthorne and the others believe it's from the Fae Realm ..."

Grandma's brows knit together. "There have been swan cults for as long as there have been independent beings, Harper. Some of the cults have been human; some have been Fae. From forever to today, they are great mysteries. I know a little. They provide bridges between opposites ... water and air ... the Fae and Earth Realms ... the Great All to worlds below. I would say if they have seen fit to materialize in Whippoorwill Gap, there is great need. Though what the connection may be to your mirror, to the murders, or to Walt, if any, I cannot say. But that Bryan's grandfather Austin could have owned something like this ..." she shook her head. "Well, suffice it to say, it fills me with wonder."

Harper tucked the mirror back into her pocket. "No matter why he did it, I'm glad he gave the mirror to me. It reminds me of the one you gave me that I carried for so long." Afraid of sounding regretful, she added, "I'm happy for you to have that back now. Your kingdom is safer now that you have it. But I have to admit that I've missed it. And now, holding this one helps me feel more secure, if that makes sense."

Grandma straightened. "Well, Darling, I see no harm in that."

For a time, they sat peacefully side by side, Harper inhaling the loamy scent from the ground, safe behind the giant green leaves that shielded them from the disordered world beyond. If she could, she'd stay there forever. But finally, Grandma stirred beside her, pulling Harper from her reverie.

Harper stretched. "I know I need to go home, Grandma, but I don't know how to get there." She gestured around them. "I don't even know where I am."

"Don't worry, Darling. You'll be escorted home. But first, I'd like to know your plan."

Harper blew out the air she'd been holding. "I don't have a plan. I want to find Walt, but I have no idea where to look. And what should I do if I find him and discover he's now a murderous monster? What if he's chosen Delaynie over me? Either way, I lose."

Only then did she remember what had upset her so after she'd left his treehouse that afternoon. She searched Grandma's face for sympathy. "I remember now why I panicked. I found another pellet near Walt's treehouse." She shuddered. "I could see it contained a human skull." Then she lowered her head and added the most disturbing bit. "Walt's shoe was beside it."

"I see." Grandma closed her eyes again, this time for so long Harper wondered if she had drifted off to sleep. But when they reopened, sparks of violet light floated from her pupils and danced about Harper's head, as though they were summer gnats, before gradually fading away.

Now the powerful yet beautiful Faery Queen stood before her. "These ancient mountains are full of dark places and endless secrets. Be careful, My Darling. You might stumble upon something for which you're unprepared."

So it would be all on her after all. Grandma couldn't help. Harper's fear and grief returned, threatening to overwhelm her. She answered painfully, through her tight throat, "I will be careful Grandma. But I must do what I can."

Grandma placed a hand underneath Harper's chin, sweeping her up in her light-filled gaze. "No one is saying you shouldn't help him, Child. But if you wait for guidance, things will stand a better chance of a successful conclusion. Trust that when the time is right, help will come, likely from an unexpected source." She gestured to the pocket which held Harper's new mirror. "That came to you when you needed it, did it not?"

Harper ran her thumb over the raised swan and nodded without speaking.

"Have faith, My Darling. Have faith in your friends. Have faith in Walt. But most of all, have faith in yourself. You managed to save me and your friends not so long ago. You had no plan then, but you put yourself in the right place, at the right time, and were led to take the perfect actions."

She stared deeply into Harper's eyes. "What matters to you more than anything else at this moment, Child?"

Harper closed her eyes, gripping the mirror tightly. "Walt. I want Walt to be safe and happy." She opened her eyes again.

The regal figure inclined slightly toward her. "Well then, focus your love and attention on Walt, then wait. Your next move will come to you. Remember your Fae inheritance. And allow your friends to help. They want nothing more."

Harper hung her head. Did Grandma suspect she had been distrustful and neglectful of her friends of late? She promised herself she'd call on them when the time was right. But now her heart filled with sadness, knowing the time had come to part. "I love you, Grandma. I would stay here with you forever if I could. But I'm needed in Whippoorwill Gap. How can I get home from here?"

Queen Sophia pointed to a gap in the branches at the edge of the clearing. "Go past that crooked branch. Keep walking. Don't turn back."

"Goodbye, Grandma. Will I see you soon? Can I call for you again if I need help?"

Her grandmother began to shimmer slightly. "That will depend on many things. Even I am barred from some locations. But I promise we will meet again one day. When the time is right." She leaned down and kissed Harper on top of her mottled hair. "But now, the time has arrived for you to return home."

Harper bowed and closed her eyes as the golden light surrounding the queen grew too bright for her eyes to bear. Once she sensed its fading, she turned away to walk through the deep purple shadows toward the gap her grandmother had indicated. Past its branches, the air became electric with a threatened evening storm, and the light changed from faded gold to deep green-gray.

But to her delight and relief, out of the gloom, two small familiar figures with long dark hair came walking toward her. Once before her, each reached up to take one of her hands in their own. Only then, with Piper on one side and Ash on the other, did she start down the mountain.

Chapter 23

THE NEXT MORNING, HARPER felt dejected to a degree she had not felt since her move to Whippoorwill Gap. While the time with her grandmother had been blissful, she now experienced an equal drop in spirits as though she were on a teetertotter. The conversation with Grandma had left her with so much to mull over. The fact that she had dated Bryan's grandfather had been a shock. Why did Bryan's dad have a Swan Clan artifact in his attic? Though Grandma hadn't specifically said it belonged to them, she hadn't rejected the idea either. To Harper, that spoke volumes.

The restless night before, Harper had flipped repeatedly from one position to another in an unsuccessful attempt to relax, struggling to come to terms with what it all meant. When her mind tired of that conundrum, the more emotionally charged mystery of where Walt might be had thrown her into an endless maze of baffling and disturbing conjectures.

At the first sign of light, she trudged, exhausted, into her empty kitchen to start a pot of coffee. Once she washed a quick peanut butter sandwich down with a cup, she planned to drive to the trail head and hike up the mountain to collect Walt's journal and notes.

She pondered Walt's last journal entry, feeling sick at heart. Something terrible had happened, of that she had no doubt. But did it involve Delaynie? She hadn't read enough of the journal to know if he'd mentioned Delaynie at all. Was it possible he feared the Swan Clan?

He'd appeared disturbed at the trumpeting call on the night of their last dinner together. Then, too, yesterday was the second time she'd seen the woman in the white cowboy hat near his place. Convinced that the woman was connected to the Clan, she wondered if the mysterious group was as benign as was commonly thought. Swans could also be fierce. She shuddered on remembering "Leda and the Swan."

She carried her nearly empty mug into her bedroom where she slipped on quick-dry hiking pants and a t-shirt. Back in the kitchen, she poured the rest of the coffee into a travel mug to drink on the drive to the trailhead.

Three hours later, she walked back through the door with a stack of folders and Walt's journal stuffed into her backpack. She greeted Piper when the faery welcomed her home with worry etched on her brown, acorn-shaped face. But she made no attempt to discover where Harper had been, so Harper gratefully kept the conversation light as she devoured a bowl of steel-cut oatmeal with honey, blackberries, and almonds, which Piper had laid out for her on the table.

Once finished, she pulled off her hiking shoes and socks before settling into her office armchair, where she concentrated intensely on the notes Walt had made. She still hadn't committed to reading his journal. The thought made her uneasy; it felt like such an invasion of privacy and trust. Perhaps she would save that until she had no other options to pursue.

Dinnertime found her still riveted there, having barely moved all afternoon. She jumped when Piper appeared to ask if she wanted dinner brought to her office or if she'd rather eat it in the kitchen.

Unfortunately, she was no closer to discovering where Walt might be. In fact, the notes had left her even more confused about what might be happening. He'd mentioned the Swan Clan and the Tskili'. He seemed concerned and uneasy about both but failed to spell out why. Her frustration left her near tears.

When she sat down to eat the tofu ramen bowl Piper had made her, her phone pinged; she saw a message from Bryan asking if she'd like to meet at Gap Park for a walk. After sitting for most of the day, an unpleasant restlessness had settled over her body. She decided fresh air and time with Leda couldn't hurt. Besides, she wanted to ask if Bryan had suspected their grandparents' unexpectedly close relationship. And with any luck, she might jog his memory about the mirror in her pocket.

An hour later, she pulled into the parking lot where once again, Bryan and Leda watched for her from beneath the picnic shelter. This evening, the park was nearly empty. A smattering of other walkers dotted the trails. A group of teenage girls played a friendly game of softball. And children squealed on the playground. Nonetheless, it all looked desolate to Harper. They hadn't gotten far down the trail when Bryan asked if something was bothering her.

Her throat constricted as she looked around in panic. Tears threatened and she couldn't bear the idea of crying in front of strangers. She spotted a lonely little gravel path that headed toward the river and turned down it. Bryan and Leda followed silently behind.

They followed the path around a curve until the trail ended at the riverside, near a secluded picnic table. Harper sat on the bench closest to the river and struggled to get control of herself by deeply inhaling the scent of rolling water, pine, and something minty coming from a nearby patch of weeds.

Just as she began to feel calm, they heard a loud trumpeting. Harper stopped short, recognizing the harbinger of the woman in the white hat. As she turned her head this way and that, hoping to see the woman's tell-tale hat, she was surprised when Bryan stood bolt upright as though struck by lightning. "Did you hear that? My God! What was that?"

Leda began to whine, then swiped a paw at his knee, keeping her eyes trained on Bryan. Harper, too, took to her feet on seeing the hat floating between the trees along the hillside on the opposite side of the river.

"Bryan, do you see that?" She pointed toward the hat, but he seemed not to hear her. Instead, he stood as though transfixed.

"Harper, what was that beautiful sound?"

"Huh?" What was he talking about? To Harper the trumpeting sounded extraordinary. She could think of many adjectives to describe it: unnerving, disquieting, or perhaps alarming, but beautiful wasn't one of them. "Forget the sound, Bryan! Do you see that white thing floating along between the trees?"

He looked toward where she pointed, but while Harper could still see the blob of white floating behind the leaves, Bryan shook his head. "I'm sorry, Harper, I don't see what you're talking about. But you did hear that music, didn't you?"

She sat back down on the bench with a thump. The hat had vanished.

What just happened? she wondered. Bryan couldn't see what she'd plainly seen. And apparently, she couldn't hear what he'd heard. But then, she guessed, if the woman herself were from the Fae Realm, it would make sense Bryan couldn't see her, not being Fae himself. Perhaps the sound she'd heard sounded lovely to human ears.

After they'd sat quietly for a spell, both lost in their own thoughts, she recalled what she'd wanted to ask him.

"Bryan, do you have any idea how close your grandfather and my grandmother were? I mean, do you have any memories about that at all?"

He took a seat beside her, staring thoughtfully at the rushing water. "I've told you all I know, Harper. I know they were good friends. I got the feeling Grandpop really liked your grandma. But best I can remember, they were always very polite and formal with one another. Why do you ask?"

How should she broach this? She could hardly admit she'd spoken to her grandmother only yesterday and learned disturbing new information. But before long, a means of broaching the topic came to her. "I've been thinking about the framed picture of Grandma that's in your office. I've never seen it before. It's odd that she would have given a picture like that to an acquaintance."

Bryan patted Leda absently on the head. "Gosh, Harper. I never thought of that. But you're right." He shrugged. "But then, she could have been friends with Me-Maw before she died." His face turned red. "You can laugh. That's what we all called my grandma. She died when I was three or four—that would have been, what? Two or three years before your grandma disappeared."

Harper looked at him, nearly giddy with exhaustion, but she couldn't let this pass. "Seriously? You called your grandma 'Me-Maw'?"

He laughed. "I was one of the younger grandkids, so I didn't come up with it. Everyone in the family, even my parents, called her Me-Maw."

Her laughter helped Harper relax for the first time in days. "Okay, that makes sense. I've just never pegged you as the 'Me-Maw' type."

They sat quietly for a few minutes while Leda ventured down to the river's edge, then got in the water halfway up her legs, still sniffing about as though for possible danger. Bryan grew thoughtful. "I really don't remember anything that would make me think they were closer than friends. Would you be upset if they were?"

Harper rubbed her face with both her hands. "I don't know. Maybe? The idea that Grandma could have had a secret life bothers me. I know it's silly. After all, what kid ever really knows the adults in their lives?"

Having accepted that Bryan knew less than she did, she changed the subject. "Are you expecting a big crowd in your store this weekend?"

"Not any bigger than normal. Why do you ask?"

"I've heard some big sci-fi and comic book convention is going on outside town at The Cardinal Inn. Quinn told me about it. He said I might get some extra traffic from old customers of Frank's. But I guess that wouldn't affect your shop like mine."

"Frank really did attract those folks, that's for sure. Yes, you might get some of his old devotees. Nostalgia can be a big motivator for people. Back when Frank owned the Robin's Nest, it was a sort of pilgrimage for many of them. But hey, anything that's good for business is a good thing, right?"

Harper nodded, but instead of excitement over the impending bump in traffic, she felt melancholy as memories surfaced of Walt and all the help he had given her during the Robin's Nest's Grand Opening last fall. Suddenly, with her emotions so overwhelmed, she became unable to speak.

"Harper?" Bryan looked at her with concern. "What's the matter? Seriously. You've seemed upset ever since we got here."

"Oh Bryan." She burst into tears.

He scooted beside her and wrapped a strong arm around her shoulder, giving it a squeeze. He let her cry for a minute, then said softly, "Tell me about it."

"I ... I miss Walt!" His arm stiffened. She felt sure he would get up now and leave her here to cry alone. But that's not what he did.

Instead, he turned toward her. Placing both arms around her back, he pulled her face to his shoulder, cradling the back of her head in one of his hands. "It's okay," he murmured. "I completely understand."

It felt so good to finally release her pent-up fear and sadness that she cried for a good, long time. He never backed away or let her go. Neither did he shush her nor attempt to distract her from her outburst.

When the tears finally ended, she wiped her face on her t-shirt. Then Bryan miraculously pulled a tissue from his shorts pocket and handed it to her. She blew her nose then gave an embarrassed chuckle.

In the rapidly draining light, she turned back to the river. He did the same, pulling her close with one arm while they watched night descend over the water. Neither said a word. Finally, beginning to feel chilled, she stirred. "I need to get back."

He took his arm from her shoulder and stood, holding out a crooked arm for her to hold. "My Lady ..."

"Thank you," she answered with a grateful smile. Then he and Leda escorted her back to her car. When they got there, she stopped, feeling sheepish at her loss of control. "Bryan ..."

"Don't worry about it," he answered. He closed her truck door for her, then knocked twice on the door with his fist. "I'm here for you whenever you need me."

She shot him a look of gratitude, then said goodbye to Leda, cranked her truck, and headed for home. If he didn't mind that she loved someone else, they could certainly remain good friends.

✦⁚✦

CLOSING TIME COULDN'T ARRIVE soon enough for Harper on the following Sunday. As expected, since Friday, the shop had been overrun by customers nostalgic for Frank's atmospheric shop. A few claimed to be happy with the changes she had made, most were noncommittal, but some complained bitterly.

Harper understood their disappointment. But she had never wanted to turn the shop into a memorial for its previous owner. Nevertheless, handling the extra traffic with no help had been exhausting. As an added bonus, it had taken her mind off last week's events.

Now she felt in desperate need of time to process all that had happened. First was the visit to Walt's, then the talk with Grandma Sophie, and finally the time with Bryan down by the river. Harper cringed at the memory. She'd have to think through that episode later. She hadn't intended to use him to make herself feel better, but she had to admit to herself that it had turned out that way.

Grateful that the shop had emptied, she counted the day's cash and receipts with five minutes to go before closing time. At one minute to six, as she pulled out the key to lock the door, Bryan walked through the door, holding a glossy burgundy tote bag emblazoned with a white swan on the side. Leda followed at his heels. Visible from the top of the bag was a wine bottle and a loaf of French bread. The sight brought a wave of apprehension from deep in Harper's gut. She eyed the wine bottle warily.

Instead of looking directly at her, Bryan stared at the counter. "Hi Harper! I know you're open on Monday mornings, but I wondered if I could interest you in a quick dinner tonight. I've brought noodles, a jar of my homemade pesto, and a fresh tossed salad. Oh, and I snagged a bottle of that cab you liked so much when we were at dinner in Asheville. You can put your feet up and sip your wine while I get it all ready." He smiled. "I have another surprise for you, too. What do you say?"

While she could think of no way to refuse without hurting his feelings, Harper felt annoyed that he hadn't checked with her ahead of time. After she'd gotten so emotional down by the river, she supposed he now felt entitled to stop by without an invitation. She supposed she had no one to blame but herself.

As she led the way upstairs, she worried that Piper had left dinner waiting for her, as was her habit, or that Alida and Lily might be hanging about to chat while she ate, as they sometimes did. She talked loudly and rattled the keys as she entered the kitchen a few steps ahead of Bryan. But they must have caught sight of Bryan themselves. The kitchen stood empty and neat.

On the counter by the sink, Bryan emptied the bag's contents, which included a scroll of thick, handmade paper, tied with a satin ribbon, a pair of wine-colored roses tucked beneath it. The sight spurred her to action. She pointed at it, wide-eyed. "What's this?"

Bryan glanced up from the cabinets from where he searched for pots and pans. His tanned face deepened a shade. "That's the other surprise." He looked up and met her hazel eyes with his autumn-sky-blue ones. "I wrote a poem for you. I thought I would read it to you after dinner."

The web of dread snaked across her chest. "Oh. Well, that's sweet, but ..."

"Well, don't say it's sweet until you've read it." His voice grew husky. "I can't pretend it does my feelings justice. But first, let me pour you a glass ..." He handed it over, then filled one for himself and raised it. "There. Let's have a toast."

Harper looked around desperately for anything to lighten the mood. She'd told him plainly that she loved Walt the other night. How could he have misunderstood?

"Let me get a bowl of water for Leda. She needs to be a part of our toast, too."

She quickly pulled out Biscuit's bowl and filled it with water, careful to keep her eyes on Leda and off Bryan. "There! Good Girl!" She patted the dog's silky coat. "We wouldn't dream of leaving you out, would we?" She crooned over the dog while she cast about in desperation for a way to bring Bryan down gently. One day, she might possibly want this. But not now.

She sat back down, ignoring her glass to watch the dog while she cast about for another line of conversation. Whatever happened, she needed to be honest. But she also wanted to be kind.

Bryan looked in confusion at Leda, then at Harper, the smile fading from his face, as spots of red blossomed on his cheeks.

"Bryan ..." she began.

"Don't." A few seconds went by, then he added in a lighter tone, "Let's just eat our dinner." He looked directly at her then, his Adam's apple bobbing as he swallowed. "I guess this was a bad idea. I should have called first. My mistake ... let's not make it worse."

Harper felt terrible but could think of no way to gracefully change course. "I appreciate your friendship," she continued softly. "But I thought you understood—I'm still in love with Walt. If he doesn't come back, things may change with time. But right now, I'm in no shape to start a romantic relationship with anyone else. It's not you. Honestly, Bryan, I do value your friendship."

He gave his chin a quick bob, his back to her as he stirred the now boiling pasta. She watched him as she took a tiny sip of her wine, followed by a crashing sense of wretchedness. Alarm drowned the sensation as he picked up his glass and gulped it dry, before placing it gently back on the countertop. After that, he stared out the window in silence until he dumped the noodles into a colander in the sink.

Then he turned to her, wiping his face on his shirt, again refusing to meet her eyes. "I'm not hungry after all. How about I leave this here? You can have it for dinner tonight, then enjoy the leftovers later this week."

Her face grew hot, remembering how kind he had been to her. She jumped to her feet and placed a hand on his arm. "Bryan, I'm so sorry! I wasn't trying to lead you on, and I wasn't trying to use you, either. I do care about you, but I'm not in a good place to start a relationship yet."

At that, the tension abated. He poured himself another glass of cabernet and held the bottle toward her. She took it, adding a tiny amount to her nearly full glass. After putting spaghetti on their plates and topping it with fragrant pesto, he offered her some grated parmesan cheese, which she accepted. Then he sat down across from her and sighed. Instead of taking a bite of his spaghetti, he took another gulp of wine. Then he forced a smile. "Rest easy. You'll never lose my friendship, Harper. You're right, you have been honest. This is not your fault ... In my defense, 'hope springs eternal,' 'old habits die hard,' and all that."

Her tension abated further as she squeezed the mirror in her pocket. "Let's just enjoy getting to know one another, for now, Bryan. I can't promise things will change. But to be honest with myself, as much as with you, I can't promise they won't either. Right now, that's the best I can do." She held up her glass and sought his wine-glazed eyes. "To you, Bryan. And to friendship."

One corner of his mouth turned up as he tapped his glass to hers. "To you, Harper, my fellow swan and lifelong soulmate."

Lips tight, she lowered her glass and pushed her plate away.

He leaned forward, a contrite expression on his red face. When he spoke, his words were slightly slurred. Half the bottle was gone, and Harper had drunk very little. "Hey, Harper, that was a stupid thing to say, but I meant it. I would rather have you in my life as a friend than not have you there at all. Please don't be upset. I know you didn't ask for this." After using a fork to stab a black olive in his salad bowl, he smiled at her. "Don't you worry about me. I'm a big boy. I'll be fine. Let's just enjoy our dinner. How did your weekend go? Did any of Frank's old customers stop in?"

With Bryan clearly buzzed, Harper stuck to safer topics. First, she filled him in on her weekend. They laughed together over some of the more incensed of Frank's customers before sharing some of their elementary school experiences in Winterfield. Relieved that he never returned to his feelings for her, Harper tried to stay upbeat.

Later, when he left, swaying a bit, she watched through the front window as they made their way across the parking lot across the street, Leda sticking close to Bryan's side. Harper was happy to see they had walked to the shop rather than driven.

Returning to her apartment landing, she noticed the roses from the scroll lying on the floor outside. She had no idea if he had dropped them accidentally or left them there on purpose. The scroll was nowhere to be found. As she sat on the small landing, holding the roses in her hands, she wondered miserably how she'd made such a mess of things. Then suddenly Earl Grey materialized at her side.

"Hello, Lassie. You wouldn't have a pint of that porter to spare for a friend, would you?"

Harper was so happy to see his good-natured face that she jumped up and led him into the kitchen, where she grabbed a half-pint glass and filled it from the growler she kept in her fridge. "I'm so glad you stopped by Earl Grey! Please, have a seat.

You drink your beer, and I'll make myself a big mug of lavender tea. Then, we'll have nice visit."

Harper bustled about, elated to have something to distract her from the painful and thorny dinner. The gnome became cheerier the closer he drew to the bottom of his half-pint glass. Once there, he pointed to the growler and raised his eyebrows in question. Harper happily poured him another. Then she continued filling him in about events over the past week. Knowing that deep down, he'd forgive her anything, she even confessed to the scene by the river with Bryan.

"What do you think I should do?" she asked as she concluded with the evening's dismal dinner. Earl Grey's little cheeks turned bright red as his bright blue eyes examined hers with keenness.

"Well, Lassie, as for Bryan, just you follow yer heart. Ye can't pull fresh water from a sea cucumber, or somethin' like that."

Then his manner grew serious. "But about Walter, I'd say our Queen Sophia was right. Don't go searchin' for trouble. On the other hand, I say don't run from it either. I've been lookin' for Walter myself, but I've run up against a blackness I cannot seem to penetrate. Whether he's hidden of his own volition or not, I cannot tell." He put his empty glass on the table with a sense of finality. The evening was ending. "But promise me, Lass, that you won't go out searchin' for him all on your own. You'll likely need support, no matter what you find."

Harper nodded. "Thank you, My Friend. I'll remember your advice."

He stood and put a finger to the side of his nose. "You have our support, no matter what. Sleep tight, Lassie!" And with that, he was gone.

Chapter 24

REGARDLESS OF WHO WAS to blame, everything felt wrong now. No matter what happened, someone would suffer. What should she do? The magic of Earl Grey's visit had evaporated overnight. Harper prepared for her morning in the shop with a sick feeling in her stomach. If only Bryan had warned her that he was coming last night, she'd have been prepared and things would have gone better. Or maybe not. She should have seen this coming. But the truth was, she hadn't. To be fair to herself, Bryan shared some of the blame. He had insisted he'd rather be friends than not see her at all.

Once the shop closed at one o'clock, Harper planned to drive to Olivia's for lunch and a short chat-and-hike. As she entered the kitchen, Piper removed a thick slab of buttered sourdough from the toaster oven and placed it on a small plate with blueberry jam on the side. The coffee was ready. Her little friend always seemed to know exactly what Harper needed. Harper greeted the faery and seated herself at the table. Between bites of the toast, she rehashed her troubles. Piper clucked over the outcome with Bryan.

"Don't you worry about it. Sometimes things just can't be helped, Dearie. You can't squeeze sweet juice from an unripe persimmon."

Earl Grey had said something similar the night before. Harper avoided considering what they might be suggesting about her. Even so, her friend's sympathy applied salve to her nettled heart. She went downstairs feeling lighter.

After an hour of bookkeeping, she was interrupted when Olivia called for a raincheck on the afternoon's outing. Harper clucked with concern and offered to drop off a pot of soup when she learned the reason—a bout of summer flu seemed to have struck her daughter. Olivia declined the visit. Quinn was coming later to take Biscuit for a walk, she said, and he'd promised to bring her a giant bagel with butter and strawberry creamed cheese from the coffee shop.

With her afternoon unexpectedly free, Harper quickly finished her books, then contemplated what to do instead. She longed to go to Walt's, curl up on his sofa, and have a good cry. But with the woman with the white cowboy hat lurking around, she feared hanging about alone. Earl Grey had been right; she'd be vulnerable should anything happen.

To clear her head, she decided to run over to the coffee shop. She locked the door on the empty shop then walked next door to order a matcha latte to go. A plump older woman, whom Harper guessed to be in her mid-sixties, took her order without smile or comment. Her bright red hair was the imminent victor in a battle to escape the ponytail elastic that corralled it. Deanna walked out of the kitchen while the woman prepared her drink.

"Morning, Harper! Let me introduce you to the newest member of the Divine Coffee team. This is Monique Rivers. She's a top-notch cook with decades of restaurant experience who's going to be helping mostly in the kitchen. But today, she's learning the front so she can fill in out here if needed."

Deanna looked at the subdued woman in the brown Divine Coffee t-shirt. "Monique, this is my friend, Harper Wood. She runs the Robin's Nest next door."

The women said their hellos, then Monique handed over Harper's latte. As she turned her attention to the next customer, Deanna lowered her voice. "She's doing great, so far. I need some rest! If all works out, I'll be turning some of the management duties over to her, so I'll have more free time soon. Maybe you, Dashawn, and I can make another visit to the brewery one evening."

When Harper merely nodded, Deanna reached over and laid a hand on her arm. "I know you're having a tough time. I won't give advice, because I really don't know what you should do. But remember, I'm here for you anytime you need me, you hear?"

Harper gave her friend a grateful smile. "Hopefully, I can have you and Dashawn over for dinner again soon." Deanna smiled and said that would be wonderful.

As a steady stream of customers continued to walk in, Harper wandered back to the bookshop, latte in hand. She thought over her options for this afternoon. Once the shop closed to the public, she could unpack and sort boxes of books, she could search online for other used bookshops to visit, or she could go to the library and do more research. She could take a tai chi class at Yo' Chicks. But with nearly a week of dog days left, simply turning on the air conditioner and hiding out in her apartment sounded tempting.

Back on her stool behind the counter, she looked up and noticed Ash curled up in an upholstered chair reading a gigantic book, typical for him. The bookish faery seldom announced his entrances; he just got busy reading until she noticed he was there. Seeing him reminded her that she was never truly abandoned. "Hello Ash," she began. "Are you reading anything I might like?"

Ash placed a finger to mark his spot in the massive copy of The Riverside Shakespeare that pinned him to the chair. That book wasn't for sale; she kept it behind the desk for handy reference. "I'm rereading The Tempest," he said. "It's always been my favorite."

"Well, enjoy. I think I'll head upstairs at closing time to do a little reading myself."

He nodded, then his eyes fixed on the page in front of him once again.

At one o'clock, Harper locked the shop's front door and climbed the stairs to her apartment. For a while she wandered about restlessly, until she gave up. Today her safe apartment felt like a cage, not a refuge. She unlocked the balcony door and stepped out for a few moments before the hot sunshine forced her to retreat inside. On the couch, she stared forlornly out the windows at Walt's empty sycamore tree across the river.

She found herself startled from her reverie when Hawthorne appeared on the rug before her, beaver skin hat in his hands, observing her with his inscrutable gaze.

"How are you faring, Dear Harper?"

She scratched her head. "You scared the daylights out of me, Hawthorne! But it's okay. I'm pretty miserable, to be honest. Hanging about like this and doing nothing is driving me crazy. Have you heard anything?"

He inclined his head. "We've flown far and wide both here and in the Faery Realm but have found no clues. I gather you have looked as well."

It had been a while since she and Hawthorne had caught up. "Yes." She went to her office and returned with the stack of material she'd taken from Walt's. "Grandma told me to wait for a sign, but there is no way I'm going to get a sign hiding out in here. I suppose you've heard I visited with Grandma?"

"As you know, Queen Sophia contains abundant wisdom. We are behind you Harper. I came to tell you we would all like to pay you a social visit this evening, if that is agreeable to you. If nothing else, it will take your mind from your troubles."

While she was grateful for their support, she suddenly felt too exhausted to talk. Her eyes filled with tears. "What a sweet idea! Believe me, I am grateful to you all, Hawthorne. But honestly, I'm *so* tired. Even though I would enjoy your company, it would help me more to spend time alone tonight. I have a lot of thinking to do."

He swept his hat ahead of him in a low bow. "Of course. If you change your mind, you need only call." He hesitated, then looked at the ceiling and spoke as though he were addressing no one in particular. "I don't believe Queen Sophia's instructions forbade leaving the apartment in the daytime." And with that, he blinked from sight.

Harper took a shaky breath before lying back on the couch, where she fell into an exhausted sleep. When she awoke, the wall clock read ten past three. On remembering Hawthorne's last words, she sat up. He was right. She couldn't simply sit in this apartment waiting for some sign that would likely never come.

With the next two and a half days free, she needed to make wise use of her time. Grandma, while she'd still belonged to the Earth Realm, had carefully taught her *that* lesson before she started school. She'd waited around long enough. Her restlessness now made remaining still a physical impossibility. The very bones in her body prodded her into action. And she would start by searching for Delaynie or the woman in the white hat. The moment she found either of them, she'd insist on straight answers.

✦

SHE STARTED WITH A brisk sweep of Puckett's Park. The robins hopped around her in agitation, but today she ignored them while scanning the landscape for any tall, thin women. Though she knew they were anxious for her welfare, she would not allow them to stop her. She'd keep walking until she located one or the other, found some clue as to where Walt might be, or fell over in exhaustion. Grandma had said a sign would come. Well then, she was looking for a sign.

From the corner of her eye, she spotted a flash of white from the top of the hill. Snapping her head toward it, she caught a glimpse of the woman in the white cowboy hat heading up the hill, her long dark hair hanging in a braided ponytail down her back.

Hurrying after her, Harper shouted, "Hello! Wait a second! I need to ask you something!" As she reached street level, turning the corner by Divine Coffee, Harper cursed under her breath. The woman was nearing Main Street, too far away to catch. Distracted, she nearly ran into Delaynie, who walked straight toward her, uncharacteristically dressed in hiking boots, shorts, and a light t-shirt with a plain white baseball hat on her head.

Harper's mouth instantly went dry. But she had promised herself to get answers, no matter which woman she found. It occurred to her that something about the whole situation with Walt and this woman seemed off. If Delaynie and Walt were staying together, why did she keep coming to town without him? The time for politeness was over, she reminded herself.

Ignoring her doubts and her aversion to this haughty woman, she rooted herself in the brunette's path.

Delaynie raised her eyebrows before abruptly halting. "Oh, hello. I didn't expect to see you out wandering around town this time of day. Don't you have some books to arrange somewhere?" She chuckled. "All joking aside, I was hoping to find you."

Harper eyed her suspiciously. "Oh?"

Delaynie's mouth formed a pout as though Harper's response had wounded her, but when she spoke, her deep voice changed to a warm conspiratorial tone. "Yes. Walter disappeared from our little nest a few days ago. He hasn't, by chance, been by your place?" She kept her eyes hopefully fixed on Harper's face. To Harper, she appeared to be searching for signs of deception.

At this news, Harper's hostility waned. If Delaynie didn't know where Walt was, could he merely have played them both? Maybe she and Delaynie were both second and third in line behind the copper-skinned beauty beneath the white hat. Whatever was happening, she couldn't think of a reason to lie. "I have no idea where he might be."

Delaynie's squinted eyes pinned her for a few seconds more. Harper returned the stare without a waver, glad she'd been forthright. Delaynie inclined her head in a barely perceptible nod before leaning down to whisper in Harper's ear, "Well then, if he's not with you, I believe I know where he might be hiding."

She straightened, continuing in a low tone, "I took your suggestion during our last conversation seriously. I started watching him carefully. I don't want to go into it now, but I did see things"—she grimaced—"that led me to believe you may have been right about him. Something's not right. I'll fill you in on what I know later. But, since he's not with you, I have a hunch about where he might be hiding. If we both confront him together, I believe we'll get some answers." She bit her lip, then continued. "We may even be about to save him."

"Now?"

Delaynie's nostrils flared and her eyes held traces of contempt. "He may not be there in the morning."

Harper felt an agitated mixture of fear, uncertainty, and hope. She had feared that, against his will, Walt might have become a heinous monster. Had she been right all along that there was a third woman? Had this woman been the real villain? The thought that she and Delaynie together could help him proved too compelling to ignore. Surely this was the sort of sign Grandma had meant for her to follow.

Swallowing her aversion to the condescending woman before her, Harper convinced herself that to follow her was her only hope of getting to the bottom of the mystery once and for all. As an added benefit, she'd also be keeping her promise to Earl Grey by tackling the situation with the help of another. She straightened to her full height.

"Okay, I'm in. But first I need details. Where are we going? Should I bring anything? Can we walk there from here or do I need to bring my truck?"

As Delaynie shifted, Harper was startled to catch a faint whiff of mildew. She ignored it.

"Do you know the Draper's Knob Trail over near the dam?"

Harper nodded. Because of her interest in Olivia's business, she'd become familiar with nearly every trail within twenty miles of town.

"Meet me at the trailhead's parking lot in an hour. If my guess is right, we'll find him camping near there."

"Camping?" Harper asked dubiously. Why would Walt need to hide out at a campsite when he had a home so close by?

Delaynie snapped her head back, a menacing frown bridging her tense cheeks. Harper involuntarily moved a step back. She could feel the energy Delaynie exerted to keep herself under control. This obvious emotional investment in Walt's welfare convinced Harper she could trust her.

Delaynie swallowed. "Perhaps 'camping' is not the right term," she amended. "But I have reason to believe he's been staying at a particular spot. You'll just have to trust me. Are you willing to meet me there in an hour or not? As much as it pains me to say so, I'm hoping that the sight of you may bring him to his senses." She pressed her lips together. "He's made it clear, recently, that he doesn't care as much for me as I had hoped."

Her voice sounded odd. But then Harper realized she had never heard Delaynie sound vulnerable before. The thought touched her. She, too, could relate to feeling rejected. And if there was anything she could do to help Walt, she had to try.

"Would you like to ride with me instead of meeting there?"

Delaynie looked startled and her upper lip curled. "That won't be necessary. I have my own transportation."

Relieved, Harper left Delaynie standing on the sidewalk, then went inside to pack a couple of bottles of water, some fruit and nut bars, and a first aid kit. She looked around quickly but could think of nothing else she might need. Once in her truck, she tucked her phone into her back pocket, then turned onto Highway 119 toward the dam.

As SHE PULLED INTO the parking lot, Harper wondered how Delaynie had gotten there first, with no a vehicle in sight. Uber or Lyft, she concluded. Delaynie interrupted her thoughts with a dramatic, "Follow me. Once we reach the top of the hill, we'll go off trail. Be quiet. If he hears us coming, he'll likely take off."

Harper paused. She doubted Delaynie understood just how literally that statement could be taken.

As Harper pulled on her backpack, Delaynie shook her head. "You won't be needing that."

While failing to see what harm a backpack could do, she replaced it without argument, squeezed the mirror and keys into her pockets, and started up the trail, with the imposing woman leading the way. Her nerves grew taut as she considered what might lie ahead.

Another uneasy thought arose. Walt could hide out anywhere in these mountains. Why here? "What makes you think he's up here?" she asked, keeping her voice low. "You said he might be hiding. What's he hiding from?"

"You can ask him if we find him." Delaynie hissed from over her shoulder. "Just a little further now, and we'll leave the trail to hike across a boggy patch. Stay close behind me. I know where the dry patches are. There's a cave entrance near the other end. That's where we'll likely find him."

Harper's skin began to prickle. "But why here?" she asked again.

Delaynie expelled an exasperated breath. "As I've said before, you're just going to have to trust me. I've known him longer than you have, and I've certainly been spending more time with him lately."

Harper winced at the verbal slap. But while she couldn't argue, her sense of foreboding continued to grow as they reached the top of the ridge and left the trail. True to her word, Delaynie whispered for Harper to watch the ground and follow closely in her footsteps to avoid getting sucked into hidden pockets of water. After Olivia had been sucked into a bog only two months prior, Harper knew waterlogged terrain could be dangerous in these parts. The smell of wet, rich earth enveloped her as she concentrated on placing her feet exactly where Delaynie had trod. The moist ground muffled the sound of their boots.

Nearby, a loud trumpeting sounded so suddenly that Harper staggered in surprise. She stopped and started to ask if Delaynie had heard it as well. But the woman only stalked ahead of her with quick, determined steps, so Harper turned her attention back to the ground. If she'd heard it, there was no indication she found it disturbing.

When they finally reached a clearing, Harper saw a rocky outcrop through the trees. Delaynie stopped and pointed. "The cave is on the other side of those rocks," she whispered. "You go ahead. I'll follow. I think Walt would be happier to see you than me. He's not happy with me at all right now."

The trumpet call forgotten, Harper shot the woman a confused frown. Nothing about this seemed right. Why would Walt be staying in a cave, of all things, that Delaynie knew about? If he was unhappy with her, wouldn't he hide out in a place she didn't know about?

Still, neither Delaynie's demeanor nor words felt deceptive to Harper. And the thought of Walt so close proved too tempting to withstand. She crept quietly across the carpet of sodden leaves until she reached the outcrop. On peeking around the edge, she saw that Delaynie had been right. A cleft in the rocks revealed a large opening leading into the mountainside, completely hidden from the bank above.

She checked to make sure Delaynie was still behind her before taking a cautious step into the dark entryway. Once fully inside, her gag reflex kicked in as she was assaulted by dank, fetid air. She forced herself forward despite her impulse to turn and flee at the evil stench of rotten flesh, digestive juices, and excrement. Her heart began to pound as a cold sweat broke out on her upper lip.

She peered into the ashy darkness. “Walt?!” she whispered.

Chapter 25

HARPER STUMBLED A STEP or two blindly ahead. Searching for direction, she turned to Delaynie. The eyes that peered back at her looked larger and more rounded and appeared to reflect a reddish glow, which Harper assumed a trick of light. As Delaynie swept past her, Harper stayed close on her heels, while her hand tightly gripped the swan mirror in her pocket. With her ankles wobbling on the uneven floor surface, Harper moved with care, flinching at the frequent crunching of something small and brittle beneath her sneakers.

She jerked to a halt, stiffening as her ears picked up soft noises coming from deeper inside the cave. A pool of cold fear spread through her abdomen.

"I didn't bring a flashlight, did you?" she whispered to Delaynie. She pulled out her phone, but, of course, it wasn't working—she'd neglected to charge the battery. She silently cursed herself. "Do you have a light?" she asked again nervously when Delaynie didn't answer. She strained ahead on hearing another moaning sound followed by a whisper-soft rustle.

She felt a shift in the heavy air as Delaynie moved away, muttering, "Hang on a second ..."

Then Harper heard a click like a cigarette lighter, followed by a flare from a torch attached to the cave wall only six feet ahead to her left. Harper looked down at her feet to gain her bearings.

On the floor, scattered bones, some picked clean, others with bits of flesh and sinew still attached, were strewn about haphazardly. Her meager lunch threatened to eject itself from her cramping stomach. To quell the nausea, she tried to inhale, but the rank odors of the cave only assaulted her with renewed force. Doubling over, she grabbed her knees and struggled to control her impulse to either vomit or bolt for the entrance.

Terror kept her thoughts focused. At this point, only Walt mattered. No matter what, she had to know. If he was a murderer, she needed to stop him. If he was a monstrous cad, she needed to know that too. And now that Delaynie had lit the space, there was no need to be furtive. Anyone or anything inside that cave would know they were there now.

Delaynie ignored Harper's unsteady gait as she made her way along the wall, flicking the lighter to another torch. For a second, Harper felt relieved to have more light, but then a sense of trepidation seized her again. "Why are there *torches* on the wall?" she asked loudly.

Delaynie, ignoring the question, answered grimly. "I'm not positive that he's still here, but let's see what we find, shall we?"

The grease-fueled, smoky light enhanced Harper's misgivings and confusion. She cried out on tripping over a large object, though she miraculously remained on her feet. Once she'd steadied herself, horror overtook her on the discovery of another large pellet with the skeletal remains of a human hand sticking from its side, by her feet. Only the sound of a loud groan from the darkness further inside the cave returned her to her senses. She scurried past the monstrosity. Someone inside clearly needed help.

When yet another torch flared to life deeper in the cave, Harper noticed a dull but metallic glint from off to the right-hand side. Peering through the haze, she gasped on seeing an empty cage, large enough to hold a human adult. A bolt of terror shot through her with explosive force. If Walt had become this savage, how could she possibly help him? Then she realized she'd be unlikely to survive the effort.

"Harper! Back here." She jumped on hearing Delaynie's stage whisper from the dark shadows still further back. "Once I light the last torch, you'll understand why I brought you here."

Now past her ability to reason things out, Harper swiped her sweat-slick hands on her pants before following Delaynie's voice into the cave's smog-filled depths. As she gingerly placed one foot before the other, a distinctly masculine groan arose from somewhere near the floor ahead to the left. Her heart leapt. Without hearing one coherent word, she recognized Walt as its source.

While her eyes focused on the blackness ahead, she heard a close rattle, followed by an icy, clawlike grip on her ankle. Before she had time to react, a clank sounded as a cold, hard band snapped shut around it, pinning her in place. Two enormous blood-red orbs swept from the floor, stopping nearly three feet above her head, where they hung, gleaming down at her through the dark. Was it Walt? Where was Delaynie, she wondered.

Then the lighter sparked once again, followed by the flaring of the final torch. Now she saw that a metal manacle, with a heavy chain attached, held her helplessly in place. Her efforts to break free only succeeded in pitching her onto the filth-strewn floor.

The torches provided sufficient murky light to illuminate the back of the cave through the clotted smoke, revealing a stage-set from Hell. In the back left corner, a second cage jutted from the wall, but unlike the first, this one was occupied. Huddled inside, a grimy, emaciated man, crusty with dried blood from deep scratches, watched her from a half-opened pair of large, round amber eyes beneath a head of matted, mottled hair. His irregular, anguished breaths caused her own chest to ache.

"Walt!" Harper strained to reach the cage, but the chain attached to her manacle was much too short. Instead of moving closer to Walt, she gasped as her knees crashed onto the subterranean floor.

Above her, Delaynie unleashed a hair-raising peal of malignant laughter.

As the pieces of the puzzle converged, Harper's outrage erupted. "You conniving bitch! You lied to me!"

Her fury toward Delaynie paled in comparison with Harper's rage with herself. How could she have been so gullible? Even worse—why had she ever believed Walt capable of such treachery? As her wrath mounted, she couldn't decide who to hate more: the loathsome creature before her or herself.

"Oh, my," Delaynie cackled before lighting a cigarette. She inhaled then released a stream of menthol scented smoke with evident satisfaction, clearly savoring the moment.

"The look on your face! Honestly, Harper Wood, you're more simpleminded than I dared to hope." She took another deep drag, giving one foot a peevish tap. "To be honest, your gullibility has ruined a bit of the fun. I was hoping for a bigger challenge." She dropped the cigarette, stubbing it out with her hiking boot before turning to face Walt's cage. "We'll get over the disappointment, though." Her voice became syrupy, mimicking those people who change their voice when speaking to babies and pets. "We'll make sure she pays for spoiling our plans, won't we Darling?"

Harper looked at the prone figure, whose dull eyes flashed briefly at her in alarm. "Walt?" she whispered, ignoring the beast before him. "Are you alright?" When he only stared back in misery, she licked her dry lips and tried again. "What happened? How did you get here?"

She watched, confused, as he looked above her and shook his head while pushing himself back into the cage's wall with a whimper. The light behind her dimmed and the shifting shadows from the torchlight stilled. Her gut turned to water as she turned to behold the source of Walt's terror.

The starkly beautiful Delaynie had vanished. In her place, a massive owl, easily eight feet tall, towered above them. Enormous tufted horns crowned the top of its head. "Welcome to Camp Tskili'," it screeched in tones that evoked the infernal abyss. Then came an equally demented snigger. "We're sure you'll love it here, right, Dear Brother?"

Brother?! Harper's head began to spin. Remembering the legend the Fae had shared with her, she could only gape. Could this hideous mutant be Walt's sibling? If that were the case, no wonder he didn't like to talk about his past. She turned to him aghast. "Walt? Is she lying? Or is this really your sister?"

He coughed weakly, then closed his eyes, giving his head a nearly imperceptible shake. "No," he whispered, his voice as dry and insubstantial as dust.

What did he mean? Was the creature not lying? Or was she not his sister?

The beast before them swayed from side to side, a ghastly grin beneath its beak. With the inflections of a playground bully about to pummel a victim, she said, "Now Walter. We've had this conversation before. Let's not waste time on it again."

It turned to Harper. "Silly Boy. Allow me to explain, Chickie. We were raised side by side in the same nest. Our mother adopted him when he was too young and weak to survive on his own." The creature addressed Walt again in a voice that grew more bellicose with each word. "She housed you and fed you. Without her, you would have died. And how did you repay her?"

Walt said nothing, so she reached through the bars of the cage, pinioning his shoulder with her claw as she screamed, her breath nearly flooring Harper with its ghastly combination of rot and hate, "How did you repay her??"

As she pulled her claw from his shoulder, he slumped against the floor, writhing in pain. She glared at him for a few long moments before settling her ruffled feathers and turning back to Harper to continue with barely controlled fury. "Your boyfriend here ... Walter ... murdered our mother."

She swept her claw forward, slashing his cheek before turning to Harper again. "That is how he repaid her kindness! So I ask you, Harper Wood ... who's the monster here?! Ungrateful wretch. On the night of my first solo hunting trip, I returned to the nest, so proud to show mother my accomplishments. But as I dropped in my prey for her to admire and share, I found my mother dead and my brother gone."

Her menace, along with her feathers, spread again. "For almost two hundred years, I searched for him, near and far, so I could have my revenge, but he'd somehow remained hidden. I've been biding my time, contemplating how to pay him back for far too long. But now that I've found him, revenge has been sweet." Her voice took on an ominous softness as she nodded, then continued as though speaking to herself. "And it's not over yet."

Harper looked at Walt, blood trickling from the gash Delaynie had left. One more scar to join the others, Harper thought. Insanely, she wished for a bottle of peroxide. Without tending, the wound would fester. Delaynie interrupted her musings.

"You haven't a clue how much I've enjoyed these past weeks. Dangling my victims before this milksop has proved more fun than I'd imagined. Observing his agony at watching me devour them while they pathetically begged for their lives. It's been delicious! Mother would have approved. It has truly been all I've dreamed of. But then, once I understood how much he thought of you ... That's opened whole new avenues with which to torment him. You're the proverbial icing on the cake!" She leaned forward, leering at Harper. "Believe me, Chickita, we're just getting started."

Harper gripped her mirror while the screeching voice continued, "Oh, I've told him all about your new beau. That beautiful curly-haired man with the elegant dog ... Walt knows all about your dates ... even how you were snuggling together only a few nights ago down by the river ... don't you, Sweetie?"

Harper turned to Walt, the lump in her chest eclipsed only by the one in her throat. "She told me you wanted to be with her, Walt! I thought you didn't want me anymore. But I needed a friend. Bryan and I ... we've never been lovers. A few nights ago, I was telling him about how much I've missed you ... how much I love you." She added the last bit quietly, looking at him, desperate for him to believe her.

Though the eyes in his blanched face remained closed, she thought she saw a barely perceptible nod of his head.

"Whatever." The monster broke in, briskly. "He's unlikely to make it much longer as things stand now anyway. Pity. I've so enjoyed myself."

She looked at Harper, tapping a claw on the floor. Apparently reaching a conclusion, she suddenly straightened. "The best thing to do before he expires would be to make him watch you suffer. Or hear it, if he can't keep his miserable eyes open. Makes little difference to me. That," she chuckled, "will be the proverbial cherry on top of the sundae, will it not?"

Walt struggled to sit up, his voice raw. "No."

The Tskili' laughed again. "Oh Walter. Somehow, you've convinced yourself you're so good. So brave. So strong. But fact is, you're nothing but a weak owl shifter. You're no match for me. You never were. And neither is your little girlfriend." After sneering those words, she reached over and plucked at Harper with a claw, snatching her from the floor. Harper cried out in pain as she felt the inch-thick tip of the claw penetrate her right side, just below her ribcage.

"But before I do anything she can't recover from, you can watch me toy with her like I've played with you." She unhooked Harper from her chain, then carried her to the empty cage near Walt's, where she opened the door and threw Harper inside, slamming it shut behind her. "We'll start by letting her watch us feed so she'll know what's in store for her. What fun! And you'll enjoy knowing that you will be the last meal Walter ever watches me eat."

With that, the creature gave a hoot that ricocheted off the walls before flying to the cave's entrance.

Once it was gone, and Harper had regained her breath, she called out, "Walt? Do you have any ideas how we might escape?"

In response, Walt only coughed faintly, then groaned. "I'm sorry, Harper. I'm so sorry. I should have warned you, before she took me. Sadly, I believed until it was too late that I could outwit her."

Frantically, Harper looked about, searching for some way to get out of the cage. Her first thought was to turn herself into an owl. If she could manage that, she could slip through the bars, then release Walt. Perhaps they could fly out together. If he wasn't strong enough, she'd hide him in the forest until she could get help.

But first, she thought it would be wise to call for help. That way, the Fae would be on their way when she and Walt broke free. She focused her mind, calling silently to Grandma, then to her Fae friends. But after several attempts, she'd gotten no indications that anyone had heard her. Next she called aloud for help. But once again, nothing happened.

With no idea how long they had before the creature returned, she focused her energies on changing into her owl form, but frustratingly, nothing changed.

"Walt? I'm trying, but I can't take my owl form. Can you?"

"No, Harper, don't waste your energy, it's useless. I've tried many times. The cages are enchanted. Our magic won't work as long as we're inside."

She slumped next to the bars, berating herself. Why hadn't she shut up and listened to him before wasting precious time? She'd allowed her panic to interfere with her thinking. Of course Walt had already tried every possible means of escape. If it were easy, neither of them would be here now. She grasped the swan mirror tightly. Its reassuring heft presented another option. Maybe when the monster returned, she could hurl the mirror toward the monster's head. With luck, she would knock it senseless. She'd wait quietly until the cage door was open, then spring into action.

No matter what happened, she promised herself soberly, she would save Walt, even if the effort killed her.

Chapter 26

WALT HAD CLOSED HIS eyes, sinking into an exhausted stupor. Harper propped her back uncomfortably against the cage's bars and examined the injuries she suffered when the monster hurled her inside. After patting her bones and moving slowly about, she didn't believe anything was broken, though her shoulder and wrist felt weak and tender. She thought it likely a few tendons had stretched too far.

As her eyes roamed the cave's repulsive, dim interior, she estimated the entrance to be thirty feet from Walt's cage, in a long straight line down the dark path littered with obstacles to trip up the unwary.

On her exit, Delaynie had extinguished all but one burning torch above Walt's cage. Its light illuminated scattered bones and piles of heavy chains. The décor aesthetic was clearly modeled on medieval torture chambers in B-movies.

She turned her attention back to the gaunt, heartbreaking sight Walt made in his nearby cage. Clearly she'd been completely off base in her assessment of his relationship with Delaynie. She wondered briefly about the woman in the white cowboy hat. Why had that woman, Fae creature, or whatever she was, been lurking about Walt's place? She caught herself on the verge of asking but fought back the impulse. At this point, what did it matter?

Instead, she poured out her heart. First, she told Walt that she loved him. Her pride now in the trashcan, she confessed that the last time she had seen Walt, he had been in the park talking to Delaynie. She finished by telling him she was sorry she ever doubted him and that, had she suspected even for a minute that he was in trouble, she would have searched until she'd found him. "I'm so sorry," she'd ended lamely, shame burning in her chest.

He'd lain there silently on his bed of rags listening as she spoke, his chest rising and falling in barely perceptible motions. If he never spoke to her again, it would serve her right, she thought. But finally he took a deep, quivering breath, then said, with a ragged voice whisper, "It's okay, Harp. What else could you have thought? I never have, and never will, stop loving you." His speech done, he slackened. Harper wondered whether he was still conscious.

Of one thing she was certain: If either of them was to make it out alive, it would be up to her. Due to his starved and battered condition, she could expect no help from Walt at all. In fact, she'd probably need help to get him out of his cage. Fear and hopelessness arose in her chest in tandem with despair. She shook herself. This wasn't over. She refused to give up.

Once again, she closed her eyes. To calm herself, she silently called out for help from her grandma or from F-Troop. She focused on each of their faces, one by one, but she felt no change in her energy and no connection. With each effort, her hope extinguished a bit more. When she focused on Grandma, she found herself unable to even picture Grandma's face, neither as the Faery Queen nor as the Grandma Sophie from her childhood. She could only conclude the enchantment Walt had mentioned earlier, or maybe the cave itself, had completely severed her spirit from those who loved her best.

Since changing into her owl form was impossible, she squelched the urge for another attempt. She needed every ounce of her remaining strength to fight once Delaynie returned.

She lifted her head on hearing the strange trumpeting sound, now so familiar. On looking at Walt to see if he, too, had heard, she found him completely still, likely unconscious. The sound faded away, then returned, much louder, as though coming from just outside the cave's entrance. She sat up, breaking into a cold sweat, wondering if it were Delaynie returning with a victim.

Bracing herself, she clung so tightly to the mirror in her hand, she felt sure the raised metal swan would permanently imprint itself into her palm. Her body flooded with tension as she waited, ready to spring, but after an exhausting minute, all fell silent again. Perhaps it had been a trick of sonic waves playing off the cave's walls. No matter its source, she needed to come up with a plan to deal with the monster on its return. And she needed to do it now.

Finally, she sketched a desperate strategy. When Delaynie returned, Harper would play dead. After all, the fiend hadn't checked to see if she was okay after it hurled her into the cage. The force might have broken her neck. She positioned herself as far from the sides as possible, hoping the Tskili' would be forced to open the cage door and step inside to check on her. And when it did, Harper would move quickly, first slamming the mirror into the creature's face as hard as she could, before scrambling from the cage to transform herself into an owl. From there, she'd be much better equipped to fight the beast with her claws.

She psyched herself as much as possible to feel strong and ready to explode into action when the time came. She felt sure she could summon any Fae forces in the area from outside this cursed cave. With luck, the others would arrive in time to save

Walt, if not herself, from the demoness forever. It wasn't ideal, but it had to work. The plan was their only hope.

Her taut nerves neared the snapping point as footsteps came from outside the cave. Fighting to control her jagged breath, she lay motionless, muscles tensed, the mirror gripped tight, and ready for battle as soon as the beast drew near. Through slitted eyes, she focused intently on the cave's entrance, preparing for the worst.

Through the gloom, a figure, much too small to be the Tskili', appeared, then hesitated. Taking halting steps, pausing after each crunch of bone beneath its feet, it moved forward into the interior. As the sounds of cracks and crunches drew closer, Harper's fears began to calm. The movements were too tentative and unsteady to be Delaynie. A jolt of dread shot through her at the thought that it might be a victim, feeling its terrified way inside. Hold still, she told herself. The basic plan must still be followed. But as the figure stepped inside the murky circle of torch light, her plans fled her mind, and she found herself sitting bolt upright.

Of all the beings in two worlds, Bryan Greene was the last she'd expected to see. Horror swept over her as another dreadful thought entered her head. Had Delaynie used Harper to lure Bryan for her next victim? Was the monster following close behind? With no time to lose, she hissed through the bars. "Bryan! What are you doing here?! Get away before the monster returns! For goodness' sakes, go!"

Bryan peered through the meager light. Clad in a sensible ensemble of loose hiking pants and a long sleeved, quick-dry sun shirt, topped with a bucket hat, he blinked through the smoke, unable to pinpoint her exact location. "Harper ... Where are you?"

"I'm in the cage up ahead to your right. Walt is locked in one further back on the left. What are you doing here!?" She was torn between an insane hope he could save them and terror that his remains would comprise Delaynie's next pellet.

As he reached her cage, he crouched down, resting a hand on her cheek through the bars. "I was driving by the trailhead on my way back from a trip to Boone. They've opened a new shop ... never mind. That's not important. I saw your car and pulled into the parking lot. Then I heard that beautiful music. You know, like I heard that night by the river? It was coming from up the trail, so I followed it until it led me here. Are you okay? How did you get here?!"

"Didn't you see the monster?"

He shook his head. "Monster? What are you talking about? No, but funny thing, you know you asked me about seeing something white when I heard the music that night down by the river? This time, I saw something white too. It was this tall woman with long straight black hair, and it looked like she was wearing an enormous white cowboy hat! I followed her and the music, and it led me right to this cave."

He held up a long, silky white feather. "I found this by the cave's entrance."

"Okay, fine. I believe you, but please leave—now. I'm not kidding. A monster, and I mean a monster, Bryan, will be back any time now! Those pellets—it's the monster that's making them."

He smiled at her as he pulled a multipurpose tool from his pocket. "Yes. I was a Boy Scout. Not going anywhere 'til the prisoners are sprung."

She shook the bars in frustration. *Men! Why won't they listen?* "Bryan, you don't understand! You don't have time to spring me from this cage, and you have no idea what you'll be up against."

She huffed as he calmly unfolded his metal implement. "Look. Just leave the tool with me. I'll figure it out. But you need to get out of here, now!"

"No can do." He shook his head as he found the opening to the cage door and began to cooly examine it, tool at the ready. "Odd," he mumbled. "There doesn't seem to be a lock. But there must be some sort of release mechanism."

She wanted to scream. "If you are going to insist on sacrificing yourself, go get Walt out, and take him to safety first. He's the one she really wants to hurt." Knowing he'd be unconvinced, she added, "As a matter of fact, without him here to torture, she'd probably just let me go."

He continued to examine the cage door with exasperating calm. "Nope. But I promise I'll get Walt out too, once you're safe." He waved the tool before her face. "You're the fair maiden in this tale. You come first." Once again, Harper heard the mysterious trumpeting call from just beyond the cave's entrance.

If Bryan heard the noise this time, he didn't respond. But as the sound faded, he began to gag. "Gah! It stinks in here! What *is* that smell?"

If Harper could have, she'd have jerked the tool from his hand. "It's bones and rotting flesh, Bryan! Why won't you listen to me? As insane as this sounds, that woman I told you Walt was seeing is the one who's been leaving pellets all over the place." When he didn't respond, she raised her voice to a yell. "How can I make this plain? You need to get out of here ... now!! This isn't some romantic fairy tale you've wandered into!"

She could sense determination radiating from his blue eyes through the dim light. "Yelling at me won't help, Harper. I'm not leaving without you ... or Walt."

He was right about one thing. Yelling wouldn't help. She softened her voice. "That's sweet of you, Bryan. And don't think I don't appreciate it. But if you don't leave soon, all three of us are going to die."

"I swear I'll protect you with my life."

"Seriously? May I remind you that you're a poet, not a warrior. What are you going to do, distract her with your verse?"

Bryan chuckled, but at that moment, the light from the cave entrance went out, followed by a chilling screech.

Together, they froze as Delaynie came slinking down the length of the cave through the darkness. "She doesn't look like a mons ..." Bryan began. But he stopped speaking, his eyes widened in horror, as Delaynie morphed into the heart-stopping, eight-foot-tall Tskili'.

The girlish giggle she emitted made a nasty contrast to the booming metallic voice. "Nice! I owe you two lovebirds a thank you. I could hear you blathering from over a mile away. I cut my hunt short, sure I'd find fresh meat waiting for me here. Oh my! Mr. Handsome! The love triangle! How absolutely delightful. You thought you'd play the hero, did you? Well, I guess it's your unlucky day! Looks like you'll be playing victim instead."

She circled around, placing a foot-long claw on Bryan's shoulder, pinning him in place. "Don't even think about slipping away, Pretty Boy."

Bryan sputtered, "Pretty Boy? I'm hardly a boy! I'm in my fifties. You've ..."

"Shut up!" Her smile disappeared. "I couldn't care less how old you are."

Then she chortled again. "It simply doesn't get any better than this! A feisty knight in shining armor! Now Walter can watch his lady love while she watches her hero die before her eyes. Angst on top of angst like a luscious layer cake! And after that, he can watch me enjoy her for dessert! I couldn't have planned a better grand finale. Once I've enjoyed my final meal, my work here will be done. I think I'll just sail away into the night, leaving my beloved brother to contemplate your destruction until he starves to death. At this point, he's not worth the trouble of consuming anyway."

She leered at them. "The time has come. I haven't eaten in days. It's time to feed."

As her claw bored into Bryan's shoulder, he yelped in pain. In her pocket, Harper felt the mirror in her hand grow hot as her body filled with strength.

When she heard the trumpeting once again it clearly came from inside the cave. Bryan's beatific smile was more suited for a poetry slam. "That music ..." he muttered.

In disbelief, Harper watched behind the monster as the tall woman in the white cowboy hat came gliding out of the gloom. As Harper watched, the hat expanded while its feathers lengthened, and the woman morphed into a giant swan. Its feet left the floor, and then it rocketed toward Bryan with a resounding cry.

Before the Tskili' had time to react, the swan reached Bryan. As it touched him, a white light flooded the cave with such intensity Harper was momentarily blinded. When she dared to open her eyes again, Bryan and the bird appeared to have melded together, forming one massive swan, equal in ferocity and size to the demoness. In the ferocious battle that followed, she lost track of their movements.

Harper watched incredulous as the bird, which appeared to be made solely of light, towered over the prostate form of the Tskili', battering the monster about the head with its lethal beak.

Then, with a gruesome shriek, the Tskili' ceased its struggle and lay motionless on the cave's floor. Then Harper closed her eyes as the swan's glow took on an unearthly brilliance. A blast of wind scoured the cave, the scent of fresh roses and river water obliterating the smells of death, decay, and rot that had pervaded before. As the intense light faded, the giant swan vanished, along with the cages and the chains. Nothing but smoke-filled air separated her from Bryan, who lay unmoving on the floor.

When Harper reached him, she found Bryan lying on a pile of downy white feathers, with a severe gash from his chest to his knee. Harper put a hand to his clammy face. She could feel his breath moving faintly in his chest. He opened his blue eyes, now the color of a lake blue crayon. "Harper. I was wrong. All my life, I've misunderstood. It was her. I first felt it when I saw you, but it was the swan who called me. Now I know what I am."

Alarmed by the strange light in his eyes, Harper whispered, "Don't move. I'm going to get help."

As he continued to stare at the ceiling, he murmured, "Beautiful."

Then Harper watched in wonder as a thin stream of mist seeped from the top of his head. The wonder changed to awe as his body, too, became insubstantial, dissolving as it floated above. On looking up, Harper saw two ghostly swans hanging near the ceiling. Then with trumpeting cries, the two figures soared to the cave's entrance where they exited with one last joint, trumpeting call.

Bryan was gone. Unable to grasp what had happened, Harper sat unmoving until Walt stirred behind her. "Harper?" he groaned. "What happened?"

"Walt!" Harper scrambled to him on her hands and knees. "Shh." She stroked his hair. "We're safe now, My Love. I'm taking you home. I'll take care of you until you're well."

In response, his body grew rigid as his eyes went wide. Harper felt a fresh, sharp ripping of the flesh between her neck and shoulder, which then made an agonizing slash downward, scraping the bones of her back ribs. As she screamed in pain, the odor of rotten flesh swept over her and the metallic voice assaulted her ears once more.

"Well, well. Did you really think I'd go down that easy?"

Chapter 27

A SURGE OF RAGE instantly combined with Harper's desire to protect Walt. Without a thought, Harper transformed into an enraged great horned owl, poised to battle the monster to the death. But, in a surge of agony, her resolve was thwarted. The monster's claw had severed her wing, leaving it painfully unhinged and worthless.

Despite the blood streaming from its beak and patches of attached feathers hanging askew, the hideous creature grinned at her. With her stomach churning, Harper regretted she wasn't a vulture shifter instead, so she could launch her stomach's contents at the creature's malevolent face. She felt quite confident the acid content was high enough to do serious damage.

"How marvelous! I hadn't suspected you and Walt were two of a kind. But your big round eyes should have provided a clue. Had I known, my strategy would have been quite different. But no matter."

Though the creature swayed from side to side, it showed no signs of pain. "Perhaps," it chuckled with malicious pleasure, "I'll get more joy out of making a meal of Walt while you watch. He's hardly worth the effort at this point, skinny as he is, but your suffering would make it worthwhile. I doubt you have the strength to resume your human form again. But it will be gratifying to see the hope extinguished from your big pumpkin eyes. Afterward, you'll make a nice little snack. The two of you together should provide me with strength enough to heal."

Harper, nearly insane with anger, lost all connection with fear. "Taunt me again!" she spat. "You're so funny. Honestly, Delaynie, I think you missed your calling in life. You should've been a bit actor in Monty Python skits."

For a second, the creature's menacing leer was replaced by a puzzled expression. "What's a Monty Python skit?"

For a second, the monster looked thoughtful, then shook its mighty head. "That was quite the spell you and Pretty Boy pulled off. It's a shame he didn't survive it, but really, all that matters is that I pulled through. It's odd, though. I had no idea you had Fae blood. I can usually tell. But then, you're such a mousy little thing." She leaned forward with a scowl. "But after all, that's what makes life so exciting isn't it, Girlfriend? Learning new things?"

As Harper recalled saying those exact words to Delaynie only weeks before, a fresh surge of impotent fury flooded her. If only she could fly, she'd bury her claws in the monster's eyes.

But before she could think of a suitable retort, the monster yelped, then whipped around, its back to Harper, and released a shriek of hurricane force. It took Harper a second to realize something must have hit it from behind, though what, she had no idea. Taking advantage of Delaynie's distraction, Harper raced forward on her sturdy little legs and clamped her sharp, hard beak on one of the monster's massive limbs. Then she held on with all her strength.

The kicks the beast used to shake her off slammed Harper into the wall. Once her head cleared, she found the impact had shocked her back into her human form. While she struggled to sit, Harper's ears rang and her eyes saw double. But through the pain and shock, she discerned flashes of red and brown as hundreds of robins flew about the head of the Tskili', with a sparser but still hefty contingent of owls on the periphery. Together, their screams created a wild cacophony. As she watched helplessly from the cave's floor, the swarm of birds became so dense that Harper could no longer see the monster at all.

As they forced the monster to the ground, the sounds of chanting began, low at first, then strengthening in volume and intensity. The sounds seemed to be coming from the floor, the sides, and the ceiling of the cave itself. Then, with a flash of golden light, her grandmother appeared in her fearsome form of the Faery Queen. As she raised both arms, her resounding, majestic voice commanded, "Be gone back to the hell that spawned you!"

As gusts of air swept through the cave, Harper crawled on her belly to Walt. Sticks, leaves, and bones whirled past her as she made her way to him, coughing in the dust. Once she reached his body, she draped herself across him to protect him from the flying debris. She had used the last of her strength to join him; now everything went black.

When she opened her eyes again, a vase containing sunflowers interspersed with purple coneflowers filled her vision. As she turned her stiff neck to look around her pale blue bedroom, relief swept over her: there was Piper, sitting in a kitchen chair by the bed just as she'd been the first time Harper saw her over a year before. The faery looked up, then gently laid aside the book that had been open on her lap.

Harper knew something significant had occurred, but she had no idea what it might have been. Squinting in confusion, she asked, "How did I get here?"

"Hallelujah!" Piper exclaimed. "What a joy to see you stirring, Dearie! You've had a nice long nap, you have. And a good thing too. Don't go getting yourself into a snit just yet. All will become clear with time." The small creature's brown brow furrowed. "How are you feeling?" Now at the bedside, she squinted anxiously at Harper.

Harper collapsed against her pillow, giving the question serious consideration. How did she feel? Still not remembering what had happened, she asked herself how she was supposed to feel. She moved and stretched as much as her body allowed. A dull ache spread through her upper back around the shoulder blade, through to her clavicle and down her side. Though everything felt tender, the pain was bearable.

Then the memories flooded in ... the cave ... Walt and ... oh no ... Bryan. As she fought to sit, Piper laid a hand on her arm. "Don't rush yourself, Dearie. I promise all is well. You mustn't exert yourself too much just yet."

But now too agitated to lie in bed, she swung her legs from the side, crying out as her back seized, making further movement impossible. Struggling to catch her breath, she looked at Piper in consternation. "Where is Walt?"

Piper stroked her forehead. "Rest easy, Dearie. Your Walter is in the next room. We've been fatting him up, we have."

A large reservoir of Harper's tension drained. She detected humming from the kitchen, along with murmurings of soft voices. On seeing her eyes shift to the doorway, Piper added, "In fact, Olivia and Deanna are cooking vittles for Walter right now. Do you feel well enough for more company?"

Harper nodded eagerly but remained on her back. She didn't want a painful reminder of her injuries just now. "Oh, goodness, Piper yes ... I'd love more company."

"Mom!" Olivia appeared in the doorway, a tray in her hands. She came in, quickly setting the tray atop the dresser, before rushing to the bedside. Her cool, slim hand felt wonderful as it touched Harper's forehead. "Thank goodness you're awake! You've been out for weeks, Mom! We've all been so worried!"

"Weeks?" Harper turned to Piper, whose solemn expression underscored the truth of her confirmation.

"Nearly three weeks, all told. We've done our best to heal you up. It's true you were in a sad shape when we brought you here. But with lots of rest and a bit of magic, it seems you will recover."

Olivia leaned over and planted a kiss on the top of her head. "We've all been so worried about you, Mom! Walt's incredibly weak, but at least he was awake." She bit her lip. "He was nearly starved. But for the past week or so, he's been well enough to come look in on you every day."

A tall, thin form limped into view, then hesitated in the doorway. "Walt!" In Harper's eagerness to reach him, she rolled from bed but found her legs too weak to hold her. But as she hit the floor, Walt was at her side. He eased himself down to join her on the floor.

"Easy there, My Tweet," he said in his husky voice. "Let's hold off on the workouts until you get your strength back." He propped her against his side, wrapping her in a secure hug with a long arm.

She laid a hand on his thigh. "Tell me what happened."

"You don't remember?" He pulled her tighter. "You saved my life, that's all."

"I didn't ..."

"Oh, yes, you did! Didn't she, Piper? If she hadn't been so brave, neither of us would be here now."

Harper shook her head, wondering how to bring this up. Didn't he remember? "But it wasn't me, Walt ... it was Bryan." She looked up in horror as the part Bryan had played came flooding back. "Without Bryan, we'd both be goners. And he's …"

Walt stroked her hair. "I'm sorry, Harp. Yes, Bryan's gone. I wish, more than anything, that I could have helped him, but I could only watch. Honestly, if I hadn't seen it, I wouldn't have believed it. One regret I'll live with for the rest of my life is that I didn't get to know him better. There was more to him than I'd ever imagined."

Harper's head reeled as tears spilled from her eyes. "I don't understand …" She tried to find the words.

"It's all right, my love, neither do I." Walt tucked her head beneath his chin, rocking almost imperceptibly from side to side. "What's important now is that we're going to take care of you. And one day, we'll be ready to revisit everything that's happened."

Her attention shifted to other areas of her life. "The shop?"

Piper answered, "We've put a sign on the door saying you were temporarily closed. Olivia spread the word that you've taken a long vacation. We'll change the sign to 'Reopening Soon' as soon as you're well enough to return to work. Don't worry, Dearie. All is under control." She turned at a soft clicking sound from the hallway. "And, we have another nice surprise for you."

At that, Leda padded into the room, walked straight to Harper, and settled on the floor, whining softly at her feet.

As Harper leaned forward to hug the dog, her sore ribs brought on a fit of coughing, but she held on to her for as long as she could manage. "Leda! My sweet girl! I am so happy to see you!" She looked around. "Who's been taking care of her?"

Everyone exchanged smiles. "She's been a group adoptee! Deanna and Dashawn have helped, too." Deanna walked into the room with a tray covered with a blue and white napkin. "Welcome back, Harper! When Olivia and I realized you were awake, I got a few goodies together for you, if you feel like eating them. And as for Miss Leda, she's been a delight to care for. On top of that, she and Biscuit get along great!"

Piper nodded. "She's scarcely left your side."

Harper stroked Leda's head, which now lay in her lap. She couldn't look at this lovely dog without thinking of Bryan. She rubbed her silky fur before addressing them all, "I'm so glad you all remembered her. I may still need to call on you occasionally for help, but from here on out, she'll be my responsibility. Won't you girl?"

In response, Leda licked her, then she took to her feet and gave a small, happy bark, her entire body rocking back and forth in tandem with her tail.

Chapter 28

FOR THE NEXT FEW weeks, Walt spent hours every day sitting by Harper's bedside. Gradually, with love, care, and nourishing meals, she began to take steps that led first across the room, later to the kitchen, and then to the living room. Within a month of awakening, she felt strong enough to leave the apartment.

Before reopening the Robin's Nest, she hired Nate to help her after school and on weekends. Deanna willingly let him go, knowing his heart lay with the bookstore, not with the coffee shop. Harper only regretted not hiring him last fall when he'd done such an excellent job helping with the bookstore's Grand Opening. In addition to his excellent knowledge of science fiction, of which Harper was cheerfully deficient, he was also an artist. He'd painted the murals in the "Good Folk" room, which she'd dedicated to F-Troop. Now Harper was happy for him to design displays and paint more murals, enticing customers with his distinctive take on books and literature.

One October afternoon, Lily and Alida flitted into the apartment bearing the day's mail, which they'd collected from the box beneath the mail slot in the shop's front door. Among the catalogs and fliers, Harper found a letter from a law firm on Main Street. She was shocked to read that they'd been informed Bryan had moved to an undisclosed location in South America. But before he'd gone, he'd left legal documents on file at their office, bequeathing his house and his business to Harper to use or sell as she saw fit.

The notice left Harper mystified. Why would Bryan have taken such a step? Had he already planned to disappear at some point? They said the official letter informing them of his decision to renounce his life in the United States had been postmarked from Knoxville, Tennessee. Who could have sent the letter to his lawyer? She had watched him disappear with her own eyes. Still, the disturbing letter gave Harper hope that Bryan might still be alive somehow. She knew firsthand that miracles do happen.

No matter where Bryan might be, Harper took managing his estate seriously. On going through his house, she found bound copies of his original poetry, published decades before. These she brought home to read. Though she'd never enjoyed poetry, she found many of his accessible and poignant. Reading them opened entirely new perspectives on life. She regretted never asking him to share this part of himself with her.

To her surprise, when Walt read them, he confessed to sharing Bryan's obsession with beauty. He intuitively grasped the root of Bryan's obsessions. He explained to her that Bryan had projected his finer impulses onto her as a child. Bryan believed the beauty was all in Harper—and Walt said he couldn't find fault with that—but the real inspiration was Bryan's own inner self. Harper accepted Walt's interpretation as a mystery she'd never grasp.

With time, she came to see that being herself and living her happiest life was all she needed. And so many things made her happy. Running the bookstore, for instance, helping Olivia, but spending evenings in the company of Walt and her friends most of all. Realizing this, her guilt about Bryan began to recede. Writing his poetry had made him happy. And for him, it was enough.

One October evening, as she enjoyed a quiet evening in her living room with Walt and Leda, she pulled out the swan coffee table book that Bryan had given her. What had happened in the cave with Bryan still eluded her. And she wanted desperately to make sense of it all.

As they looked through the book together, she remembered the Swan Clan and the woman in the white hat. She laid the book aside and looked at Walt. "There was a woman that I saw, several times. Like when I went to your treehouse to see if I could find you. Remember that night just before you disappeared when we had pizza at your house? We heard a trumpeting call. You seemed troubled at the sound, but we never got to discuss it."

With no wish to cause him pain, she stopped, unsure how to continue. He squeezed her cold hand with his warm one. "When I heard that call, I suspected it was a member of the Swan Clan. Anytime one of them appears, trouble will be on its heels. They don't cause the trouble; instead, they seek to restore balance. That night, I was already worried that Delaynie showed up, but I didn't want you to worry, so I didn't say anything. I had no doubt she'd come after me soon. But keeping you safe was my first priority. So while the call of the Swan Clan reminded me of the coming trouble, I also knew help was on its way. That helped me feel just a little better."

"But the woman ... the one in the white-feathered cowboy hat. She looked like one of the Cherokee or at least one of the native tribes from hereabouts. I'm embarrassed to admit it, but I wondered if you had taken her as a lover."

The muscles in his jaws tightened, but he shook his head. "No, Tweet, I never saw her until we were in the cave and she came to join forces with Bryan. I'm not sure why you saw her at my place, but she was likely looking for Delaynie. I suspect she had a dual purpose here; one was thwarting the Tskili' and the other was bringing Bryan into the Clan. But this is all just my guess. Still, we do know she was involved in the resolution of the whole affair."

Harper stopped speaking as she let this sink in. "The Swan Clan must have had something to do with Bryan and I becoming friends. Not long after you disappeared, he stopped by one evening to give me a mirror. I'd show it to you, but I never saw it after he and the woman joined forces in the cave. Anyway, the mirror looked a lot like Grandma's." She looked at him for validation. "You do remember Grandma Sophie's mirror?"

He nodded, giving her his full attention.

"Well, he told me he found the mirror at his father's house. It had a swan on it with the letters 'SC' above. I kept it close; since it was so much like Grandma's, it was comforting to me. But then, F-Troop told me it was likely of Fae origin like hers. Nothing about Bryan suggested he had any relationship with the Fae Realm. If he did, I feel sure he didn't know about it."

Walt squeezed her hand. "I was never around him enough to get a sense of that myself. But people can fool you."

"Isn't that the truth? I don't know if you heard her, but Delaynie told me in the cave that she had no clue I had Fae blood either. But back to the other woman. I first saw her the day Bryan gave me the mirror. Later, I spotted her walking around town, then near your house. She even showed up across the river from here one night after the Fae found a couple of Delaynie's pellets there. Do you think she was looking for Delaynie to try and stop her?" She asked the question because, though she'd given the subject a lot of thought, she was far from convinced her instincts were right.

Walt nodded. "That's my thought, too. But it's even more fascinating to me that she had a connection with Bryan as well."

"Yes." Harper sat thoughtfully. Leda walked over and Harper rubbed her silky coat. "I said he was just a normal guy, but there were odd things about him. Bryan was fascinated by swans. He told me it was partly because I danced the lead roles in Swan Lake in high school. Anyway, I found out later that his grandfather had courted my Grandma Sophie back in Winterfield when we were kids. I had no idea! And I talked to Grandma while I was searching for you ..."

He nodded again. "Yes, Earl Grey filled me in on some of that. I'm so touched that you tried so hard to help me, Harp."

She leaned over to kiss his cheek. "I'd do it all again today. But Grandma told me she had dated his grandfather ... his name was Austin. Is it possible Bryan's grandfather Austin had a connection to the Swan Clan? Do you know if the Clan has connections to humans?"

"Many of the Fae have connections with humans. It depends on whether or not they want to. Sometimes these connections are helpful and sometimes they are harmful. And, as you know yourself, Fae can interbreed with humans too. So it's possible Bryan's grandfather could have been a part of, or descended from, the Swan Clan."

Harper suddenly sat straight with a new thought. "Walt! Do you think it's possible that the swan Bryan was so obsessed with was the part of himself that belonged to the Swan Clan? He said, before he disappeared, that he'd misunderstood. It wasn't me, he said, it was the swan. All along, he was in love with a part of himself he didn't understand ..."

"And he projected onto you. Yes, Harp. I think that's it. They are a fierce and beautiful force, the Swan Clan. Though," he squeezed her shoulder, "you're pretty fierce and beautiful, too."

Harper stared out the balcony door at the rising moon. No wonder Bryan had been a poet. No wonder he seemed lonely. He'd never fit in with the people around him. But he'd said he was happy now. She felt so grateful to know that.

✦⁘✦

Two weeks later, on Halloween night, Walt and Harper pledged their commitment to one another in a beautiful, late-night Harvest Moon ceremony in Olivia's long, secluded backyard. With hay bales for seating and muslin draped around for atmosphere, everything looked magical in the moonlight. Bowls of apples and grapes sat among platters of cheese and fresh bread and butter for everyone to wash down with lager and wine. Though out of season, swarms of fireflies arrived to lend their sparkle to the event. Dressed in a gauzy dark green dress, with a garland of leaves and dried flowers around her multi-hued head, Harper had never felt lovelier.

As the ceremony ended, Grandma Sophie made a brief, but magnificent appearance to bestow blessings on the marriage. She paused above the couple and wished them a happy union. Then she laid a hand on each of their bent heads before vanishing, leaving behind a diffusion of champagne-gold light.

While those in her set who had the Fae sight understood the real source of the twinkling lights, those without, like Dashawn and Ida Barker, commented on how long it must have taken to string all those twinkling lights between the branches and other decorations. And they had all speculated on the lightning flash and thunder at the moment Grandma Sophie showed up. Most felt it a miraculous, but favorable coincidence.

Her happiness only increased when, during the post-ceremony dancing and dinner, Olivia and Quinn stood together to extend the assembled company an invitation to their wedding on Old Christmas Day in January. Harper had begun to suspect there was more to her daughter's friendship with the folklore scholar long before Olivia admitted it to her. While the wedding announcement didn't surprise Harper, learning that Olivia had told Quinn the truth about her Fae inheritance as far back as last spring did.

Walt had decided to move in with Harper. He would keep his treehouse as an office and workshop and use it for writing and other projects. Besides, he told her, everyone needed a private space.

In the months following, the darkest of the year, the Fae returned to their normal routines. The brownies kept the building in tiptop shape. Ash devoted his spare time to keeping Harper's book collections in perfect order, while Piper managed the kitchen and oversaw the wintering flora in the park. Ivy monitored the safety of all beings within their domain. Lily and Alida joyously recommenced their watery frolics, indoors and out, cavorting with bugs, birds, fishes, foxes, and other local fauna to their hearts' content. Meanwhile, Earl Grey and Hawthorne debated the meaning of life together while smoking ancient pipes in warm corners, both lending a helping hand whenever and wherever they were needed.

Shortly after the Thanksgiving holiday, Harper visited Bryan's lawyer. After weeks of earnest thought, she'd decided to turn Bryan's lovely home on Poplar Street into a nonprofit Arts Council, for Whippoorwill Gap and the surrounding county, with guidance from the National Endowment for the Arts. When it was ready, they'd hire someone, preferably from within the community, to run it. As a result, Bryan's legacy would support local artists, celebrating the region's rich artistic and cultural heritage.

She sold Whippoorwill Gap Books to one of Bryan's former employees, who wanted it to remain a bookstore. She had the proceeds from the sale divided among Bryan's siblings with a special bequest for Autumn, the niece who'd kept him company.

One Tuesday evening in November, after dinner was over, she and Walt sat side by side on the couch in her living room, with all of F-Troop gathered around. They had assembled for their newly recommenced weekly sessions of readings, storytelling, and music, the first since before Harper had gone searching for Walt last summer. Piper's honey oat cakes were still warm from the oven, and Harper prepared peppermint tea and hot chocolate. Though the night was cold, they'd left small openings in the windows to allow the bracing fresh air to circulate.

Everyone felt jovial now that law enforcement had officially wrapped up the case. The Fae had succeeded in delicate operations to redirect the attention of the media and police departments. Even the FBI, who had all previously been deeply involved in reporting on or solving the case.

With a few selective but well-placed enchantments, memories were "corrected." Once the records had been slightly amended, everyone agreed that the whole affair had been the unfortunate work of one lone individual who had been living in a cave near Draper's Knob Hiking Trail, near the dam. They had found the remains of the perpetrator inside. DNA testing had revealed that it was an unknown person from outside the area, probably a transient individual who was now out of commission. The community could once again rest easy.

Though Walt had never revealed what had happened to Delaynie's mother, the fearsome Tskili' that Hawthorne remembered from his early days in the North American wilderness, Harper couldn't bring herself to ask him. She'd gathered from Delaynie's ravings that he'd been adopted by the loathsome creature, so he'd either been orphaned or stolen when young. Somehow he had escaped, and, in the process, the creature had perished. Even though Harper was interested in the details, she could not bring herself to put Walt through the pain of reliving it for the sake of relieving her curiosity.

Tonight, in the glow of her present company of friends and beloved Walt, she decided it didn't matter at all. He'd been a child pitted against a monster. Whatever had happened had not been his fault.

Most of the assembled company had been thinking for weeks of their contributions to the soiree. In addition to the usual poetry recitations and prose readings, musical numbers were presented solo and in groups, and skits, some involving props and costumes, were performed. Each performance was followed by loud rounds of applause and raucous shouting as bows were taken.

Once the shows were over, the company settled down to an impromptu round of riddles and jokes.

"What do you call a cow who can no longer give milk?" Tarryfoot asked, looking about expectantly.

When no one answered, he hooked his thumbs beneath his belt. "An udder failure!" he shrieked as the rest of the company groaned, before a smattering of polite applause sounded.

Suddenly, Leda stood and paced to the balcony's door, whining softly. She stared intently through the door's glass and began wagging her tail, the silky fur catching the light as it swished from side to side.

"What is it, Girl?" asked Harper, moving to the sofa's edge.

All conversation ceased when, through the barely open windows, they heard the trumpeting call of a swan. As they jumped to their feet, faces to the windows, Walt threw the balcony door wide. Then together, they peered through the dark toward the river. There, against the backdrop of the full Cold Moon, the outlines of two enormous swans arose from the river and flew north, over the treetops, out of sight.

Let's stay in touch!

Keep up to date on L.C.'s latest happenings, and get a **free** short story, **available only to newsletter subscribers**! You'll also get freebies and exclusive insider information.
In addition, provide your input for future writing projects!
Sign up at https://lcmaxie.com

***

Audiobooks of the Whippoorwill Gap PWF series coming in 2026!

About the Author

L.C. Maxie pursues a magical life. After the former librarian published two guides to excellent nonfiction books, *Library Lin's Guide to Superlative Nonfiction* and *Library Lin's Biographies, Autobiographies, and Memoirs*, both featured in *Booklist*, she ventured into paranormal women's fiction. The Whippoorwill Gap PWF series is set in the town of Whippoorwill Gap, North Carolina, where faeries cavort alongside the human residents. The series novels are *The Robin's Nest, Book One; The Lady Slippers, Book Two,* and *The Swan's Song, Book 3.* When she's not writing, L.C. bakes goodies and takes walks in Virginia's Blue Ridge Mountains with her husband Roger and their captivating canine, Dusty Marie.

Connect with L.C. Online:

https://lcmaxie.com

facebook.com/LibraryLin
youtube.com/@teawithl.c
pinterest.com/lfmaxie

Also by the author

Whippoorwill Gap PWF Series:
The Robin's Nest
The Lady Slippers
The Swan's Song

Nonfiction:
Library Lin's Curated Collection of Superlative Nonfiction by Linda Maxie
Library Lin's Biographies, Autobiographies, and Memoirs by Linda Maxie

Acknowledgements

My heartfelt thanks go out to everyone who has read, reviewed, or recommended my books—your support means the world to me.

I'd like to extend special thanks to several people who went above and beyond to make my last novel, *The Lady Slippers,* a success.

My favorite bookseller, Traci Morton hosted a fantastic launch party for *The Lady Slippers,* Book Two in the series. Her encouragement and enthusiasm have proven invaluable.

The beta readers of this book were super-helpful. Of these, Emma Babbitt has been there for all three novels in the series. Her ear for writing is impeccable, and she's gifted at providing valuable feedback without squelching my confidence. She's a wonderful writer and a gem of a human being. Kim Carter, Julie Moore, Anne Pyles, and Mary Smith rounded out the beta readers. I learned much from all of them and valued their feedback. I took suggestions from each and every one of them.

The following have been cheerleaders who have encouraged me to persevere when the going got tough: Bobby Fisher, Carol Hopkins, Tammy Ussery, Rebecca Flippen, Nancy Bryant, and Audra Eckert. I could never thank you all enough.

Without the astute input of my editor, H. Louise Sianni, this book would have been much less pleasurable to read. She has never failed to draw my attention to needed fixes, and her "ear" for good writing is spot-on.

In this series, cover designer Karen Dimmick of Arcane Covers has been a priceless member of the book production team. While her work speaks for itself, I still highly recommend her to anyone in need of a fantasy or paranormal book cover.

And I thank you, Dear Reader, for staying with me to the end of the book. I hope that the experience has been both enjoyable and rewarding. Feel free to contact me with comments.

Cover Design by: Karen Dimmick at Arcane Covers

Editing by: H. Louise Sianni at Sianni Editing

First edition 2026

ISBN 979-8-9859234-8-3 (paperback)

979-8-9859234-9-0 (ebook)

www.ingramcontent.com/pod-product-compliance
Ingram Content Group UK Ltd.
Pitfield, Milton Keynes, MK11 3LW, UK
UKHW021650190726
13853UKWH00001B/169